Leap the Wild Water

Jenny Lloyd

Published by Jenny Lloyd

To my ancestors.

For surviving and inspiring this story.

Preface

In a society where women are neither equal nor free, Megan Jones strives to carve a life of her own choosing. As her secrets and lies begin snapping at her heels, there seems no escape from a past which threatens to destroy her life.

Set in early 19th century Wales, within a religious community as harsh and unforgiving as the landscape, Leap the Wild Water is a dark tale of treachery, secrets, and what it means to be free. Weaving past with present, the heart-breaking stories of Megan, and her brother, unfold towards a terrifying conclusion.

Chapter 1

Morgan

My sister is a scheming whore. I should have seen it coming, that day I saw Eli ride away from our house, and Megan wasn't going to tell me he'd been here. And the day she came home late, looking like a tramp, her hair a tangled mess, and her arms full of bunches of stinking daffodils. I know, now, that she had been with him. All the signs were there, but it did not enter my head that she'd play that game again. I'd have thought she'd learned her lesson.

She always was a sly one. Not a word does she say about it until it's all but done and dusted. Just hours ago, she comes up to the field where I'm sowing oats, to break the news. I'd been up in that field for most of the day; rain one minute, sunshine the next. My legs and arms felt fit to drop off, on account of all the walking and raking over I'd done. So I was not in the best of humours when I see her walking over the bare ground, her boots caked with mud and her skirts trailing in the dirt. She paid no heed to where she was walking, trampling all over the tilth where I'd just then scattered the seed.

Twisting her apron in her hands and looking at the ground, she says she has something to tell me. I carry on walking and scattering the seed, thinking she's going to say she's burned our supper or something like that. She trots along beside me, struggling to keep up, stumbling between the furrows.

"Me and Eli are courting and we're getting married two weeks from now. The banns are being read on Sunday."

She comes out with it straight, all in a rush, not pausing to take breath.

That stops me in my tracks for a second. Then I carry on walking and scattering the seeds. I can't think of one damned word to say in answer to her. From the corner of my eye, I see her stand for a moment before she turns and heads back to the house. What a schemer! I don't know why it comes as such a shock. It's not like she hasn't done it before; gone courting behind my back, as if I have no right, as her brother, to tell her what she can or cannot do.

I pace up and down between the furrows, repeating her words in my head, until they have properly sunk in. She did not waste any time. Mam only recently dead and Megan is up to her old tricks. Was Eli dull in the head or what? I presume she's told him what she got up to in his absence. She'd have had to. He must be soft in the head to take her on. I can't think of any other man that would; and him with the pick of the bunch, silly sod.

The moon is already out of bed, hovering over the top of our hill before the sun has even set, so I carry on sowing. I can smell more rain on the wind and want the job done before it arrives. I also don't want to go down to the house until I've had more time to think of what I can say or do to keep Megan from marrying.

When I do go down to the house, my stomach snarling with hunger, the moon is sailing high in the sky, peeping in and out of racing clouds. I think, she'll be tucked up in bed by now, so I'll have time to myself, to think. What the hell am I going to do if she goes? I can't run a farm and a house on my own. I'd have to give up this farm, which I've worked since I was a boy. I don't care how much she wants to marry Eli, I'm not giving it up for her sake.

I don't see her sitting there, waiting by the light of the fire, until it's too late and I'm taking off my coat. I think about turning round and going back out the door, but I want my supper. She gets up straight away and hurries to the pot above the fire where my meal is keeping warm. She starts up talking as soon as the first spoonful is heading towards my mouth.

"We have to talk, Morgan," she says, standing over me.

"Can't a man have some peace to eat?" I bark at her and she shuts up then.

She goes to the fire with a candle, lights it, and comes back to place it on the table beside me. I give her no more than a glance while I eat. I note she has her hair tied in some gaudy ribbon. If Mam was still alive, she'd throw it on the fire and follow with a lecture on the pitfalls of vanity. I feel like doing it myself, for I'll wager that Eli gave her that. I can't think where else she would have got it. Mam always said that Megan was far too proud of those long, chestnut locks of hers.

She sits down opposite me but I cannot look at her, so mad am I at this latest betrayal. I look instead at the dresser against the wall behind her, with Mam's best plates lined up along its shelves. Megan continues to wait while I eat, and I let my gaze wander around the flickering shadows of the room. It alights on Mam's empty chair inside the inglenook, and a pang of grief threatens to engulf me. I push my plate away. First Mam, and now my own sister is planning to abandon me.

She starts up again, the minute I push my plate aside.

"Morgan, we need to discuss what will happen when I'm gone," she says.

"You're not going anywhere," I say, "I'm the head of this household now, and I get to say who will marry or not. And you're not marrying anyone. You can tell your Eli that from me."

You have to remind women, every now and then, of their place in the order of things. I have made a big mistake in letting our Megan have a loose rein again, since our Mam died. It's time to rein her in and remind her who's in charge.

"You can't stop me, Morgan," she says, her voice quiet.

"Just watch me," I throw back.

"No, Morgan. You are my brother but you're not my keeper."

"We'll see about that."

We glare at each other across the table.

"All my life I've looked after you and Mam. I've had no life I can call my own. This is my one and only chance, and not you or anyone else is going to stand in my way."

She does not raise her voice, but talks with a determination I've not seen in her before. But I'm not beaten yet.

"What about the little one? You've forgotten all about her, I suppose," I say, knowing full well my words will hit her as hard as any slap.

She does not know what to say for a moment, then I am treated to an outburst which surely made Mam turn in her grave.

"How do you dare say that to me? Forgotten her? Have you no idea what it is like for me, to go on living without her? You stupid, ignorant…"

She bites her lip and closes her eyes. I know of only one way to stop her from marrying Eli. It is time to play my trump card.

"Let's fetch her home then, Meg. We can go tomorrow, the two of us. You don't have to live without her a day longer."

Since Mam died, I have thought of little else but bringing home the daughter we stole away from Megan. But Megan's reaction is not the cry of delight I had imagined. She opens her eyes to stare at me, her eyes black with contempt.

"You're six years too late in saying that, Morgan Jones. Why now, and not when I begged you? Because you'll do or say anything to stop me marrying, that's why."

"My hands were tied before, you know they were. She is my responsibility, now Mam is gone, and I say she comes back where she belongs."

"Do you, now? You're the one ordering my life now? And what about your reasoning for stealing her away? You and Mam couldn't face the shame it would bring on you, to see me shunned by the whole parish for what I did. You'd see me shamed now though, would you, rather than see me marry Eli? "

She gets up from the table and snatches up my plate. I watch her carry it out to the scullery, kicking the door open with too much force so that it flies open and bounces back towards her, knocking the plate out of her hands. It lands on the flagstone floor with an almighty smash, the pieces flying in all directions. She stands for a moment, tight-lipped, and with her hand clasping her forehead. Then she stoops to pick up the shards, tossing her hair over her shoulder and muttering all the while.

"Thanks to you and Mam, I'd be a stranger to her now," she says, getting down on her hands and knees to retrieve a shard of plate from beneath the dresser.

She gets up, grasping the small of her back and wincing. She waves the shard of china at me, while ranting on about how there is another woman who her daughter calls mother now, the only mother she will remember, and how it would be cruelty to wrench her away again.

I think of the poor little girl living in that hovel with Nesta Harding who does not love her as a mother should. It would be cruelty to leave her there. But how can I tell Megan without letting her know I left her child in such a place? She'd likely kill me and I wouldn't blame her.

"You and Mam stole her from me and now you're planning to steal her from someone else," Megan says, shaking her head in disbelief. "Why must you continue to meddle in things which are not your concern?"

"I'm trying to make amends, for pity's sake!"

She places the shards down on the table, sits back down opposite me, and takes hold of my hand, grasping it tight, with a pleading look on her face.

"If you want to do that, you'll wish me well, now, in the one chance of happiness I have. This is my one chance. Would you begrudge me even that?"

"I don't begrudge you anything but I want to do what's right for your daughter."

"Then leave her be. You can't turn the clock back. What's done is done. Too much time has passed. I'm going to marry Eli, perhaps have another little girl to love and cherish. I won't let you stand in my way, Morgan."

She takes her hand from mine and sits back in her chair, arms folded, defiant. My hope of making amends is slipping from my grasp but that is not the only loss I shall suffer if Megan goes. If Megan wanted revenge on me for what I took part in, she could not have chosen a surer route to my destruction.

"You always were a schemer. What am I supposed to do? I can't run the farm, and the house, and all. I'll lose this farm, everything I have lived and worked for all my life. Is that what you were thinking when you told Eli you will marry him?"

"You have some cheek to call me a schemer! If you and Mam hadn't stood in my way, I'd have married Eli six years ago. You may well look shocked! You probably thought I'd never find out about that little scheme of yours. Eli has told me all about the letter of proposal he sent when he had to go off to his Uncle's farm."

If I was looking shocked it was because I didn't know what she was talking about. It was the first I'd heard of it. But I wasn't surprised. Our Mam would have done anything to keep Megan here.

"I don't know what you're talking about," I say, and she makes a little snort of disbelief.

"I suppose you don't know about the letter of refusal I am meant to have sent back either, saying how I couldn't possibly marry him when I had you and Mam to look after. While I thought he no longer wanted me, you and Mam knew all along the real reason for his silence."

"I swear to you on our Bible, I had no part in any letter."

She looks at me long and hard. She has known me all my life, so I hope she knows when I am telling the truth.

"I would congratulate her, then, if she were still here, for doing her own dirty work for once."

I feel a hot flush of shame redden my face. Dirty work it was indeed that I did at Mam's behest. I shouldn't have done it, knew it then and know it now. Between us, Mam and I caused Megan more pain than any should have to suffer in this life. I, for one, shall forever be sorry for it.

I think back to that time when Eli left, how heartbroken Megan was, when she heard no more from him. Not even a goodbye, and them all but betrothed since they were children. It shocks me now, to think our Mam knew the real reason all along. Shocks me, because I remember how Mam goaded Megan about it, after he'd gone.

“That’s the last we’ll see of him. He’ll find himself a nice Cardigan girl for a wife, I expect. He can’t hope to run his Uncle’s farm without a wife.”

That’s what our Mam said after he’d gone. We were sat here by the fire, and Mam addressed her words to me but they were meant for Megan’s hearing. Megan didn’t lift her head from her sewing but carried on as if she hadn’t heard.

“You’ve missed your chance there, my girl,” Mam adds.

At the time, I thought Mam was no more than tactless. It never entered my head that she was being deliberately cruel.

To Megan’s credit, though her heart must have been breaking, she didn’t give our Mam the satisfaction of seeing it. If she did any weeping, which I’m sure she did, she did it in those of her few private moments, away from Mam’s prying ears and eyes. But her unhappiness showed in other ways she could not hide. She became quiet and withdrawn, not taking part in conversation with us and only speaking when spoken to, and the light went from her eyes. I’ve seen that happen in horses, when they’ve had enough of the toil that is life.

Women are no different to horses. They need a tight rein but they also need to run free sometimes. Too much control is as bad as too little, it makes them unmanageable. You have to get the balance right. Megan was too spirited and proud for Mam’s sort of handling. The tighter Mam drew in the reins, the more Megan would pull against them. Our Mam knew that well enough, but she could never resist forcing Megan to bend to her will.

So it's not like I don't understand that our Mam pushed Megan too far, with her taunting and controlling. And now I know that it was Mam herself who prevented that marriage, while rubbing Megan's nose in it, it makes it all the worse. But Megan pulled too far and we've all paid the price for that.

Megan places her hands on the table and winces as she pushes herself up out of her chair. She's as thin as a willow branch these days, but there's strength in her arms; brown and tough they are, like her face.

Megan announces that it is very late and that she is going to bed. I watch her walk stiffly across the room and slowly ascend the stairs. She is only twenty eight years old but hard work is already taking its toll. Her back troubles her greatly, I know, and her hair is peppered with grey too soon. I can't blame her for wanting the easier life she'd have with Eli, but she can't go, and that's that.

Chapter 2

Megan

Since I was twelve years old, I have fed and watered that brother of mine. I've milked the cow, made the cheese, and churned the butter; with so much sweat dripping from my brow I had no need to salt it. Every morning, as soon as it's light, with the yoke chafing my shoulders, I've carried the pails of water up from the gorge below our house. I've scrubbed the floors until my back felt it would never unbend again, while Mam sat there in her chair by the fire, pointing to the places I had missed or not scrubbed hard enough.

Morgan would have me do all this, and more, until I fall willingly into my grave. And what would he do then, poor thing? He would find a replacement, that's what he'd do. He'd marry at last, or get a maid to live in and carry on as if I'd never been. Yet he would keep me here; prevent my marriage to Eli, while knowing all this toil has made me old before my time.

Morgan claims he knew nothing of the trick that was played on Eli and me. I wish now that I had gone to the dresser and taken down Mam's precious Bible and made him swear on it. For now the great, glowering bulk of him is not sat in front of me, and I lie in my bed reflecting on our conversation, I am no longer sure I believe him. I think to myself, a man that is capable of stealing away his sister's babe is a man capable of all manner of trickery and lies. That he would again try to prevent our marriage, tells me he thinks as little of me now as he did back then, and he is not to be trusted.

I will not let him stand in my way again. Even when I was just a child I believed I would marry Eli. It was as certain a point in my future as growing to be a woman. As natural as the dawn after darkness, and as spring follows winter. Yet, now it is to happen at last, I am not happy! For my waking hours are haunted by the dreadful secret I have not told Eli, and my heart is filled with hateful rage, against the mother who will never answer to me now for all her vile treachery against me.

If I were as good and pious a woman as I am meant to be, I would trust and be satisfied that Mam would, at least, have to answer to God. But I don't know that I believe in God anymore, certainly not the God she taught me to believe in, and who she quoted every day of my life. Nor the God in whose name she claimed to act and who guided her in all things.

She was always too much to bear. Yet I did not truly know how she weighed upon my very soul until they lowered her coffin into the ground. As the earth finally bore the weight of her, I felt my own body become so light that I felt myself lift from the ground. So dizzying was this sensation that I grabbed Morgan's arm, lest I be carried away on the breeze.

How strange are the twists and turns of fate? Within a day of her dying, I heard that Eli had returned, as if he had been waiting in the wings. In the week running up to Mam's funeral, it seemed to be all that everyone was talking about and wanting me to know; all the neighbours who made the long climb up our hill, on foot or on horseback, so that Morgan and I were rarely alone.

Every evening, when the sun went down and their chores were done, they came from far and wide. At any one time, there were two or more neighbours sitting with us, or with Mam where she lay in her coffin, on the table in our front room (which to my memory had not been used since father died, and then for the same purpose). They come with gifts of food for us, and go to see Mam for the last time, before the lid of her coffin is nailed down. We have not had so many visitors inside our house for as long as I can recall.

The womenfolk come with their sewing, or knitting, and sit by the fire beside me. By the flickering light of fire and candle, they sit in companionable silence, or talk of who they saw at chapel, who is courting who, whose child has died and whose child has been born, to the rhythmical clickety-clack of their needles and the crackle and hiss of the fire. And they talk of Eli's return, and how he is all alone down at Wildwater farm. They stay until it is bedtime, trusting that horse or lantern will guide their way home in the dark.

In the midst of our neighbours' company, I am reminded of what mother once told me; you cannot survive in this world alone. She was sat there, in her now empty chair, with her ever present bible on her lap when she spoke.

"Everyone needs to belong somewhere. You need people just as you need food and water," she said. "You are no different to the sheep on the hill. Isolate one from the rest and it does not last long."

I thought I did not care if I belonged, thought I would rather be alone in this world than live a life of her choosing.

The men of our parish come in pairs and sit with Morgan. On dry evenings, they sit on the bench outside the front door, with a storm lantern for light. They talk of the weather or the prices fetched at market. They bring with them their whittling knives, to occupy the hands which are unused to being idle for long. Little piles of wood shavings collect beneath their feet, which I will sweep up in the morning. The older men fashion shepherds' crooks or axe handles, practical things they cannot live without. Their sons carve intricate love spoons for the girls they are a-courting.

Morgan sits stiffly among them. He keeps his head down and his shoulders hunched. He smiles and nods when they speak but he only speaks when directly asked a question. His grief is wrapped deep inside himself. He hugs it close to him, for it is all he has, now, of his precious Mam.

It is during the first of these fireside vigils, when I hear the news I had long since ceased to hope for. Jane, of Oak tree cottage, and her sister Bess, have come to sit with me. They sit side by side on the settle, knitting stockings. So small of stature, their feet do not reach the floor, but swing in time with their knitting. Neither of them had married and their parents were long dead. They were middle-aged now and the stockings were their only source of income. The stocking man comes once a month, to collect and pay them for what they have made.

"Did you hear that Eli is returned home for good?" Jane asks Bessy, as if I am not there.

"Never! No, I hadn't heard that!" Bessy says, wide-eyed with feigned surprise, while I have all but stopped breathing.

It was plain from their expressions that they had rehearsed this conversation before coming, and that it was for my benefit.

"It is as true as I am sitting here. His uncle has died, so he's sold up the farm and come home. I suppose, with his parents gone, he's inherited that too."

"He's a wealthy man now, then. Remind me, who did he marry?"

"He never did marry, Bessy! What's happening to your memory?" Jane scolded.

I try to feign disinterest in their conversation, while struggling, in the poor light, and with trembling fingers, to pick up the stitch I have dropped in my knitting.

"Well it's about time he did marry! Perhaps he's come home to find himself a wife!" Bessy goes on.

From the corner of my eye, I see her nudge Jane with her elbow and nod in my direction. I get up from my seat to hang a full kettle of water over the fire, praying they will change the subject. Water spills from the kettle spout, hissing and spitting in the flames, and sending a flurry of ash into the air.

"Steady with that kettle, Meg!" Jane admonishes me, standing up and flapping her hands about as the white ash falls about her.

I apologise for my clumsiness, sit back down beside them, and take up my knitting again. I am longing for them to change the subject, for I know where it is leading.

"Meg here is unattached. Perhaps Eli will be coming a-courting, Meg!"

I feel myself blush and brush away the suggestion with my hand.

"And what would he be wanting with an old maid like me?" I say, with false gaiety.

Dear Bessy, she has no idea how undeserving I am of her good-hearted intentions. If she, or any of my neighbours, knew the truth about me, they would not be sitting here with me now. I am a pretender amongst them and it grieves me to be so, for I know it is a betrayal of their trust in me.

"Old maid indeed!" says Jane. "You're younger than him, anyway."

"Wouldn't it be grand?" says Bessy. "You don't want to be looking after your brother for the rest of your days, do you?"

"I'm sure if Eli were to marry, he would be looking for someone who can provide him with a son and heir. It's a bit late in the day for me, don't you think?" I say, the tremble in my voice betraying the feelings their conversation is arousing in me.

"Heaven's above! You're young still! There's still plenty of time," Bessy carries on, unaware that I am close to tears.

"Perhaps we shouldn't be talking about such things just now," Jane says to Bessy, and gives Bessy a warning look. Bessy glances at me and falls silent.

"I'm so looking forward to the spring, aren't you? Winter is almost over!" Jane says cheerily, tactfully changing the subject.

But the evening is spoilt. It is all I can do not to weep. For all that I try, I cannot lift myself from the dark reverie their conversation has pitched me into. When they speak to me, I respond as cheerfully as I can muster, then find myself staring into the fire, my thoughts pulling me back into a past that I never want to resurrect. They chatter between themselves for a while longer, before saying their goodbyes. I can see by their faces, they do not understand why I am so aggrieved. Why would they, when they do not know what I have done?

When they were gone, I sat thinking how cruel it was that Eli should return now. Mam was dead, but that did not mean I was now free to marry Eli or any other. I had ruined my chances of ever doing that. Besides, Eli had gone off to his Uncle's farm without a word of goodbye. Bessy and Jane were very much mistaken if they thought he had come back for me, I told myself. He did not want me then. Why would he want me now?

Then, just days later, he rode up here to ask me if I would change my mind, now, and marry him. I did want to tell him what I'd done in his absence and all because I believed he'd jilted me. I did try to tell him I no longer deserved him. Then he told me how hurt he'd been by my rejection and, now Mam was gone, there was nothing to stand in our way. And I thought; if I refuse him now, then Mam would still be getting her own way, even after death. And I couldn't let that happen, could I? So I decided that he need never know, and that what he didn't know could not harm him. So, I shall have to carry the burden of my secret to my grave, and do all in my power to make myself a worthy wife to Eli.

If Morgan is speaking the truth, when he says he played no part in the trick Mam played on Eli and me, then surely he will see now, how unjust she always was in her treatment of me. Surely, he will see how wrong it would be to stand in our way? When Mam was alive,

Morgan always took her side or made excuses for her. She doesn't mean to be cruel, he said back then, when I told him how she had continued to taunt me about Eli. Can my brother not imagine how I feel, to know that while she taunted me, she knew she had tricked Eli into thinking I did not want to marry him?

"Morgan tells me you are troubled because Eli has left," she said, closing her Bible and placing it carefully on the table beside her.

It was a sure sign that she was planning a long conversation, and she had chosen her moment well. It was baking day, when I would be tied to the kitchen and her company for most of the day. I'd been up since dawn to light the bread oven, for it took hours to get it hot enough to bake the week's bread. I could have kicked Morgan's shins for telling her. Always fond of carrying tales he was, though he knew what she could be like if she got hold of something like that.

"Is that what he said? Well, I'm not in the least upset, so you need not worry your head about me," I said.

In truth, I was devastated by Eli's continued absence and silence. I was desperate to see and speak with him. I had not seen him since he last came to chapel before leaving for his Uncle's farm in the next county. I was haunted by that last sight of him, and the cold way he had looked at me as Morgan drove me away on the cart. I could not fathom why he had not come the very moment he knew he would be leaving. I thought he had given up waiting, for Morgan to get himself married so I would be free. Morgan wasn't even courting because he wouldn't think of doing anything without Mam telling him to. And she was hardly likely to tell him to do that.

Of course, I didn't know about Eli's proposal, nor that he'd said I could bring Mam along to his Uncle's farm if I would be his wife.

While I kneaded the bread dough, I had to listen to her cruel words.

"You'd have thought he'd have come to tell us himself, wouldn't you? But then, from what I've been hearing, he has more important things on his mind than us."

Though she said 'us', she meant me, he had more important things on his mind than me. Do not listen, Megan, I silently told myself, she is just trying to goad you.

"I daresay the next time we see Eli Jenkins it'll be with a pretty, young, Cardiganshire wife on his arm. I've been hearing rumours," she went on, drawing me in.

"What rumours would they be?" I ask, wiping the sweat from my brow with a flour covered arm.

"Nothing for you to worry your head about," she said, mimicking the very words I had spoken to her, moments before, "there's probably no truth in it anyway."

She picked up her knitting and began to knit, as if that was the end of the subject.

"No truth in what?" I ask, trying to hide my alarm.

"Well, if you *must* know, they were saying, after chapel, that a neighbour of his Uncle Eben has a *very* beautiful daughter, and Eli is *very* taken with her."

I pause and watch her turn her knitting needles to begin another row of stitches. Back and forth her needles went, her finger winding the yarn, back and around, with each stitch.

"I don't know how people seem to know such an awful lot about Eli, all of a sudden, especially as they never see him!" I say, punching the air out of the dough.

"Whatever gave you the idea they never see him? He comes back regularly! Ask Morgan if you don't believe me."

This news came as a terrible blow for it confirmed my fear, and the shock must have registered in my face for she gave a short, derisive laugh at my ignorance.

"Oh! Of course! I suppose you thought that because *you* hadn't seen him in months, nobody else had either!"

"No. I never said that."

"He makes a lot of visits, apparently, on his trips back to Wildwater, does the rounds of all his old neighbours and friends."

Everyone but me, it seemed. I placed the dough in the earthenware bowl and set it to rise by the fire. How could he be so cruel, I asked myself, to reject me so entirely?

"Her father's a wealthy farmer, by all accounts."

"And what if he is?" I snapped, opening the bread oven door to throw more fuel in.

"She's a cut above the ordinary peasant girls, is all I'm saying, dresses very smart and all that, you know. But then he's a very smart man, himself. They sound like the perfect match, if you ask me. He'll be wanting to show *her* off, mark my words."

"I don't know why you're telling me all this as if I care," I snap at her, and begin scrubbing down the kitchen table with treacherous hot tears threatening to well up in my eyes.

"I was just making conversation. Why would I think you'd be troubled by anything Eli Jenkins does, anyway?"

"I really can't imagine why you would think that," I said, though I knew very well that she had always been perfectly aware of my feelings for Eli, and his for me.

"You didn't think he'd want you, did you; him with his own farm, and all? He wouldn't be interested in the likes of you when he can pick and choose!" she said, and laughed at the ridiculousness of my hoping for such a thing.

I couldn't bear to be in the kitchen with her a moment longer. I took myself off to the dairy, on the pretext of fetching some butter. I did not know whether I wanted to cry or scream. The trouble with our Mam was, she could not resist an open wound, so long as it was someone else's and preferably mine. She would dig and delve until she'd find a soft spot, then, like Morgan's dog with a bone, could not leave it alone.

Standing alone, within the cool walls of the dairy, I felt my anger cool and become resolve; it was as hard and tempered as the blade of Morgan's scythe, honed beneath the blacksmith's hammer. She had gone too far, this time. She was too cruel to bear, taking such pleasure from my pain. No more would I try to please or appease her. She had no sympathy for me, so I would no longer allow myself to feel any for her. Should I feel myself weaken and feel sorry for her, I would only harden my heart further. All my life, I had questioned myself, looked to my own shortcomings for the reason she did not love me as other mothers loved their daughters. Always, I had thought the fault lay with me, until now, when I realised I did not deserve, had never deserved, to be so cruelly treated.

If I had known then, that she had orchestrated Eli's estrangement from me, that all the while she taunted me, she knew why he had not come to see me, I am certain my feelings of dislike for her would have turned to hatred. I am certain of this because that is what I feel for her, now I know the truth.

Later, when I was milking the cow, Morgan came to find me, to impart two pieces of related news. First, that a neighbouring family was being turned off their farm because they had fallen behind with the rent, and secondly, he said we would end up the same if the price for wool kept falling while the price of grain kept rising.

"What's wrong?" he asked, when he realized his little speech had elicited no response from me.

I was still angry with him for having betrayed my feelings to Mam. I turned my head away in a fit of pique and rested my cheek against the cow's warm flank.

"What do you care? You come and go as you please, off to the hill, the market, the mill. You have no idea what it is like for me, stuck here, day in and out, with Mam. Why did you have to go and tell her I was upset over Eli going?"

"She asked me if you were, that's why. I couldn't lie."

"It's all she's talked about since he left. She is too cruel."

I took the full pail of warm milk from under the cow and carried it over to the dairy, with Morgan following behind.

"She doesn't mean to be cruel," he said, standing inside the dairy door.

I cast him a withering glance but he was oblivious. He was gazing around at the shelves, where I had dozens upon dozens of cheeses ripening. The past two summers had been so good; the cow had put out oceans of milk. The result was more cheeses than we would ever be able to eat ourselves.

"I was looking in here the other day, and I got an idea."

"That's right, change the subject. Never mind about me," I said, skimming the cream off the milk to make butter.

"If you would just listen, you would know I'm not changing the subject. I'm thinking we should start selling your surplus cheese and butter at market; eggs too, if you can spare them. A lot of farmer's wives and daughters do it to make extra money, and we're sorely in need of that, I can tell you."

"Oh, I see. So while I'm stuck up here making all this cheese and butter you're going to sell, you'll get an extra day out at the market. Very clever, Morgan!"

"You must think I don't have enough to do already. You try running a farm single handed and see how much time you have for trips to market. I'm thinking you will go do the selling, you daft woman. It'll get you out of the house for one day a week, anyway."

My heart was fluttering like the wings of a young swallow, about to fly for the first time. A whole day out on my own, every week! I hadn't been to market since, one winter, when we were still growing up, and Mam got ill, so ill she took to her bed for a month or more, coughing, endlessly coughing and almost too weak to walk. I think Mam had feared she was close to death that winter. Though she recovered from that illness, she was never the same after. She handed all the work over to Morgan and me, and took to sitting in her chair by the fire, seeking refuge in her bible. Our weekly jaunts to market came to an end and, from that time onwards, I had to shoulder the burden of all the work that had to be done in the house and dairy. How I had loved market days, the excitement of going, the hustle and bustle, the stalls and the crowds of people. For me, market days were bound up with the free and happy days of youth. I hardly dared believe that Morgan's suggestion was anything more than a dream.

"It will never happen," I said, returning to skimming my milk.

Morgan leans against the door jamb and folds his arms across his chest.

"It will happen. I've set my mind on it. We have to find extra money, somehow, and it's all I have come up with. I thought you would jump at the chance."

"Oh, I would Morgan, I would. But I don't want to go getting my hopes up, only to be disappointed. I don't think I can bear any more disappointment," I said, swallowing hard on the lump that has risen in my throat.

"If you're about finished here, we'll go and tell Mam," he said.

"You can be the one to tell her!" I say, with a splutter of disbelief. "If she hears it from me she'll say no, straight off."

Despite my determination not to hope for the best, a flurry of nervous excitement was building inside me as I followed Morgan over the cobbles to the house. I followed him inside and stood behind his chair where he sat down at the table, as nonchalant as you like. He wasted no time in broaching the subject.

"Like I said earlier, Mam, we need to find extra money from somewhere."

"Pray and the Lord shall provide, Morgan," she said.

"Praying hasn't helped our neighbour and, anyway, doesn't the Lord help those who help themselves?" he said.

Mam opened and closed her mouth, lost for an answer to him, so Morgan carried on.

"I've thought of a way we can make more money, quite a bit more, in fact."

"Oh, aye, and what might that be?" she says, her expression hardening.

"We're going to start selling all our surplus cheese, butter, and eggs at the market. A lot of the farmer's wives and daughters are doing it and they can't produce enough to meet the demand. There's a small gold mine sitting there on Megan's shelves in the dairy."

"And who do you think is going to buy it? Who in this parish does not make their own?"

"I wasn't talking of selling it locally. I was thinking of selling in the market town of Dinasfraint."

"And where will you find the time to do that? It's a good ten miles from here," she says to him.

"*I* haven't got the time but Megan has. She could go one day a week."

"Could she now? And what about me? Have you thought about me? How am I to manage if she is off at market?" she says, raising her voice in protest.

"Come now, Mam. I'm sure you can manage without her for one day a week," he says.

"So I'm to be a servant in my own house now, am I? I'm to do Megan's work?"

So that's how she sees me, I thought, as an unpaid servant.

"Don't talk daft, Mam, a servant indeed! You won't have to *do* anything."

"No, you won't," I speak up, silently damning the plaintive tremor in my voice. "I'll prepare food for the day, for you and Morgan, the night before. All you will have to do is put it over the fire."

"All I will have to do? I see! You've got it all planned out between you! Behind my back, and all! My own children! Conspiring against me! Is this how I am to end my days?"

Her voice became querulous, rising to that pitch which always preceded a tantrum.

"I'll put it over the fire myself, then!" Morgan shouts at her. "I'll not lose this farm because you don't want to warm my damned dinner!"

"Lose the farm? Lose the farm? What are you talking about, lose the farm?" she says with a look of alarm.

Morgan stands up then and punches the table with his fist, our meek and mild Morgan who had never before raised his voice to our Mam.

"Does nobody listen to me around here? This isn't about you, Mam! This is about our survival! We're in trouble. We were barely making ends meet before the rent went up. How long do you think we can last with our costs going up month on month? You must know what I'm saying is true, Mam. You're the one holding the purse strings, after all."

Until then, I thought he'd come up with this idea for *me*. I thought he had seen my despair and seen this as a way to gain me a little freedom. But he spoke with such passion, I realised our plight was real. We could lose our place at Carregwyn, the farm we had toiled so hard on since he was little more than a boy. Morgan's words filled me with fear and I saw, looking across at Mam's face, she felt it too.

"Well, why didn't you say that in the first place?" she said. "Megan shall have to pull her weight from now on. She shall have to work a bit harder, whether she likes it or not."

I let it pass, her inference, that I was not pulling my weight already. I who did everything, while she sat in her chair by the fire, complaining and criticising about all that I did or did not do. I let it all pass; because I felt I was not standing there beside Morgan, but flying. My whole being felt like it was soaring free like the skylarks above our heath. One day of the week, one precious day, was to be all my own.

Morgan feels I betrayed him, for it was him that set me free, never knowing what that freedom would lead to. He thinks I orchestrated everything that followed. He believes I went chasing after the first man that came along, and got myself with child, as an act of revenge on Mam and Eli. But truly, I did believe Eli was not coming back, or that if he did, it would be with another girl as his wife. I admit I did not want to be a spinster when that happened. But it is not as Morgan says. If they had only let Eli marry me back then, none of what followed would have happened.

Chapter 3

Morgan

"I've been thinking, Morgan," Megan says, tracing a crack in the table-top with the tip of her finger. "You can get a housekeeper to live in. I thought Beulah, from the village, would be suitable. I hear she is recently widowed and has no means to support herself, other than knitting stockings. She'll be looking for a post."

Megan's face is all lit up, as if she thinks this is a wonderful idea.

"Beulah?!" I say in disgust, though I have nothing against her, she's nice enough, but that's a far cry from wanting to live in the same house as her.

"Yes, Beulah," she says, as though she is speaking to a child, "she's not so young as to be inexperienced but old enough to know how to run a house. She's only a couple of years older than you, in fact. She's nice, sensible, and easy to get along with."

In my mind's eye, I see me sharing this house with a woman I barely know, and the thought fairly makes me want to hang myself.

"I barely know her."

"That's not true. And anyway, you'll soon get to know each other well enough."

"I don't want to get to know Beulah. I want things to stay as they are."

"I'm sorry, Morgan," she says as if she means it, and reaches out to place her hand on my arm.

I snatch my arm away. I don't want her bloody sympathy; I want her to stay in this house.

"I hope you can find it in your heart to be happy for me. It would mean so much if we were to have your blessing."

As if I am going to give her that, when she is prepared to run off and leave me to fend for myself. Anyway, once I give her my blessing, I'm done for. She'll be off without a backward glance.

"Mam is proved right, yet again. You don't think of anyone but yourself."

She ignores this insult and carries on as if I haven't spoken.

"I'll go and see Beulah, tomorrow, ask her if she can start right away, so I'll have time to show her the lay of the place before I leave."

She has no right to do any of this. She forfeited any right she had to marry Eli, or anyone else, when she went bedding a man she was not married to. Why Eli is taking her on after that I do not know, he must have taken leave of his senses. I've a good mind to go to the preacher and ask him to remind Megan where her duties lie – with me.

Megan has always been headstrong, and no matter what she has, it is never enough for her. Our Mam was right about that. Mam tried to keep a check on Megan, but I see now that she had her work cut out. From the moment Megan began going off to market, each week, she was beyond Mam's control. Megan loved her trips to market, would come back with tales of the friends she'd made, and brimming with pride that her customers came back, time after time, full of praise for her cheese and butter. Why wasn't that enough for her?

You'd think she would have been content with that, but no; she had to go chasing after some ne'er-do-well behind our backs and almost bring ruin on us all. That was the thanks we got for letting her go off to market. It felt like she'd thrown it all back in my face, every good turn I'd ever done her. Now, she'd have me condemned to live with a near stranger, while she swans off and marries the sweetheart of her youth, and never mind the child she brought into the world.

Six years ago, Megan wanted to keep her baby and never mind the shame, but it was too much for our Mam. Mam couldn't bear the humiliation of people knowing. That's why the baby had to go. Begged us to let her have the baby back, Megan did. Now, I'm saying she *must* have her back, and face up to her sin, like she should have back then, and now Megan says no because she wants to marry Eli. It seems to me, I am the only one thinking straight around here, and the only one thinking of that child. But then Megan does not know what I know. It's easy to turn your back on something, easier to sleep at night, if you don't see what I see when I close my eyes.

I don't know why I believed that a woman who takes in bastard children for money would also be doing it out of the kindness of her heart. But that truly is what I believed. I am haunted by the possibility that I believed what I wanted to believe; what was convenient for me to believe. In retrospect, it would have been right and wise to go and see the woman first and establish that she was of good character and reputation. In truth, she was the only person we knew of who would take the child in, it wasn't like we could pick and choose. It seemed like a better option than leaving it on the steps of the nearest poor house, or worse.

It was one year after taking Megan's baby away, when I went to pay Nesta Harding her annual fee, that I first discovered how the poor child was living. When I arrive at Nesta's door, I can hear the baby crying inside. It was the fractious, frightened crying of a baby left on its own too long. It was sometime around late morning. I knock several times in the space of some five minutes before that woman answered the door. Then it is clear from her appearance that I have disturbed her from sleep. She stands there in the doorway, almost as wide as she is tall. Her face is as round as a pumpkin with folds of wobbling fat beneath her chin. Her sleep-tangled, greasy hair is all over the place and there are pillow creases on her fat face.

"Whadayawant?" she asks, squinting up at me, clearly not recognizing me.

"It's Morgan Jones. I've come to pay the money for the little one." I nod my head in the direction of the screaming child.

"Oh. Ta."

That's all she has to say for herself, while holding out her grubby hand.

"I'd like to see her," I say.

"Suit yourself. Little sod hasn't shut up for more than an hour since."

She stands back to allow me to pass into the 'cottage', which is no more than a one room up, one room down, cramped, smoke-filled, mud-floored hovel.

"As you can see, it may be small but there's no lack of warmth and comfort," she says from behind me.

I wheel round, thinking she is having a laugh at my expense, but there is no sign in her face that she is joking. A lump of peat smoulders in the small fireplace. I have not been in the room more than a couple of minutes but my eyes are beginning to sting. I go over to where the baby is sitting on a filthy, excrement covered blanket, inside a makeshift cot.

I pick up the screaming child who I cannot believe is Megan's baby. Her face is filthy, and it is clear she has been lying in her own filth for some time for it has dried on her. Once she is in my arms, she stops screaming and begins to furiously suck at her fists.

"She's crying because she is hungry," I say to Nesta.

"You an expert are you?" the impudent cow says back to me, but I bite my tongue, for I know I cannot afford to pick a fight with her.

"No, but we pay you to look after her, not to leave her go hungry."

"I was just about to feed her when you arrived at the door," she lies.

She goes to the corner at the back of the room and comes back with some bread soaked in milk. The dish she has put it in has not been washed since the last time she used it. I say nothing but take the dish from her and offer the food to the little one.

"Don't let her eat too fast! She'll be sicking it back up!" Nesta says, standing over us with her hands on her hips.

The child is so hungry she grabs the chunks of milky bread and crams them into her mouth. When she is fed, she becomes quite sociable. She reaches out to pull at my hair and tries to poke her fingers in my mouth. All the while, she makes nonsensical, chattering noises, as if she is trying to talk. She has short chestnut-brown curls and deep brown eyes. She is the image of Megan. I think of how Megan doted on her, how Megan would never have left her baby go hungry or dirty.

I feel my treacherous heart shrink as I hand her over to Nesta and take my leave.

"Don't you worry, dear, I'll look after your little one for you," she says with a wink, as if it is our secret, just between the two of us.

Poor child, poor little child. That's all I could think all the way home. I paced up and down in the barn until I saw Megan leaving the house. Then I went in to speak to our Mam.

"Megan's child can't stay with that woman. She's not being looked after properly," I say.

"And what would you know about that? When did you ever look after a baby?" Mam says with a scornful laugh.

"She was in bed, that woman, late in the morning, and the baby lying in her own filth and screaming the place down with hunger."

"For goodness sake, Morgan. Perhaps the woman was unwell. And babies scream when they're hungry. It does not mean they're not being looked after."

"But she was filthy. She looked as though she hadn't been washed in days."

"Oh! I remember when you were a little one! No sooner had I cleaned you than you were dirty again. You can't be washing children every hour of the day!"

"But the place is filthy. It's a hovel. The air in there is thick with smoke from the fire."

"So it's no different from the homes most children grow up in. Did you expect she would grow up in a palace? For if you did, you've gone soft in the head, boy."

I thought back over that morning and began to think perhaps I had been mistaken. I had expected, I don't know what, exactly - that because Nesta was being paid to do the job, she would do it as well as Megan? She hadn't met up to my high expectations. That didn't mean she was the worse than useless I'd felt her to be. I had jumped to conclusions. Like Mam said, that I found Nesta sleeping late while the child screamed could be due to her not being well. I had been too quick to condemn Nesta as idle and careless.

So I let it go, left the child to her fate. Even if I were right, what could I do? Mam wouldn't have her back, there was nowhere else to put her, and I could hardly confide in Megan.

A short time after I took her baby away, Megan went from fairly constant pleading and begging to not speaking at all. She barely spoke two words to either of us, from morning till night, and then it would be no more than yes, or no, to a question. She'd come and go from the house, milking the cow, collecting the eggs, her work in the dairy, doing the laundry. Her face was a stiff and unchanging mask, its expression never altered. It was one which spoke of a woman who was just getting on with what had to be done in the time between now and when she died. She closed herself up and shut us out, as if there were just Megan living here alone, and we were no more than unwelcome ghosts, existing in those places that lay on the edges of her vision, glimpsed but not attended to. How else could she cope with having to go on living with two people who had so betrayed her? We were the daily, living reminders of all she had been robbed of. We must have been exceedingly painful for her to behold.

Meanwhile, I was an annual observer to her child's neglect. The next time I see her, she is a walking, talking two year old, who hides behind Nesta's voluminous skirts. It cuts me in two to see her peering out at me, seeing me as a frightening stranger. The little dress she is wearing is filthy and torn. Her hair is a tangled mess of growing curls, and her face and bare feet are as dirty as her dress. It was plain as day; of the money Nesta was paid, there was little of it spent on the child. I thought our Mam would have cared about what she was getting for her money, at least, but she didn't want to know.

"The child is lucky to have a home at all," was her answer.

It seemed to me that having denied Megan the right to raise her child, the least we could do was ensure that she was being raised as Megan would have wanted. Over the years, I witnessed her being treated no better than a scivvy. It was clear that Nesta had no maternal feelings for the child. By the age of four, Nesta had the girl fetching and carrying for her. If it wasn't water from the brook below the house, it was fuel for the fire. While Nesta sat like a queen on her fat backside, in the chair by the fire, getting fatter each year that went by. And the child doing as she was told without a word of complaint.

That Nesta ordered the child about in my presence, told me that Nesta saw no wrong in using the child for her own ends.

"She's a lazy little sod. Won't do a thing without my boot up her backside," Nesta said to me, the last time I was there.

I wanted to grab Nesta by the hair, and tell her that Megan's child was too good for the likes of her; that we didn't pay her so that she could use her as a free housemaid. But I had to swallow my words, and my anger, for my hands were tied. It was our Mam that held the purse strings, our Mam who dictated what was to be. Our Mam didn't have to trouble her conscience because she didn't have to witness the consequences of her decision at first hand. And me, my conscience was troubled alright, but while Mam was alive I could tell myself it wasn't my fault because it wasn't me that was insisting that the child remained in that filthy hovel.

How easy it is to do wrong when there is someone else to blame. Though it was me who walked away from the child's plight each year, shaking with impotent rage, I could tell myself I wasn't to blame, it was our Mam's decision to leave her there. And ultimately, the two of us could always lay blame at Megan's door for having the child in the first place. So when I came away from that hovel, hating myself for walking away, and frustrated by my inability to do anything about it, I could always turn it all onto Megan. And I would take it out on her with ease, for wasn't it all of her own doing, and so no less than she deserved.

Now, I have the opportunity to rescue the child from that place. It is I, not our Mam, who is in charge now. I can't tell myself it is Mam's decision, or go on laying blame at Megan's door. There is plenty of blame attached to Megan, but the life her child endures is not down to her. If I do nothing, say nothing, then it will be for my conscience alone. I am the only person on God's earth who can act in this. I must make amends, and Eli Jenkins can think again if he thinks he is going to marry my sister.

Chapter 4

Megan

I was to travel to market each Friday. Morgan said I would need to take the pony and small, two-wheeled cart, for it was too far to walk and carry my wares. I had never, in my life before, driven the pony and cart. So, that week, every evening, Morgan took me out to teach me. He assured me the pony would do whatever I asked of it; I just needed to learn how to 'speak' to it through the reins. His assurances made very small roads into allaying my terror when he urged the pony forward then placed the reins in my hands. As we lurched forward, and the cart creaked and rolled from side to side, I was certain the whole thing would overturn, crushing us both beneath. In my terror, I gripped the reins so tight, the pony came to an abrupt halt and we were pitched forward, and almost thrown from our seat.

"What did you stop her for?" Morgan asked, incredulous. "We'd only just started to move!"

"I thought we were going to overturn!" I said, wiping the sweat from my brow with the back of my sleeve.

"Overturn?! How many times have you ridden in this cart? Did you ever once know it to overturn?"

"No, but you know what you're doing, I don't. And you needn't look at me as if I'm the village idiot. Carts do overturn. Look what happened to our Da."

"Da's cart overturned because he steered the pony too close to the edge," Morgan says.

"Well, there you are then! You tell me I can trust the pony to know what it is doing, and now you're telling me a pony can be steered too close to the edge. If it can happen to our Da, it can happen to me."

"Well, unless you're intending to get drunk when you are at market, Megan, I really don't think there is much chance of you doing the same."

Our Da had been a drunkard; down the tavern every night, and liked the women that frequented there, too, by all accounts - in the days when there *was* a tavern, down beyond the mill, before everyone converted to the Chapel. It was after Da died that Mam converted. Morgan and I stood, hand in hand, on the river's edge, sobbing with fright as the preacher pushed Mam under the water. We didn't know she was being baptized, we thought he was drowning her. When she clambered out of the river with the water pouring from her hair and clothing, we ran to her, crying, but she looked right through us and beyond us, her eyes gleaming.

From that day forward, her bible became her constant companion, and fear of hell's fires became a constant in our lives. In that bible, Mam found all the reassurance she needed that our Da was suffering in the hereafter for all the humiliations he had heaped upon her. There, she found confirmation that all those who crossed her in this life would be punished by God. There, she found a lifetime's source of threats which she could use to terrorize and keep us in check.

I urged the pony forward, as I had seen Morgan do a thousand times, and put my faith in Morgan's judgment that I would not overturn the cart. When we reached that part of the track where our Da had gone over, I curled my toes and gritted my teeth, but refused to hand over the reins.

Morgan let me drive the cart along the narrow country lane which wound through the valley, and soon I was urging the pony into a full trot and feeling as free as the wind that blew through my hair.

"Oh, I love it!" I said, laughing.

"Aye, well, don't go mad," he scolded, but he was laughing too. "I'll teach you how to turn her, tomorrow, and then you're away to make us our fortune!"

A few days later, and I was riding along the lanes towards market, enjoying the sound of birdsong and the cold breeze playing on my face and hair, and remembering our long ago trips to market. I loosened the reins and the pony picked up speed, trotting along, with her mane rippling in the breeze.

"We're off to market, pony!" I shouted to her, and I felt a lightening of my spirit for the first time since Eli had left.

The pony tossed her head as if she understood, and I no longer felt I was on this adventure alone, we were venturing out together. I sat back in my seat. I began to take notice of the scenery which unfolded before me, scenery I had not seen since I was a girl. It was a bright and crisp winter's morning, the ground white with frost. The sky overhead was the palest blue, with a few thin, wispy clouds. Occasionally, light flurries of snow dusted the stone walls and grass verges.

The narrow lane twisted and turned through the countryside. The winter sun was low in the sky, struggling to rise above the naked trees which were like black fingers stretched against the pale yellow-grey of the early light. The icy air stings my face and nostrils, but my body is cosily wrapped in a hooded cloak which Morgan and I once fashioned from sheepskins, its seams roughly stitched together with twine.

We passed through whitewashed farmsteads where hens scattered on our approach. Ganders chased after us, hissing, their long necks extended, and ducks slithered atop icy ponds. Farmers and their families were already out and going about their chores. Their breaths making clouds in the air, they pause to wave to me. I wave back, smiling and proud; an independent young woman, off to market all on her own. I will show that Eli Jenkins, I say to myself. If he comes back, with his pretty wife, he won't find me brooding over him. He will find me managing very well without him.

An hour later, I passed a milestone where the road forked, which told me I was just two miles from my destination. Soon, I was approaching the little town of Dinasfraint and saw that, though I had set out at the first light of dawn, there were many arrived before me. The verge of the road approaching town was lined on both sides with ponies and carts. I pulled my pony to a halt alongside. I had to break the ice in a stone water trough so she could drink. Then I tethered her to a post and pulled a nosebag of oats over her head. From there, I carried my baskets of cheeses down to the market square and stood dithering over where to set out my wares amongst the traders already there. I chose a small area between a wizened, old gentleman selling willow baskets and a woman, who stood with her two daughters, knitting and selling stockings.

I laid a fresh linen cloth on the ground and displayed my cheeses on this. I felt self-conscious as I worked under the watchful gaze of my neighbours. When I finally stood up, to await my hoped for customers, the stocking knitter and her daughters stepped up to introduce themselves.

"I'm Myfanwy and these here are my daughters, Blod and Elenid," the mother said, without pausing in her knitting but nodding at the two girls who also carried on knitting while nodding and smiling at me.

Blod and Elenid were the spit of their Mam with her perfect round of a face, deep red cheeks and twinkling blue eyes. They all bore mischievous expressions, as though they knew some juicy piece of gossip which they were bursting to share. As I got to know them, over the months to come, I discovered this was often, in fact, the case.

"We haven't seen your face at market before. Come a long way, have you?"

I introduced myself, and told her where I came from, and explained I had not been to market since I was just a girl.

"Well then, you must explore before you go home," Myfanway said. "And I'll tell you who is who. I've been coming so long, I know them all, I do."

Myfanwy nudged me with her elbow and nodded toward my space.

"You've got your first customer!" she said with a wink and I took up my place once more, my heart racing in anticipation of making my first bit of money.

My customer was a woman of about my age, but smartly dressed. I eyed her clothes while she inspected my cheese. Not a patch or worn hem on her skirts, I noticed, and wondered if my rival for Eli's affection dressed like this. No make-do shawl or sheepskin cape for her but a long cloak of fine worsted.

"I'll have this one," she said, holding a large round cheese in one gloved hand and passing a handful of coins to me with the other.

Flustered, I counted the coins in my hand, recalling how much Morgan had told me to charge.

"I shan't pay a penny more. You can take it or leave it," the woman said.

"I'll take it," I said, quickly.

She had paid me quite a bit more than Morgan had expected I would get.

I watched her place her cheese in her basket and stroll off to browse the other stalls with a dignified, almost haughty air. That's just how she'll be, I thought, returning once again to the subject which dominated my waking thoughts. Are you going to think of nothing else? I admonished myself. My own thoughts seemed to have become as great a torment to me as Mam's words.

"She's a good payer, that one. You'll be laughing if she comes back to you regular, which she will if she likes what you're selling. Only the best for her, mind. Wealthy cattle-trader's wife, she is. Wouldn't be seen dead and buried in my stockings, mores the pity!" Myfanwy said with an exaggerated sigh, making me laugh.

"I'm sure that's not true!" I said.

"Oh it is, I'm afraid. I don't fool myself, do I girls? I know our stockings won't make the grade for the likes of that one. She bought one pair, when she first came to market, and never stopped at my stall since."

Before much time had passed, the little market square was a bustling throng and there was no more time to talk as there was a constant stream of people strolling by. Myfanwy's customers were mostly single men, young or old, she explained to me later, "them who hasn't a woman at home to knit for them", she said. Whereas those who stopped at my stall, to look or to buy, were generally better dressed than the average.

"Not poor people, like us, who has to make our own or go without," she explained.

Within an hour or so, my leather purse was half full and I had sold more than half the cheeses I had brought with me.

"You'll be sold out by mid-day. Then you and me will have a wander," Myfanwy said to me.

A short while later, a middle-aged gentleman approached my stall and asked to taste before he bought, taking a sharp knife from his pocket and cutting a slice of cheese for himself.

"I'll take two," he said. "and I'll take two every week so long as they're all like this."

I blushed with pride at the compliment, and blushed again when he paid me top price for them. He said he would buy butter from me too, if I brought some along, so long as it was of the same quality as my cheese.

Myfanwy sidled over as he left.

"Well done, girl! He's the owner of the coaching inn over the way! Those cheeses of yours must be good for him to say that!"

As Myfanwy had predicted, I sold my last cheese before the town clock struck twelve.

"I'll leave the girls to look after things and take you for a walkabout," Myfanwy said.

Standing in the middle of the square she pointed out various traders to me.

"That there is Rhys, the cobbler. He's deaf and dumb," she said, pointing to a young man who sat over a last, repairing people's boots and clogs.

"Born that way, he was, and his parents both dead now. Must be an awful lonely life for him. The quiet! I know I do complain, about the noise my girls sometimes make, but I fear I should go mad if I never heard a thing."

"Then there's old Martha, the herbalist, or witch as some do call her. Call her what they like, she can cure just about anything with those potions of hers that she makes."

Martha sat on a low milking stool, amidst an array of small bottles and jars. Her aged face was swathed with wrinkled folds, out of which peered two small, brown, sunken eyes. She peered up at me, and nodded without speaking, when Myfanwy introduced us. Then she reached about her, her clawed and wrinkled hand fumbling, before finally alighting on what she searched for. Then she smiled at me and croaked.

"This be what you need."

It was a potion made from Heartsease, for mending broken hearts. I blushed to the roots of my hair while Myfanwy scolded Martha for having embarrassed me.

Martha shrugged her shoulders and said; "I was only saying the truth."

“Come on, Meg, don’t take any notice!” Myfanwy said, and steered me away with a hand on my elbow, into the path of a young woman carrying a basketful of brightly colored ribbons.

“This here is Eleri. How are you, girl? This is Megan. She’s come to sell cheese.”

Eleri was a sullen looking girl who looked at me sideways, her eyes slyly taking me in from head to toe. It was quite obvious she was not impressed by what she saw, though I did not think I was any more shabbily dressed than her. She did not deign to say hello to me, but spoke to Myfanwy, sighing and rolling her eyes in an exaggerated way.

“Mam’s in the family way again, and Da gave her a beating when she told him. As if it wasn’t him that put it there, she said. And I’ve sold next to nothing today, so he’ll be in a worse temper when I get home and he has no money for his beer.”

“Megan here will buy some ribbons off you, won’t you Meg? They’ll pretty up your hair, no end.”

I hesitated. Mam would have one of her fits if I came home with coloured ribbons in my hair. But I could wear them when I was at market, I thought, and she would never know.

“Blue! Blue would look lovely against the chestnut of your hair,” Myfanwy said, and I was persuaded.

“Here, take off that hat and I’ll tie them into your hair for you!”

I took off my hat, and stood patiently, while Myfanwy decked my hair.

"There! Now isn't she as pretty as a picture!" Myfanwy said to Eleri, who shrugged again and arched her eyebrows with disdain.

"Take no notice of her, either! She's a jealous one, she is!" Myfanwy said, when she had steered us out of earshot. "And no better than she should be, either, if you know what I mean."

I did not know what she meant, but did not have time to ask, as Myfanwy had stopped again and nodded towards a middle-aged woman, dressed all in black, who stood with baskets of linen for sale.

"She's one of them hellfire and brimstone, Baptist lot. Doesn't have anything to do with us. We're not good enough for the likes of her, even though we do sometimes go to church of a Sunday. Just look at the face on it, sour as the mix I put in my bread dough."

I looked at the woman who was Baptist, like me. It was a shock to hear one of my own described as one of those 'hellfire and brimstone', Baptist lot. I'd had no idea that was how other people thought of us. I could and should have said, well, actually Myfanwy, I'm Baptist too. But I instinctively remained silent, because I did not want Myfanwy and the rest to judge me as they judged this woman dressed in black. I wanted them to like me for who I was, not reject me, without knowing me, on grounds of my religion. To declare my religion with pride, because it was so much a part of the me I wanted them to like, did not enter my mind.

A fiddler struck up a tune then, and Myfanwy stopped to listen, clapping her hands and tapping her feet, a smile breaking out on her round face, creating dimples in her rosy cheeks. Mam had raised us to believe that music was the devil's work. I knew that Twm, Hillside cottage, had been a fiddler in his youth and that his fiddle had lain under his bed, gathering dust, since his conversion. As I listened to the strange music, and saw how it cheered everyone to hear it, I found my own feet tapping too. Then before I could object, Myfanwy took my arm in hers and reeled me, first this way, then that, with me stumbling over her feet, as well as my own.

"Anyone would think you'd never danced before!" she said, laughing at my clumsiness. I did not have the courage to tell her I was not allowed to dance, for fear she would think me strange.

"Oh! I've always been a hopeless dancer!" I say, and Myfanwy says she and the girls will show me how to improve.

Myfanwy continued her tour of the market place with me. She knew everybody, and a great deal about each of them. I met a woman who made traditional hats like those which most of us wore, but also the prettiest of bonnets, bedecked with flowers she had made from brightly coloured, felted wool. I lingered a long while, admiring these, and wishing I could own one for myself. Then there was the lace maker, a widow, who sat with a horsehair pillow on her lap, weaving intricate patterns like spider's webs, from threads which were wound onto fine, wooden bobbins. In a basket by her side, were lace trims for cuffs, and whole collars, which I yearned to wear.

"Her eyes are failing. The Lord only knows what she will do when she goes blind. She'll end up living on parish relief, or in the poor house, I expect," Myfanwy whispered to me, with her hand shading her mouth, as we passed on.

"My Blod has one of those! Her young man bought one for her," Myfanwy said, as we passed by a man carving love spoons.

"They'll be married soon. You ought to see them, like a pair of doves they are, cooing over each other."

I wondered if Eli had carved a love spoon for his new love. He never did carve one for me.

"I've told them to be careful, you know, until they are properly married. Martha has given Blod one of her potions, just in case she gets caught."

"Caught where?" I asked. So ignorant I was.

"In the family way, of course. But I'm sure it won't be needed. I've told Blod a trick or two to stop the babies from coming, until she has a ring on her finger. Because you never know, do you? They're in love now, but they might be out of love before long and decide not to get hitched."

I'm sure my shock must have shown in my face though I tried to conceal it. I could not quite believe what I was hearing. Myfanwy's ways were a world away from the ways I had been taught. I had liked her, the instant I met her, but I now discover she is a person I knew I should not keep company with. What she was speaking of was a sure road towards the hell fire and brimstone she'd spoken of earlier.

"We'll start packing up now, girls, there won't be any more customers today," Myfanwy said, as we arrived back at her stall.

Only a few late-comers now strolled around the square, looking but not buying. We said our goodbyes, and I made my way back to the pony and cart with my full purse of coins heavy against my side. I looked forward to telling Morgan that I would be able to sell as much cheese and butter as I could churn out. I smiled to myself as I walked along, thinking of his delight when he saw how much money I had made.

On the journey home, my thoughts dwelled on Myfanwy's revelation. It was as if I had stepped into another world for a day, a world as different as could be from the one I had grown up with; a world in which young women were not shunned or condemned for 'knowing' their young men before marriage; a world in which wronged young women would never be shamed and turned out, as they would be in our community; a world in which there was forgiveness, tolerance, kindness, yet a world that would be deemed 'ungodly' in my parish. I had discovered there were very different ways of living, and believing, from those which Mam had taught us to live by.

When I reached the turn up our track, I remembered the ribbons still tying up my hair, and stopped to remove them and hide them in my pocket. I wished my day out did not have to end. I wished I did not have to return home. As the pony pulled the cart up the hill, I found myself feeling something akin to dread.

It's not as bad as all that, I told myself, but I could not prevent my spirits from sinking. The contrast between how I had felt that day, and how I felt now, at the prospect of returning home to Mam, brought home to me the depth of my unhappiness. Perhaps that was why Mam never wanted to let me go; she didn't want me finding out how much I was missing, and how different my life might be.

When I entered the house and saw Mam's face, set rigid with disapproval of whatever she imagined I had been getting up to at market, it was Myfanwy's words which sprung to mind - 'sour as the mix I put in my bread dough'. Mam did not ask how my day had gone and I offered no information. I hope I never end up like you, I thought, as I went about preparing our supper and doing all those chores which Mam had chosen to ignore while I was gone.

While I worked, an idea blossomed in my mind. I thought that, seeing as I was expected to do all the work, while Mam sat there in her chair, and seeing as it was the fruits of my labours that were making us all this extra money, then surely I was entitled to some of it. That day, I had seen other women spending money, and for the first time in my life, I'd spent money from my own purse. And why shouldn't I have a little money of my own, when others clearly did?

When I had done the evening milking, I went in search of Morgan, to show him how much money I had made, and to broach the subject of my having some of it. I found him in the stable, sitting by the light of the lantern, sharpening and oiling his scythe in readiness for the next season.

"Well, this will more than cover the rise in rent," he said, his face lighting up.

"And I could have sold that amount, twice over."

"I said that dairy of yours was a gold mine, didn't I?"

"Aye, you did. And I was thinking, it's only fair, seeing as it's me that puts all the work into it, and it's me who will have the extra to do now we're selling, well, I think that some of that money should go to me."

"What in God's name would you be wanting with money?" he said, with a look of horror on his face.

"There's plenty of women have money of their own. I saw them in the market. It's really not so unusual, you know."

"But what would you want with it?"

"That's for me to know. It's none of your business."

"Well if you can't even think what you want it for, I won't even consider letting you have any."

"Won't consider letting me? I made that money, not you!" I snapped at him, my anger rising at the cheek of him talking to me like Mam did.

"And I make the money on the rest of the farm. You don't hear me saying; you can't eat the food on the table because it was me that earned it!" he says, wiping the blade of his scythe with an oiled rag.

"I do my share. Inside and outside of the dairy! And if you can't let me have one little bit of that money I earned, for myself, then go hire yourself a dairymaid and see how much profit you have left then!"

I was hot with temper. No one, not even our Mam, could get my gander up like Morgan when he tried to lord it over me.

"Now then, Meg, there's no need to talk like that. I'm sure we can come to some arrangement," he said. "So long as you spend it wisely, mind."

"It is none of your business what I spend it on," I said.

"Why won't you tell me what you want it for? I'm sure if you were to ask Mam…"

"I don't want to have to ask her for what I want. Besides, you know very well, she always says no to any request of mine, while if you want something from market, it's of course Morgan, here you are Morgan. "

"That's different. When I want something, it's for the farm. I had plans for any that was spare, myself."

"Oh. I'll wager you did! I'm not asking for all of it. I'm only asking for a small share."

"But what for?"

"All right then. I'll tell you. But only if you promise me you will let me have a share."

"I promise."

"Right. Ever since Eli left…"

"Oh, Eli!" he says, rolling his eyes to the rafters of the stable.

"Aye! Eli! Ever since Eli left, all I have heard from our Mam is how he has met this beautiful, young woman over there, how smartly dressed she is, and how it won't be long before he is back with her on his arm as his wife. All I want is not to be shown up. I want him to see I can be smart too, without him. The next time the travelling dressmaker calls, I want to be able to pay her to make me something that will show him just that. So when he comes back to show off…"

Morgan interrupts "…I had no idea! He's met someone else? He didn't waste much time, did he? Oh, Meg! I'm sorry. No, you're quite right. We'll show him all right. You take what you need, just so long as you leave me enough, mind."

"You mean it?"

I never imagined he would understand; my infuriating, wonderful brother.

"Aye. We won't have him showing you up. I can hardly believe it, you know. What a thing to do to you. I thought he was better than that."

"Thank you, Morgan," I said, feeling again as though I were flying.

"I don't know how you're going to persuade our Mam, though," he said, bringing me sharply down to earth.

I am silent for a moment. "What she doesn't know can't hurt her," I said, looking him right in the eye, willing him to agree.

"Be it on your head, then, if she finds out. I don't know anything about it."

Mam would find out soon enough, when the travelling dressmaker called again and I placed an order with her. She could say what she liked, I wasn't about to let her stop me. As long as it was something sensible, like a smart winter cloak to wear to chapel, she would not be able to find any reasonable grounds for objection. She wouldn't be able to taunt me about how smart Eli's young woman was, when I was a match for her. I could well imagine the lecture Mam would give me, about how 'pride comes before a fall'. What I didn't imagine, was that she would be proved so very right.

Chapter 5

Morgan

Megan is like a runaway horse with her plans for marrying Eli. My only hope of reining her in is to tell her how her daughter is living, but I have not yet found the courage. I have wondered if it would be better to broach the subject with Eli himself, reason with him, man to man. It's not like Megan is the only eligible woman in the parish. He would soon find another. I have not found the courage to do that either. Meanwhile, Megan charges on with her plans for me, and due to my own procrastination, I fear I am being hurtled along into a future that is not of my own choosing.

It is but two days after Megan tells me I am to get a housekeeper, and here comes Beulah with the grand sum of her belongings tied up in a shawl slung over her shoulder. The weather has improved, so I'm in the middle of rounding up a small flock of sheep and lambs, to take up to the top hill. I pause to watch Beulah coming up the track. I should have offered to go fetch her in the cart but that would have given Megan the wrong idea. She'd think I was coming round to the idea of having Beulah here.

Beulah is a tall, big jawed girl with broad hips. The way they sway from side to side puts me in mind of our carthorse. If she's no good in the house, maybe I could persuade her to pull the plough. A big strong girl like her should be more help on the farm than Megan, at any rate.

I'll want to get my money's worth, if I'm going to have to pay her for what Megan does for nothing. Though, by the way she is puffing coming up the track, I'd say she's not used to much in the way of physical work.

I have been counting the cost these past few days. The way I see it, I'm always paying the price for Megan. Megan doesn't seem to have thought how her marriage is going to cost me, in the form of having to pay Beulah. That's on top of what I'm already paying for Megan's mistake, while Megan swans off and marries one of the wealthiest farmers around without paying a penny. Seems to me, she's playing me for a fool.

As for her beloved Eli – everyone makes a big thing of how he owns his own land, like that makes him better than the rest of us. They choose to forget how his grandfather came by it. He won it from our landlord's grandfather, over a bet on some race between their horses. Or was it that Eli's grandfather bet he could outrun the landlord's horse, and won? I can't remember the details exactly. But isn't gambling meant to be a sin? So doesn't that mean Wildwater is ill gotten gains?

Beulah holds her skirts in her hands, to keep them from trailing in the mud churned up by the recent rain. It's a bright, late-April day with a nice breeze blowing, a few clouds scudding overhead, their shadows chasing across the hills. It's not what I'd call warm, but Beulah takes off her bonnet and wipes the sweat from her brow with the edge of her shawl. Her hair has the colour and sheen of crow feathers and it gleams in the sunlight.

I watch as she leans forward into the hill, climbing the last stretch of our track. Her skirts bunched in one hand, she fans her face with the bonnet, and juts out her bottom lip, directing her breath upwards to cool her face. When she reaches the gate, she stops to lean on it and catch her breath, before walking the last stretch to the house.

"Hullo, Morgan!" She bellows across the yard when she sees me, and waves her bonnet, her big grin as wide as the barn door.

I nod and raise my hand, seeing as I'll have to be nice to her, unless something happens to prevent my impending doom. Perhaps Eli will fall off his horse and break his neck. Or our Mam will return from the dead to give Megan what for. Maybe Megan will take pity on me and change her mind. Perhaps hell will freeze over.

When I go in the house at mealtime, they are clucking away to each other about everything and nothing. When women get together, they become as noisy as a gaggle of geese. The only breaks in their conversation come when Beulah pauses to ask where she will find the plates and Megan pauses to answer. Then they're off again. Cluck, cluck, cluck.

Beulah is put to sleep in Megan's room, because Beulah 'doesn't want to sleep in a recently dead person's room, no disrespect intended'. She's a nice enough girl, but if she slept in the barn it would not be far enough. She snores so badly that I'd be forgiven for thinking the pigs have broken out of their sty in the night and trotted right up the stairs. To be fair, the woman has a streaming cold, so perhaps, and I do pray this, her snoring is a temporary condition.

Beulah was the grand-niece to an old woman who once lived down the valley, near the ruin where we played as children. Suzzanah, the old woman's name was. Nobody could say exactly how old she was, for there was not one person left alive who knew when she was born. She'd be seen walking about the place, leaning heavily on her stick, her back so stooped that her chin was about waist level. Her face was as deeply carved by time as the bark of an old oak tree. Never married, she lived alone in a tumbledown cottage sitting in a couple of acres of land. Suzannah is long dead, and nothing but a moss-covered heap of stones is left of the cottage now.

Suzannah kept a goat for milk, a few chickens for eggs, and a couple of sheep for wool. She survived by knitting stockings from the wool of those sheep. A hair shirt would be less torture to wear, and the stockings did not last a season, but all of us neighbours would swap some bread flour from our store for a pair of them, when Suzannah brought them to our door. It kept the old woman in bread, and meant she never had to suffer the indignity of accepting parish relief.

When Suzzanah got so frail she couldn't walk the hills anymore, Beulah would go there from the village to help her out, and go door-to-door for her with the stockings. Beulah was just a child then, but her grand-aunt had taught her to knit, and you'd see Beulah, walking the lanes and footpaths, knitting as she walked. Twenty years on and Beulah is still knitting. If her hands aren't busy at something else, she's knitting. She says it comes as easy as breathing.

So Beulah is not a complete stranger, but I would never have thought that, all these years later, I'd be living under the same roof as her. She recently lost her husband, when they hadn't been married more than three months.

"Didn't stay alive long enough to make me a baby to cwtch," I hear Beulah tell Megan, during one of their 'not for men's ears' conversations, out in the scullery. Megan speaks in loud whispers but Beulah couldn't keep her voice down if she tried. It is a loud, clattering thing, like cart wheels over cobblestones. I couldn't help but overhear if I'd been over in the barn, let alone sat here in the next room, whittling by the fire.

"Dropped down dead on his way out of the door, going off to work. One minute he is saying goodbye, the next he's lying at my feet, as dead as that door post. Terrible shock it was."

I hear Megan click her tongue.

"And do you know what?"

"No. What?" Megan says.

"After William died, his mother tells me his father did the very same thing. Though his father did stay around long enough to father William, which was one good thing his mother could say for him. I wish someone had told me before I married William. I'd have thought twice about saying yes if I'd known he was going to go and die on me."

"You don't mean that, Beulah. Better to have been married a short time than never have married him at all, surely?"

"No indeed, I'm not sure about that. Though, I suppose I made the last few months of his life happy ones. For he was terrible happy when I agreed to marry him, and a more cheerful soul I could not have wished to meet. But I would have liked one child to show for it. I would have liked that, at least. Didn't leave me so much as a pot to piss in. Oh! Do excuse my language!"

There is a prolonged silence and I have to stifle a laugh. What I would give, to have seen Megan's face on hearing Beulah swear. One thing I'll say for Beulah, she's plain speaking, though I don't know how she will go down with the neighbours' wives.

"Well, it's not too late to marry again! Look at me!" Megan says.

"Aye, well, but you're made to be a rich farmer's wife. Not like me. A maid is all I'll ever be now. To tell you the honest truth, I only said yes to William because I thought that, if I didn't, I'd end up like my grand aunt Suzannah."

"Don't be daft! Beulah! You're a good looking woman still! I can't believe William is the only one to have asked you."

I roll my eyes at the ceiling. Why women have to flatter each other so is beyond me.

"Well, I'll tell you the truth. There was another, and I'm not saying his name, for he's married to another now, and not a million miles from here. And he was a farmer's son, and all. He was very sweet on me, and I on him. But I was looking after Mam and Da at the time and couldn't leave them. And he couldn't wait. So that was the end of that. But never mind. It wasn't meant to be."

"Oh, Beulah. What a shame!" I hear our Megan say, in a hushed 'poor you' voice, as if something a hundred times worse hadn't happened to herself.

"Oh, well. Can't be helped. I'll be alright. This job is a godsend, I have to say that. I was to be turned out of our cottage next week. With no William's wage coming in, I couldn't afford the rent. I didn't know where I was going to go. I've got a cousin over the border, but I don't suppose she'd have been over the moon to see me, turning up at her door without a penny. She's got six children and they struggle to make ends meet as it is. I'm very grateful to you for asking me, Megan, indeed I am."

"I'm only too thankful you accepted the post. Goodness knows how poor Morgan would have managed without you."

I take note that Megan doesn't say "I would have had to postpone my marriage if you had said no". She was going to leave me high and dry, whether Beulah had accepted or not. That's nice that is.

"You never know….." I hear Megan say, and then she whispers something to Beulah which makes Beulah whoop with laughter. I've only got to hear that woman laugh and I find myself wanting to laugh too.

"Oh, no, stop it! Megan! Honestly! Though I have to say I wouldn't say no if asked!"

Another whoop of laughter, then the both of them in fits. I imagine they must be doubled over, holding their sides.

When they've calmed down, they come back in the kitchen, dabbing at their still mirthful eyes with their pinafores. Their faces break into smiles when they look at me. I frown at them, puzzled. Then they're off laughing again, tears running down their faces.

"Stop it!" Beulah is squawking at Megan, but Megan laughs all the harder.

They're so weak they have to sit down, with much sighing and oohing, by the time they have laughed themselves out. I still don't know what it was all about. Women are beyond my understanding, sometimes, most of the time, in fact.

Megan says Beulah is like a breeze of spring air. Myself, I would liken her more to a gale blowing through the house. Though, I have to admit, there's been more laughter in this house since Beulah arrived than there was in all the years before. Not that I let either of them know I find Beulah in the least bit amusing. I like Beulah well enough; I just don't want to live on my own with her.

Megan is so happy having Beulah around, I wonder if she might change her mind about Eli and stick around. I thought I might suggest something along those lines. I know Megan has found all the work too hard over the years. With Beulah's help, life would be a lot easier on Megan. If Megan were to start selling her cheese at market again, that would pay Beulah's wages. Though, it would be on the understanding that Megan would have to behave herself this time round.

I wait until Beulah walks to the village, to see an old friend, and Megan and I are on our own, up on the top hill, gathering peat for next winter so it has the summer long to dry out. I cut, Megan carries and stacks. We're almost done when I broach the subject with her.

"Don't be daft, Morgan! What did you think I would say to Eli? I'm sorry, Eli, I've changed my mind, I want to live with Beulah instead?" Megan says, when I suggest my idea to her.

I drive the long spade deep into the peat and cut another wedge.

"Well, aye, you could say something along those lines. Why not? You and Beulah are getting along so well. And just think how much easier your life will be, with her to help."

"You've never been in love, have you Morgan? I want to marry Eli more than anything else in this world. I like Beulah a lot, don't get me wrong, but she's no substitute for Eli."

Megan carries a turf and, with a lunge, throws it onto the cart.

I pause for breath and lean on my spade.

"I don't know what you want to go marrying him for. Listen! Megan! I wondered if you'd thought any more, changed your mind, perhaps, about what I said, about the little one coming home."

I regret bringing it up as soon as I see the stricken look on her face. You would think I'd slapped her.

"I'm sorry. Forget I mentioned it," I say, seeing her fighting to keep control of her emotions.

I go back to the job in hand, but Megan continues to stand where she is, the wind snatching at the tendrils of hair that have escaped from her bonnet. She is silent for some time before she speaks.

"Is this how it's going to be from now on? Are you going to go on torturing me with reminders, every chance you get? Why won't you let go of it? I've told you my feelings on the subject. Let that be an end to …"

She pauses, like she is choking on the words, and tears fill her eyes. Then she gives a little 'how stupid it all is' laugh.

"…… and how pointless it would be anyway. The whole reason she was stolen from me was to save me from ruin. If she were to return here now, I would face the ruin our mother so feared. It would mean that all the pain of losing her would have been for nothing. And that, let me tell you, Morgan Jones, I truly could not bear. My daughter is gone but I have carried her in my heart since the day I lost her. That is where she must stay. All that matters to me now is that she is being cared for."

I retreat to the task of cutting the peat, wondering how I'm going to tell her, before it is too late, exactly how her daughter is living.

Chapter 6

Megan

How I loved those trips to market and watching my small hoard of savings grow. Each week, I would return and hand over the bulk to Morgan, while keeping a little aside for myself. I hid it behind a loose stone in the wall of the barn, safe from Mam's eyes, should she go prying in my room. I felt something akin to happiness, for the first time since Eli left, and all because I was carving a small piece of my life for my own, and reaping the rewards of my own labours. It was a dream I had never dared wish for. When I thought of Eli, it was with defiance. I looked forward to seeing him again, so he would find me utterly changed from the peasant girl he had abandoned.

It was Mam's own cruelty that had set me free. I no longer felt I had to oblige or appease her in everything. Her cruelty had negated any debt I had felt I owed her for my existence. I pulled away from her, rebelled against her constraints, until there seemed nothing she could do to prevent me from having a life of my own. I made many friends in the marketplace, and Myfanwy and her girls taught me how to dance reels to the fiddler's music. If Eli could see me now, or if Mam could see me now, I'd think, as I reeled this way and that to the music, knowing Mam would have one of her fits if she found out.

When spring arrived early, with a glorious spell in late February, I delighted in the primroses and violets coming into bloom alongside the lanes. The market became busier than ever, the spring weather bringing people out in crowds. Flower sellers arrived, with baskets full of small posies of the same flowers I admired along the verges. I felt full of life and energy as never before, and everywhere around me, I saw others feeling that same surge of life and hope that comes with every spring. The worst of winter was behind us and there was the whole spring and summer to look forward to.

Other young ladies shed their winter cloaks and stepped out in pretty spring frocks and shawls, while I had only my grey serge dress to wear. It prompted Myfanwy and her daughters to comment upon how drab I looked, and 'didn't I have something prettier to wear than that old thing I'd been wearing the whole winter long?'

The following week they had a present to give me; a dress which both Blod and Elenid had outgrown.

"You're so small, we were sure it would fit you." Myfanwy said.

"I couldn't possibly accept it," I said, knowing that if Mam saw me in it, my trips to market would come to a swift end.

"Don't be so daft! Try it on when you get home. It might need a bit of adjustment, mind. But it's in good condition. Blod and Elenid look after their clothes, they do."

Myfanwy held the dress up against me, remarking on how the colour suited me. It was a shade of sky-blue, with an all-over pattern of small sprigs of cream flowers.

"It is lovely!" I said wistfully, fingering the little gathers around the waist.

"There! It's yours!" Myfanwy said, folding the dress into a bundle which she pressed into my arms.

I thanked them all, profusely. I could not begin to explain to them that Mam would not allow me to come to market dressed in it – not without revealing that we were 'those hell-fire and brimstone, Baptist lot' they so despised. Over the months of our growing friendship, I had revealed to them nothing about it. I had, though, told them how Eli had jilted me, and fallen for another, and that my life at home was 'hard'. I think they must have thought me even more impoverished than they, that they felt they had to provide me with something 'decent' to wear to market. I would have to wear the dress they had given me, or risk offending them.

From then on, I pulled up the pony and cart each week, to change into the dress behind a stone wall, and changed back again on the way home. It fitted me like a glove, and I felt transformed from the dowdy woman I was at home. Myfanwy, Blod and Elenid made a big fuss when they saw me in it, making me blush with pride.

"Isn't she as pretty as a picture in it?!" Myfanwy said, twirling me round in a circle.

"Oh, that does suit you, that do!" said Blod, standing back with hands on hips to appraise me.

"You'll be turning a few heads now!" Elenid told me, grinning from ear to ear.

How they cheered me, my friends, with their laughter and chatter and idle gossip. Every week, there would be some little thing they would do or say that would make me smile whenever I thought of it. Their cheerful company would lift me up and carry me from one week to the next. Hard work is so much easier when it is done with a cheerful heart. The aches and pains, that had plagued my joints from youth, did not go away but did cease to torment me during all my working hours. Even Mam's dissatisfaction, with all that I was and did, had not the power it once had to make me quietly despair. If only life had carried on like that. But, oh! Fool that I was! I let my head be turned and began to think that my new found freedom was only part of the dream I could have.

I'd woken, following a dream in which Eli had returned for me. It near broke my heart to wake and find it was nothing but that – a dream. My heartache quickly turned to defiance. What I would give to be able to tell him of the transformation in my life since he had left, and show him how happy I could be without him. I was so impatient to do so, I walked over to Wildwater farm, with some vague hope that he would be there on one of his visits home.

It was a bright spring morning and the skylarks had arrived. Their joyous warbling soon dispelled my gloom and filled me with delight. There was not a cloud in the sky, and the sun was so warm it felt more like a day in May. The grass and lichens on the heath were dry and crisp underfoot, and I noticed wild strawberry flowers already blooming amid the crevices of rocks. Looking down on the woods in the valley below, I could see a tree here and there beginning to leaf, and hawthorns and hazels beginning to green along the lanes.

Morgan had been delighting in the perfect weather for his young lambs. I stopped to watch a group of them playing 'chase', like children. They raced each other as far as an outcrop of rock, then stopped as if to confer, before turning and racing back again. There was an obvious leader, and one who always got left behind the rest, and another who didn't want to race at all, too overcome with the desire to leap and spring, instead. Their antics made me laugh out loud, but as quickly filled me with longing regret for the children I would not now have.

As I descended the hill, I passed by the field of wild daffodils, where Morgan and I would play as children. The flowers were just coming into bloom, their bright, yellow trumpets dazzling in the sunshine. I resisted the urge to pick them; knowing Mam would not allow them in the house anyway, claiming it was bad luck. I carried on down the hill, alongside the tumbling mountain spring. My footsteps crunched the skeletons of the winter's leaves, and the breeze groaned through the bare treetops as I passed through Eli's oak wood.

We used to climb the trees here, Eli, Morgan and me, a long time ago, when we were children still, unburdened by the chores and duties which were waiting to abruptly end our childhoods. Da was still alive then, and I remember him and Mam out in the fields from dawn to dusk, working the land together, and in all weathers.

Mam was a strong woman in those days. There was nothing she couldn't turn her hand to. She could plough a field as well as any man, certainly better than Da when he was too hung over. Though she could barely put one foot in front of the other for a day or two after, she'd still go and do it all again the next year. It all took its toll, eventually, and then Morgan and I had to take over. Could she not see it was doing for me, just as it did for her?

Morgan and I would be tucked up in our beds when the sun went down and Da went to slake his thirst down in the tavern. We slumbered, while Mam sat alone by the fire until the early hours, waiting for him to stumble through the door. We'd wake up then, and lie there stiff as broom handles, staring into the peat-black darkness, hardly breathing, and straining to hear what was said.

It would always begin with Da telling Mam about some woman down in the tavern; how this one was a real beauty, or that one was a 'cut above the rest'. Then Mam would start crying, and he would start shouting, asking what in hell was the matter with her now? Couldn't he come home without having to look at her snivelling face? And one of these days, if she wasn't careful, he wouldn't come home at all. He was true to his word in that.

Da was kind to me and Morgan, though. I do believe he loved us, for all his threats of leaving. He would always have time to play with us; chase, or hide and seek, that sort of thing, or he'd whittle us some toy to play with. Mam would come in from doing some work or other, and start laying into him, about how he'd be a lot more use out working on the farm. Once, I remember, he whittled a whistle for Morgan which drove Mam to distraction until she threw it on the fire.

Mam didn't shed one tear at his passing. As soon as he was in the ground, she marched off down to meet the preacher, at the new chapel that had just been built by our newly converted neighbours. I want to be baptized, she told him. While Da was alive we didn't set foot in church or chapel, except for the occasional wedding or funeral. Now it was chapel three times on a Sunday, never mind that it was a three mile walk, there and back. And our evenings were spent listening to Mam reading from her precious bible, telling us of all the human sins that would see us burn in the fires of hell.

I could hear the roar of the Wildwater river, long before Wildwater farm came into view. The violent power of it, as it surged down from the mountains, had always struck fear in me, whenever I encountered it. I followed the path alongside it, and was relieved as the path took me away from the river and up towards the farmhouse. Eli's home seemed unchanged at first. The whitewashed walls still dazzled in the sunlight, and daffodils were blooming in the orchard. But as I got nearer, I sensed the air of emptiness about it. Without human habitation, it was reduced to a lifeless shell. It was silent as the grave; the only sounds to be heard were the birdsong and, from here, the roar of the Wildwater seemed no louder than wind sailing through the trees.

So many shearing suppers we'd come to here, over the years. Grand affairs they were, too, when Eli's parents were alive. Eli had been an only and late child. He'd hardly grown into a man before both his parents died within six months of each other, leaving him to run the place alone, until some day in our future when we had been meant to marry.

I wiped the dust from a window and peered into what had been the kitchen, when Eli was here. I was surprised to see there was very little furniture within; a table, one chair and a small bed against the back wall. It was this sight, more than anything, which brought home to me the reality that Eli was gone for good.

"Hello!" said a voice, and I whirled around to find a young man had appeared on the path behind me, as if he had dropped like a skylark out of the sky.

"Can I help?" he asked, curtly, clearly irritated by my intrusion.

"No! I was ..I just ..a friend of mine used to live here …it doesn't matter," I stammered, his sudden appearance having startled and unsettled me.

"He's gone to his Uncle's farm," he said.

"I know. I just came …for old time's sake."

"I've seen you before," he said, "in the market at Dinasfraint. At last I get to meet you, Megan Jones."

He reaches out to shake my hand but holds it a little too long, so I have to pull away. This unsettled me further, as did the fact that he appeared to know who I was, while he was a total stranger to me.

"How do you know my name?" I ask, pulling my shawl closer around me.

"It's my business to know everyone's name. I'm Eli's new manager. I'm taking care of the place for him."

"And you're living here?"

"That's right. Iago's my name and I'm very pleased to make your acquaintance."

He makes a funny little bow and grins at me, his dark eyes twinkling with mischief. I try not to smile.

"And I yours, but I must go, I'm expected home."

I turn to hurry down the path, and I hear him call after me.

"I'd like to ride home with you next market day, Megan Jones!"

I do not turn round and keep on walking but I cannot stop smiling. He was so handsome! A head of brown curls any woman would yearn for, and that smile of his that could melt your heart. And he wanted to ride home with me!

The next time I saw him was indeed at market. He came along with his mischievous grin and asked to buy some of my butter and eggs. I blushed the moment I saw him, and my hand trembled as I handed over his change.

"Well! You're a dark horse, I must say," Myfanwy said as he walked away. "Who is he?"

"His name's Iago. I met him for the first time the other day," I said, watching him weaving his way through the crowd until he disappeared from my sight, leaving me wishing he had stayed longer.

"Well, he's taken a fancy to you, girl," she said, with a knowing wink.

"Don't talk daft," I say, grinning, as if I did not know it for myself.

"He'll be asking to court you before the month is out. I know a smitten man when I see one."

A couple more customers came along then, but my mind was elsewhere as I served them. I dared not hope that Myfanwy was right, but hope was rising despite me, making my heart beat faster and trying to make me smile.

"All I can say is," Martha carried on, as my customers walked away, "if only I had my youth again, I'd follow my heart, I would. Me and my late husband, now, we got along well enough, you know, but he wasn't my first love, so to speak. There was one afore him who, to this day, I will always regret not following. But there we are, too late now. He married someone else. He's dead and all now."

"I've only just met this man and you're talking about love and marriage!" I say.

"This one is the one for you, I'm telling you. I feel it in my bones. If you don't believe me, let's go and ask old Martha."

"No! No. No need," I say, suddenly embarrassed by the turn our conversation was taking.

If I had consulted Martha, who can say? Would she have forewarned me? And if she had, would I have heeded her warning? If I were given my time again, I would run like the wind from Iago, but back then I had not the wisdom of hindsight.

Iago was walking the road when I made my way home. Later, he told me he had purposely arranged a lift to market rather than take himself there, so he could ask a lift home of me. He waved as I approached, and I pulled up the pony and cart to a halt beside him. I remember him sitting beside me, talking away as if he'd known me forever, his presence filling all my senses. He sat with his arm stretched out across the back of my seat, so tantalizingly near, I could almost feel the warmth of his hand near my back. Each time I sneaked a glance at him, it was to find him gazing at me in a way no man had looked at me before.

So began our courtship. He would be waiting for me, each Friday, when I made my way home from market. I ceased to tarry and chat with the others after my wares were sold; claiming a mountain of chores awaited me when I got home, so that I could get away earlier and thus spend more time with Iago. I was the light in his life, he said, wished we could spend more time together. He was the whole light of mine. I went about my daily work with a lightness of step, and found myself singing as I worked. I had not known just how dull my days had been before he entered my life.

"What are you so happy about?" Mam asked, as if my happiness offended her.

It astonished and delighted me to be the object of Iago's attraction and admiration. In his company, I felt special in a way I had never felt before. As the weeks went by, he filled my waking thoughts, and the waiting to see him again seemed interminable. I had known Eli since I was a child and though I had loved him, it was never thrilling like this. Each time I saw Iago waiting there, for *me*, my heart would race.

Then, after a few weeks, Iago was not waiting for me as I drove the cart home. I felt bewildered and bereft, as a child would feel when a long anticipated birthday gift is snatched from the outstretched hand. I waited so long, the sun was going down before I would accept he was not going to come.

His absence evoked a dread in me that I would not see him again. How could I ever return to my life, as it had been, without him? He was funny, clever, amusing, and in me he saw qualities that nobody else had noticed. He made me feel gloriously alive and wanted. That week, following his absence, the minutes stretched before me like days, and the days seemed like years of waiting and hoping he would be there the following week. Please let him be there, please let him be there, I beseeched the sky as I rode along the lane from market.

When I saw him standing there, with his cheeky grin, my face broke out in a smile while tears sprang to my eyes.

"Where were you? I've been so worried!" I scolded him as he climbed up beside me.

"You're not cross with me, are you? I was held up elsewhere on business. Did you miss me, then?" he says, with that grin of his.

I shrugged. "A little. I didn't know what had happened to you, that is all. I was worried."

"I couldn't get word to you, could I? Not without risking your Mam, or your brother, coming after me with a loaded gun."

I flicked the pony's reins and she broke into a trot. During our conversations, I had explained to Iago how it was best if Mam didn't know we were seeing each other, because she would not approve, and how Eli had gone off without me because he wasn't prepared to wait interminably for the day when I would be free to marry.

"I was thinking this past week, I don't know if there's any point in us going on seeing each other," Iago said. "It'll never come to anything. I can't see you leaving your Mam for the likes of me."

Just a moment ago, my spirits were soaring at the sight of him returned to me. Now, I felt my whole being about to fall to the earth with a crash, as he carried on speaking, oblivious to the effect his words were having on me.

"I'm not getting any younger. I'd like to settle down and marry. Have a few kids running around the place. I'm too old to be content with a cart-ride once a week," he carries on, leaning back in his seat and looking ahead, seemingly oblivious to the panic his words are evoking in me.

It was happening again. Mam's needs coming in between me and love, marriage, children, *happiness*.

"You're wrong," I say, pulling the pony to a halt. "I'll never let Mam stand between me and what I want, never again. She can find herself a housemaid to look after her and Morgan."

"And what is it you want, Megan Jones?" he asks, cupping my chin in his hand and turning my face towards his.

"Same as you it sounds like."

I smile and swallow hard. Ask me, just ask me and I will follow wherever you want to lead me, I think.

"Marriage? Children?" He lets go of my chin and strokes my hair. "Love?"

I nod, and a solitary tear wells up and trickles down my cheek. He leans forward and kisses the tear away. Another wells up and he kisses that too. He kisses my eyes, my nose, my cheek, my brow and then he kisses my mouth, and I think I shall drown in the bliss of it. Then he reaches his arms around me and envelops me, holding me like I've never been held before, holding me in such a way that I feel I need never fear falling, for he will always be there to keep me soaring.

When we reach the turn for Carregwyn, and I pull up the cart, I am already feeling the missing of him and longing for the next time.

"I cannot bear to have to wait another week," he says. "Will you come to see me at Wildwater?"

"I will. Oh, yes, I will," I say, without hesitation, and without thinking how I was going to manage to get away.

"Promise me you will."

"I promise. I will come, as soon as I can get away."

He kissed me again then, long and tender, and then abruptly stopped, and jumped from the cart, and walked backwards away from me, blowing kisses to me, grinning all the while, leaving me laughing and feeling that my heart would burst with the love of him.

I felt so excited to be alive, so blissfully alive, that I could feel my blood singing through my veins. So this was what Mam never wanted me to feel and know. I could think of nothing but Iago until I saw him again the next day. With my chores done, and Mam's raised voice following after me, demanding to know where I thought I was going, I donned hat and shawl, and set off for Wildwater. It was early evening and the weather had brightened following a day of rain. A warm southerly breeze was blowing away the clouds, their shadows raced across the hills, creating fast moving strips of light and shade.

My stride was determined and steady as I climbed through the bracken, stepping over the curled shoots of new growth amid the crunching dead stems of old. Up on the heath, the grasses were tipped with a million jewelled dew drops, glinting with the colours of rainbows. Excitement churned my stomach. I had no thought in my head, only a vision of him waiting for me at his door. I did not think of Mam and Morgan wondering where I had gone to. I thought only once of Eli, and it was with only a twinge of sadness that this wonderful thing could not have been for us.

Like one cast under a spell, I simply did what I was bound to do, which was to be with Iago. Perhaps it was the madness of March, but the me who went to Iago that day, and to the many other meetings which followed, was wholly without fear or doubt. It was as though, in breaking free of those constraints which Mam had placed upon me, I also broke free of all caution, and all she and our chapel had ever taught me. Perhaps, it was that my new found freedom went to my head and rendered me incapable of thinking beyond the moments when I was with him. All I can be certain of, is that when I was with him I was complete, and when not with him, bereft.

He told me I was his one true love. He told me we would be married soon. I believed in him, totally, and that his feelings for me were equal to mine for him. I thought he was as helpless as I against the force of our love and passion for each other. I had not known such pleasure and joy was possible. He could not be close to me without moaning like a man in pain; a pain for which my body was the only cure.

From the first time I lay with him, I was like a creature denied water when we were apart. That April and May, I lay with him beneath the blossoming damson and apple trees in the orchard of Wildwater. I lay with him in the lush green bracken, and upon the springy bed of whinberry shrubs upon the hill. I lay with him on a scented carpet of bluebells, beneath a canopy of new green leaves, in the little oak wood above Wildwater. I could not have enough of him, nor he me. And each time I lay with him, I swear, it was without any thought that I was doing it on Eli's own property.

When it rained, we lay together upon his feather bed. Afterwards, he would read poetry to me from a book written by a man named William Wordsworth, whose poem about daffodils always moved me to tears. Then he would kiss the tears from my face and love me all over again. Only when dusk was falling did I run for home. As the weeks went by, and the days lengthened, I arrived home later and later.

Under Mam's ever watchful eye, I dared not think of Iago in her presence, for fear she would see the thrill that passed through me and made me weak when I thought of him. Mam did not know what to say or do. I was never there to share supper, and Morgan asked me, several times, where on earth I went to every evening. I told him only that I needed to be alone, liked to walk out on the hills. I've had a lifetime of being cooped up in that house with Mam, I told him, and surely you don't begrudge me these evenings to myself.

"First, it was whole Fridays at market, now it is every evening you want to yourself. How far are you going to pull, Megan?" he says to me. "Mam says you are too like our Da, that no matter how far you pull, it will never be far enough for you."

"That's nonsense. It's not as if I'm down in the tavern getting drunk every night."

I realise then, with a shock, that in any eyes other than mine and Iago's, what I am doing is a far greater sin than getting drunk in the tavern. I did pause to wonder if my Da had felt the same irresistible pull toward the tavern and its women as I felt now towards Iago. Perhaps he was as desperate as I to get out from under Mam's overbearing demands, I told myself.

I knew that in the eyes of our parish, I was committing a sin in 'knowing' Iago outside of marriage. But I had lost all respect and belief in their and Mam's judgments. Through my friends at the market place, I had discovered there were different ways of living, a world where tolerance replaced the condemnation and blame I had grown up with.

The pleasure I had taken in my trips to market, paled beside that of being with Iago. Though I continued to add to my little stash of savings, I forgot altogether my reason for doing so. I no longer fretted over the prospect of Eli returning with a beautiful young wife on his arm, for I had my own true love now and would be married myself, before long.

"I don't know what's got into you. I thought you were content now you have your day at market," Morgan says to me. "Mam blames herself, says this is all because she let you go to the market. Give her an inch of slack and look what happens, is what she says."

"Oh, for heaven's sake! I'm going walking of an evening, that's all. Where is the harm in that?"

I was soon to discover the answer to that question, and my lies would come back to haunt and shame me; when Morgan and Mam discovered the consequences of my 'walks' upon the hill.

I carried on meeting Iago each evening, but became extra cautious and kept a look out, in case Morgan should take it into his head to follow me. I never imagined it could end. I never doubted it was forever and that we would marry. Then towards the end of May, I arrived to find Iago was not there to greet me, and the door was locked against me. After waiting an hour or more, I thought he must have been held up somewhere on business, and made my way home.

Only when I found he was again not there the following evening did I fear some harm must have befallen him. There was no one I could ask without raising suspicion as to my interest. A small knot of fear formed itself in the pit of my stomach, as I sat on the little wooden bench outside his door, and I waited until it was almost dark and the moon began to rise from behind the hill. I waited there in the darkness and silence; the only sounds were the hooting of a distant owl and the breeze blowing through the tree tops. I waited until the night air became chill, and then stumbled my way home by the light of the moon with a heaviness in my heart and a sense of impending doom. To calm myself, I told myself there was nothing to fear, that he would be there the morrow, explaining the reason for his absence.

He was not there the next evening, or the next, and I was beside myself with worry. By now I was quite sure that some terrible accident had befallen him. My only hope was that he would have got word to someone at market, knowing he could not send a note to me at home. I felt physically sick with worry.

That Friday, on my journey to market, I tried not to think of what I would do if no one at the market had heard word of him.

"You all right, Meg?" Myfanwy says, coming over to me where I am laying out my cheese and butter.

I shake my head, unable to speak for the lump which has risen up in my throat at her kindly concern.

"Whatever has happened? You don't look at all well," she says, "come and sit over here by me for a minute, before things start to get busy."

I sit on the small stool she places beside her and tell her how Iago has gone missing, and of my fears.

"I'll ask around for you. But try not to worry, you're making yourself ill. There'll be a simple explanation, you'll see."

Her kindly face and words reassured me for a while, but my sense of impending doom returned when all she could glean from her enquiries was that Iago had been absent from the cattle market that week. His absence had been noticeable, for it was part of his job to be there, and questions had been raised as to why but no one seemed to know the answer.

"He'll be alright, you'll see. Perhaps he's gone to visit a family member taken suddenly ill? This time next week, you'll be wondering why you got yourself into such a state. Mark my words," Myfanwy said, her hands placed on my shoulders, her kind and smiling face close to mine.

I continued to walk down to Wildwater each evening, and each evening I found the place empty and the door locked. I continued to go, despite the growing conviction that I would never see Iago again. Each time I went there, it was with a fine thread of hope that one evening he would be there to greet me with his laugh of delight, and his moan of pleasure when he clasped me to him. I held onto that thread of hope as though it were a rope and not the fragile thing it was. I had to have something to hold on to, for I was quite certain now that I was with child.

That thread was snatched away the following week. Shearing time was upon us, and I was to discover that Iago was the main topic of conversation in our parish.

Chapter 7

Morgan

When not showing Beulah how to run the place, Megan's time is increasingly spent at Wildwater. Eli insists on walking the land with her, so she will know her new home as well as she knows this one. And she has to spend time with Gwen, the housekeeper, and the dairy maid, to get to know them a little better. The banns were read in chapel last Sunday. Megan will be married before the end of the month. Everything is happening so fast, I can't fully believe it is real.

So must the child stay where she is, until she is old enough to make her own way in life? Is it God's will that I am to be faced with the consequences of my actions, each year, until the child is grown? I am torn. One minute I think I should not tell Megan. The next, I think I must tell Megan. Day and night, I wrestle with my indecision. And I was thinking, if Eli is such a saint as to take Megan on, perhaps he would consider taking the girl, too. But as quick as this thought comes to me, I realise how ridiculous it is. It is one thing for Eli to take Megan on, while only he and she know of her sin, it would be too much for him to have another man's child in his house, or to be married to a woman whose reputation would then be publicly ruined.

So if I were to tell Megan the truth about her child, I would be forcing Megan to choose between her and Eli. I do not doubt she would choose her daughter, but it would be at a terrible cost. Mam and me denied Megan that choice once before. If I say nothing, does that mean I am denying her the choice again? Am I not just repeating the mistakes of the past?

Megan has made her decision to leave the child where she is. She has made that decision because she believes she is well looked after and loved. I am the only soul in this world who can tell Megan the truth. All I want to do is the right thing but I cannot decide what the right thing is. To tell, or not to tell, the truth? Once, it would have seemed so simple; that to tell the truth was always the right thing. But when the truth will ruin the life of another, is it still right to tell it?

If only Megan were not in such a rush to get married. She will be gone from here before I go to pay Nesta again, for what I had hoped would be the last time. If I am to tell Megan, then I have to tell her before she marries Eli. Perhaps she will be able to persuade him to take the child on, though I doubt it. Whatever she decides, surely she has a right to know how her daughter is being raised, and the right to do something about it. After many sleepless nights, that is what I decide.

Once my decision to tell Megan is made, the waiting to find a time alone with her seems interminable. The only chance I get is when Beulah gets her day off. The minute I see Beulah strolling on down the track, to visit her friend in the village, I take a deep breath and head indoors to confront Megan where she is stood at the table, peeling potatoes.

"There is something I have to tell you. You said all that matters is that your child is well looked after. Well, that is far from the case, I'm afraid."

She stops for a moment, a potato in one hand, the knife in the other, to give me a long hard stare, but she says nothing, so I carry on, heedless.

"I could not tell you, when Mam was alive, because she refused to do anything about it. But your daughter lives in a filthy hovel with a fat, idle woman who cares nothing for her and treats her like a servant. There, I've said it."

My whole body is trembling and I cram my hands inside my pockets, so Megan does not see how much they are shaking. Megan continues to stare at me in silence. I take her expression for shock at hearing the truth.

"I'm sorry, I know this comes as a shock, but I thought you should know, thought you would want to know. And do something about it. Bring her home. I'll stand by you."

I cough to clear my throat, and wait for her response, sure of what it will be. The only sound in the room is the ticking of the grandfather clock behind me. I watch her narrow her eyes, and chew her bottom lip, while she considers what I have told her. Then, before I have time to register what she is about to do, she has hurled the potato at me with some considerable force. It strikes the middle of my forehead and hurts like hell.

"You mean, selfish, hard-hearted, lying cheat!" she screeches at me. "You'll say and do anything to keep me from marrying Eli, won't you?" she says through clenched teeth, picking up another potato and hurling it at me.

This time, I see it coming and have time to shield my head. It strikes my elbow and bounces to the floor.

"How dare you!"

Another potato hits my hand.

"Get out!"

And another.

"You come in here and make up this horrible lie in the hope that I will fall for it!"

"I'm telling you the truth!" I say, ducking another potato.

"Liar! You would never have left her there if what you're saying is true. Never! Not even you could do such a wicked thing as that!"

"I had no choice. Mam would not let me bring her back! For God's sake, will you stop throwing those potatoes at me?!"

I've never seen Megan in such a fury. Of all the reactions I'd imagined, her disbelief comes as a complete surprise.

"Mam would not let you! Huh! Well, you can say what you like now, can't you? She isn't around to defend herself. Why won't you give it up? Leave me be! I'm going to marry Eli, no matter what you try to say or do to stop me. Do you understand that, Morgan?"

Her voice has risen to a scream.

"God Almighty! It is impossible to talk any sense to you while you're hurling those damned potatoes at me!"

"Talk sense to me? I'll give you talk sense to me! Making up stories to try to spoil everything, that's what you're doing! Well, I don't want to hear it! So go away, or it will be more than a potato I hurl at you."

The knife glints in her hand at this moment and I begin to back towards the door.

“Alright! Have it your own way. She’s your daughter. Just don’t go saying I never told you,” I say, and turn away to walk out the door.

Another potato hits the back of my head. If she wasn’t a woman, and my sister, I’d throw the damn thing back at her. What am I to do now? I ask myself. Other than tying her up and dragging her all the way over there to see for herself, there is nothing I can do to convince her I am telling the truth. I never imagined she would think I was making it up, though I can see why, now. She knows I don’t want her to go. Damn it to hell, I wish I’d told her before that Eli came sniffing round here. I had thought I had all the time in the world. How was I to know she would go getting herself married, no sooner than our Mam was cold in the ground?

The Sunday before the wedding, we’re all standing around in the May sunshine after the chapel service. Megan seems to have decided to let go of her anger with me, and has even been quite civil to me these past few days. Megan and Eli are the main attraction, everyone coming up to them, wishing them luck for next Sunday, saying how happy they are for them, how much they’re looking forward to the wedding, and what a lovely time of year for it, and so on.

As I look at the two of them smiling at each other, I can’t help but wonder at the blindness of love. Eli seems able to shut from his mind all thoughts of Megan’s murky past. How long will it last? I wonder. When the first light of love has dimmed in his eyes and he looks at her in the cold light of some future morning; will he not resent her then? Will he not find it a torment to think he wasn't the first, that she didn't keep herself pure for him? I can't begin to understand him. I don't know another man who would do what he is doing. I only hope, for Megan's sake, that he was sure in his mind he had forgiven her before he asked her to marry him.

The week running up to the wedding, we're all busy with getting the sheep washed, before the shearings which will be starting soon.

A sheep will not willingly jump into water. It has to be slung, headfirst and bleating, only then to discover it can swim. Six days of it we have; first catching, then slinging one sheep after another into the water to get the worst of the muck out of their fleeces. We have a thousand or more sheep between us. By the end of the week, I feel like my arms have been ripped out of their sockets, and the muscles of my shoulders and neck seem to have knotted together. There is no time to think any more about the child. No time to try again, to convince Megan I am telling the truth. Like Megan says, it is too late, years too late for the little one. And for me.

I am all done in by the day of the wedding, so tired I have barely registered that Megan is about to leave for good. She and Beulah are a flurry of activity and giggles, from the time they get up. It being Sunday, they have nothing to do but get Megan ready for the service. Eli has bought Megan a new Sunday best dress and boots to wear for the occasion. I wish I could have afforded to do that for her myself, but no matter.

An hour before we are due to leave, is when it hits me in the chest like a wagon full of hay running straight into me. Beulah has been down to the woods to pick bluebells and has just come back with them. She picked some meadowsweet, too, on her way back up, to mix in with the bluebells, and is making up a posy for Megan. It hits me then, watching Beulah arranging the flowers into a posy. I don't know why it took so long for it to sink in, but there it was, Megan would not be coming home tonight, or any other night, ever again.

Everything we'd ever done or said comes back to me in that moment, so that my mind is flooded with memories; of Megan and me growing up together, running, playing, climbing the hill. And now it was all over. And even as that thought enters my head, I think how stupid it was to think that, because it was all over, long before this moment. It was all over from the moment our Mam said 'tell your brother what you have done'.

So I cry like a boy, out in the barn, overwhelmed by the realisation it is all too late. I cry for the child and the life she could have had, would have had, if only. I weep for all that is lost and can never be put right. I cry for Megan and all she'd suffered. I cry as if my heart is being wrung out. Then I go to the pool in our gorge and wash my face with the icy cold water. Then I go to the house and dress in my Sunday best clothes. And then I am ready as I will ever be to give my sister away to the future she has chosen for herself.

She comes down the stairs in her new clothes and even I have to admit she looks grand.

"Doesn't she look wonderful, Morgan!' Beulah says, beaming with pride.

'Indeed she does." I say, swallowing hard.

"I wish I didn't have to wear black on such a day as this!" Beulah says with a tragic look on her face.

I've not seen Beulah wear anything but black since she came here, on account of her being recently widowed. She is wearing her Sunday-best, black dress, but has tied up her raven-black hair with red ribbons.

"You look lovely, anyway. The red ribbons look very striking. She looks beautiful, doesn't she, Morgan?" Megan says, turning to me with a beaming smile.

I don't think I have really looked at Beulah until this moment. She has just been Beulah, an uninvited (by me), albeit pleasant, presence in the house. Looking at her now, I can see she does have something about her, that she is, as Megan says, beautiful. In a way, if you like that sort of thing.

"She looks very smart indeed." I say, clearing my throat. "We'd better be going."

Megan goes to her wedding in our rickety old cart and leaves the chapel, by Eli's side, in his smart new trap. So it does at least look like a step up, and in the right direction. Then we all head back to Wildwater for the magnificent spread which Gwen, Eli's housekeeper, has prepared for all. The whole parish turns up to wish Megan and Eli well. There's food aplenty to feed them, and enough cider and mead for us to drown ourselves in.

I have to hand it to Eli, he knows how to lay on a feast. He's hired a fiddler and a harpist, so there's dancing and all, which was the biggest shock of all. The elders of the parish sit, tight-lipped, on the chairs which line the sides of the room. If Mam were here she'd have something to say. I can't ever remember having so much to drink. So much, that I feel myself warming to Eli as the evening goes on.

"You're a saint, Eli. A bloody saint. That's all I have to say. Megan is the luckiest woman on this earth," I say, slapping him on the back.

"Not at all, Morgan. It's I who am the lucky one. And I just want to say thank you for not standing in our way."

That's how he talks. Always so serious and correct. I cannot abide it.

"Aye, well. I just want her to be happy. God knows she's had enough trouble in her life. But that's all over now. Thanks be to God. And to you, of course. No, man, honestly, you are a living saint."

I go to slap him on the back again, and I think the bugger must have moved out of the way because I end up swiping the air in front of me.

Megan grabs my arm then and drags me away.

"He's a saint! Isn't he just!" I say, slurring, for my tongue seems to have grown too big for my mouth.

"Shut up, Morgan! You're embarrassing me!" Megan hisses, and I wonder if perhaps I may have been talking too loud.

I clamp my hand over my mouth.

"Oh, sorry! I'll keep my mouth shut. Sorry."

Next thing I know, Megan is asking Beulah to take me outside, for some fresh air to sober me up. It must be late because it's dark outside and I almost trip over the step. Beulah takes my arm and sits me down on a seat in front of the house.

"I think it would be wise if you did not drink any more cider tonight, Morgan," she says to me.

"Aye. I think you might be right," I say, for my head is spinning, now I'm out in the fresh air.

"We'll just sit out here, awhile, until you've sobered up a bit, shall we? You wouldn't want to let Megan down on her wedding night, would you?"

"No, hell, no. I wouldn't want to add that to my long list of sins."

As I say this, I feel an almost overwhelming need to cry and tears spring to my eyes. Fortunately, the blackness of the night means that Beulah does not see. I have a struggle to control myself, and try to think of something other than all the wrongs I've done. Beulah and I sit for a while, without talking, under the stars, listening to the strains of the harp and the fiddle travelling on the air. Then Beulah sighs deeply and speaks.

"I know you're not very happy about Megan marrying Eli. And I know you're not happy about me housekeeping for you. But I hope you'll give it a go, Morgan. I know I'm not a patch on Megan, but I will improve, I promise you that."

I don't know what to say to her. I'd like to say, I'm glad she's here for I'd never manage on my own. I'd like to say I even enjoy her company. I open my mouth to speak but the words stick behind the lump in my throat and all I can do is nod my head like a donkey.

"Mm. Mm." I say like a dullard.

Then she takes my arm and pulls me up.

"Come on, Morgan! Let's have a dance!"

God help me. She's a hell of a woman. I don't know how I'll manage her.

Chapter 8

Megan

Iago had been missing a week when summer arrived with a spell of scorching hot weathe,r and the parish men announced the sheep ready to shear. So began a frantic week of travelling, from one farm to the next, each day, to get every farm's shearing done before the weather broke again. Morgan and I set out each morning before the sun was up, and did not arrive home until after sunset. My anxiety now turned, each evening, to the prospect that Iago had returned and I not there to meet him.

Every evening on our return, I had to stay up late preparing food for our own shearing supper. Half a dozen of our nearest neighbours would turn up for our shearing day, with their wives and children in tow, and all of them would need feeding. I boil a great leg of bacon in the pot above the fire, and bake a huge fruitcake in the bread oven, after the bread baking is done and the oven not so hot. All the while, I struggle to quell the urge to wretch at the sight and smell of my own cooking and to put from my mind the fearful thought that I am with child.

Late on the eve of our shearing, Morgan and I went up on the heath with the dog, to bring our sheep down. The air up there was still warm and it flowed like warm water over my skin. The heath was a vast expanse of colours. The bright yellows of tormentil, cinquefoil, and bird's foot trefoil grew among the deep blue flowers of milkwort and heath speedwells, and the purples of thymes. The warm air smelt like fresh mown hay, filled with the scents of flowers and the ripening grasses. As the sun neared the distant horizon it began to glow red, setting the whole skyline ablaze with crimson light. Once was the time my heart would have sang to be up on the heath on such a night.

In Iago's absence, the spell I had been under was wearing off and I was becoming increasingly alarmed at the awfulness of my predicament should he not return. I had thrown all caution to the wind because I never imagined it would end. I watched Morgan as he directed his dog with whistles of varying notes, each conveying a different message to his dog to lie down, stand still, slow down. He would never forgive me for lying to him. I no longer cared what our Mam thought of me but it pained me to realise how badly I had betrayed my brother.

"Just look at that!" Morgan was saying to me now.

We paused for a moment, before descending the hill, and watched as the sun dropped out of sight. In the fading light, the crimson skyline took on hues of lilac and pink. The colours of the sky tinged the haze of mist which was steadily filling the valleys below. The skylarks had dropped from the sky for the night, and there was not a sound but the tremulous bleating of lambs and the low answering bleats of their mothers. The sky beyond the mountains to the east was beginning to glow from the moon which was yet to rise above them, and the first stars appeared in the sky. While Morgan stood beside me, drinking in this wonder and beauty, I felt a deep, deep sadness because there he was, so innocent, and unknowing, and so ignorant of what I had done behind his back, that my heart ached for him.

That night I got down on my knees and prayed to the God I had all but forgotten those past two months. I prayed for Iago to be returned to me. I pleaded for my madness to be forgiven and promised never to sin again should Iago only be returned to me. I was soon to discover that my prayers were all in vain and my fate already sealed.

Our neighbours arrived with the first light of dawn. The older children were set to work catching the sheep for the shearers, and the usual racket kicked up as the sheep and lambs were separated from each other in the mayhem. We women wrapped the fleeces in the barn, on makeshift tables made from old doors, working fast to keep up with the shearers. We tossed the fleeces into the waiting sack which was roped to an overhanging beam in the barn. There was little time for talk and, though we were out of the heat of the sun, we were soon glistening with sweat and the grease from the wool.

The men sheared under the shade of the barn's north-facing wall, but the sweat still poured from their brows as they worked. Mid-morning, they pause briefly to change their shirts, which stick to their backs, so drenched they are with sweat and grease. The dust kicked up from a thousand sheep's feet clings to the sweat on the mens' arms and hair. The dust fills their mouths, coats their tongues and sticks to the back of their throats. Throughout the day, they continually slake their thirst but the liquid seems to turn to sweat and pour straight through their skins before it has time to reach their stomachs.

At the end of the day, when the men are pitching Morgan's initials onto the newly shorn sheep, we women carry out the great platters of food and lay them out on some sackcloth, which I spread out under the shade of an apple tree in the orchard. We sit under the dappled shade of the tree to eat our meal but there is no relief from the heat even there. There is a light breeze blowing but the air it blows is too warm to provide any relief. Sitting among our neighbours as they chat and make jokes, and seeing that even our Mam was managing to rise to the occasion, I try to enter the spirit of things. Then the conversation turned and with my heart pounding, I discovered the truth regarding Iago's absence.

"Have you heard the latest?' Dai asks us. "Eli has sacked his manager. He can't have been here for more than a few months."

"I know the chap you mean, but I met him only once, when I went down to Wildwater looking for some stray sheep," Morgan says.

I look at Morgan with surprise. Iago never mentioned ever having met him.

"You're lucky he didn't steal them, Morgan! For that is what he's been sacked for; lining his pockets with Eli's profits." Old Twm pipes up from his perch on a low branch of the apple tree.

'I'll be damned! I'm not surprised, mind. I thought he was a strange one," Morgan says.

"Why is that, Morgan?"

Their conversation carries on, but I am only half listening, for I am quite sure I am about to fall to the ground as all my strength drains out of me.

"Oh, I don't know, just something about him. 'Well! If it isn't the great and pious Morgan Jones, himself!' he said to me with his thumbs jammed in his waistcoat pockets and his chest all puffed out like a peacock. 'I've heard a lot about you!' he went on. Smirking he was, like he was having some secret joke at my expense. I can't think what he would have heard or from who. There's not much to tell about me!" Morgan was telling them.

"Well, he didn't hear anything from me. I never met him. Never will either, now he's been sent packing," says Elgan, who has been lying on his back on the grass with his hat covering his face. He removes it now, and sits up to join in the gossip.

"He got off light, then. It's a wonder Eli did not have him up in court."

"Aye, well. You know how Eli is. He's not one to make a fuss. He sacked him as soon as he found out and that was an end to it as far as he was concerned."

"You obviously haven't heard but half the story!" says Rees, who has been quiet until now. "They say he'd been having his way with a maid from the village but denied it, of course. She was a young girl who was working as a maid for Angharad."

"Worse than that! The girl is Sian Williams, the daughter of Dafydd the Mill's cousin. Dafydd says he'll murder the man if he comes back here."

My distress was lost amid the loud gasps and scandalized outbursts, all round, from the womenfolk.

"No better than she should be…"

"Has the preacher been told? ...."

"The girl must be brought before the elders…."

"She has brought shame on the whole family! ..."

"The preacher has told her parents to throw her out but first she has to face everyone in chapel this Sunday," Martha tells us all, her eyes gleaming with anticipation.

"Well, she'll pay for her sins, now! It'll be the poorhouse for her," Twm says.

"The poorhouse is too good for her, if you ask me!" says Kitty.

"Well, I'd like to see the robber banged up! Cheating one of our own," says Twm, his knees jerking up and down with anger and the colour rising in his sunken cheeks.

"Aye, you're right about that, Twm!!" says Elgan.

I watch the spittle fly from Elgan's mouth and the circle of heads all nodding in agreement, and I stretch out a hand to Morgan as I feel the ground come up to meet me.

"It will have been the heat," Martha is saying, leaning over me and peering into my face. "Carry her up to the house, Morgan, and make sure she goes straight to bed. We can clear away these things for her."

Then I am lifted up and carried in Morgan's strong arms, but there is nowhere on this earth he can take me where I would want to be.

"What's the matter with her?" I could hear Mam asking, over and over, as Morgan carried me up the stairs and laid me down on my bed.

"You may as well lay me down in my grave," I murmur to him.

"Don't talk like that, Meg. What is it? You've been strange for so long and now this."

“The heat,” I say, turning my back to him and closing my eyes so that I do not have to see the brotherly concern in his eyes. It is a greater torture to me than the condemnation which is coming for me soon from every quarter.

I hear him walk across the room and shut the door quietly behind him.

“Hush, Mam!” I hear him saying as he descends the stairs. “Megan needs to rest.”

Oh, what have I done, what *have* I done? I silently beseeched myself. I was too stunned to weep, wanted only to close my eyes and sleep without ever having to wake again.

I stayed in my bed for the remainder of that day, unable to find the will to get up and go about my chores. Morgan came and went with plates of food I could not eat. When he entered my room I did not even raise my head above the covers to acknowledge his presence. I feigned physical illness though it was no sickness of the body I suffered. I simply could not bear to face him or anyone else. I knew that if I faced him, feeling as I did, he would see and know that some terrible fate had befallen me and would not let up with his questions until he had wrenched the truth from me. I was not ready yet, felt I would never be ready, to tell him the truth.

How could I have been so foolish, so utterly reckless? I admonished myself as I lay in my bed and in the next moment asked myself how could I have known, how could I? I had not worried about consequences because I never doubted that we would marry. If Iago were not gone we could marry and no one but God would be the wiser and only God would judge me. But I was carrying

Iago's child and soon the whole parish would know and judge me.

I felt the deep, dark pain of humiliation as I lay there and thought about Iago laying with Sian Pritchard while professing his undying love for me. When I thought of how Iago had tricked everyone, I despised myself. When I thought how he had taken Eli's hard earned money while making fun of Morgan's honesty and piety, I wanted to die. I was the leper among them and they did not even know it, yet. I was the contaminating weed that must be torn from their soil and flung into the waste.

I deserved to be condemned. It was not fear of that which most haunted me. It was that I couldn't bear for Morgan to know how I had deceived him; blatantly lied and betrayed his trust in me. I was ashamed for him to know how low I had fallen, but more than that, I could not face seeing the pain it would cause him. And Eli, any respect he once had for me would be shattered. I had hoped that when he saw me again it would be to find me transformed. I had hoped he would feel a twinge of regret at having abandoned me. Well, I was transformed, alright, into a woman he would despise.

So in my bed I remained, paralysed by shame, by indecision as to what I was going to do, and by fear of discovery. So much did my conscience trouble me, I believed that Morgan and Mam would only have to look in my face to see my guilt exposed there. I thought of taking my life; of walking the path along the Wildwater; of filling my pockets with stones and jumping in; up there where the water was a raging torrent, cascading over boulders of crushing rock; boulders under which a weighted body could remain hidden for eternity.

The next Sunday at chapel, the hushed conversations of the congregation die away as the preacher climbs the steps to the pulpit. Unusually tall of stature, up there in the pulpit he towered above us. With his flowing white hair and piercing blue eyes, he had frightened me since I was a child, when Mam converted.

He stands there, clutching the lapels of his coat and rocking back and forth on his heels, staring out at us as if he can see into our very souls. I keep my gaze averted, terrified that if he should look in my eyes he will see my guilt there. He pauses long enough to be sure he has our attention, and then he stretches out his arm, his finger pointing out into the congregation, his hand trembling with rage.

"A sinner has come among us! A serpent has entered our garden of Eden!" he shouts so suddenly that I all but jump out of my seat.

Rage had reduced the blacks of his eyes to pinheads, and spittle flew from his trembling lips, arcing through the dust filled rays of sunlight which poured through the chapel windows. Everyone else was craning their necks, trying to get a look at the poor girl who was in the line of that accusing finger. Sian Pritchard stood up and her parents stood up either side of her. To my shame, I was glad it was her and not me standing there.

"Aye! You! You know who you are! Come forward and show yourself!"

Sian's mother was weeping, with her head bowed, but Sian stood straight, her head up, looking out on the congregation with what seemed like an air of defiance.

A buzz of whispering and mumbling filled our little chapel. I looked up at Morgan but his gaze was fixed on the spectacle unfolding before us.

"Confess your sin, girl!" the preacher said then.

I sat, open mouthed, as Sian spoke without a tremor in her voice.

"I won't confess while the Da gets away with it. He cheated me!" she said, and there was a collective gasp from the congregation.

"Sian Prichard! Are you denying you are with child?" the preacher bellowed. Red in the face with rage he was at her denial.

"No. I don't deny that," Sian said.

"Are you refusing to confess and repent?" he says, his face almost comical in its contorted disbelief.

The chapel was buzzing with conversation. People were turning in their pews to share words of outrage and disbelief with their neighbours. All the while, I could not take my eyes off Sian, so transfixed I was by this spectacle, as if I were trapped inside a terrifying dream from which I could not wake. I was watching this young woman suffer this public humiliation, as I would suffer, too, before the year was out. To my right, Morgan hung his head. To my left, Mam was quietly reciting the Lord's Prayer.

Sian's mother began wailing loudly, begging Sian to please, please just do as the preacher had instructed her.

"I'm sorry, Mam, I will not take all the blame!" Sian said, shrugging herself free from her Mam's grip and hurrying down between the pews to get out, with everyone's eyes on her, condemning her.

The preacher shouted after her, quoting from the bible, his accusing finger still pointing.

"They that are without God, judgeth! Put away from among yourselves that wicked person!"

That evening, the mood at home was subdued while I felt sick to my bones at what I had witnessed.

"Do you not think it was unfair, Morgan, that that poor girl should have been treated so harshly?" I say, praying that I will find in Morgan some compassion for Sian's plight.

It is Mam who answers.

"Have you forgotten what you confessed when you were baptized? You confessed you would shun any member of our chapel who fell into sin, and you agreed to be shunned if you did so yourself. Do you not remember that?"

Mam began to quote Corinthians from her Bible, then.

"I wrote unto you in an epistle not to company with fornicators. If anyone be a fornicator, or covetous, or an idolator, or a drunkard; with such one will not eat. Put away from among yourselves that wicked person."

"You think you know people," Morgan says, shaking his head in disbelief, "but Sian is a stranger to us now and ever shall be. I don't give a damn if she confesses or not, she'll never set foot in our chapel again."

He glared at me when he said this, challenging me to dare contradict him.

"Quite right, Morgan," Mam says, "she is a sinner."

"And the way she stood up in front of us all without shame for what she's done, that's what I can't get over. I won't take the blame, she said. What kind of thing is that to say, in her condition?" he says, pushing his plate of uneaten food away from him.

"The devil has many disguises, Morgan." Mam says to him.

If there had been any hope in my mind; that I would find any mercy from either of them when I was found out, I no longer harboured any such delusion.

I barely slept, that night, as I relived the scene of Sian's humiliation in our chapel. I supposed that Iago had tricked her, too, with promises of marriage, and that was why she so bravely stood up and said she would not confess to something that was not her fault. I wondered what she was going to do and where she was planning to go if her parents turned her out, as the preacher demanded they do. Her fate and mine were inextricably linked. She was the one person in all this place who I might confide in and who would understand.

By morning I had resolved to visit her, and let her know she was not alone in her predicament. I don't know what I hoped for, only that I felt she was my only hope and that her existence meant I was not wholly alone.

I knew that her parents lived on a small farmstead a few miles north of our own, and I assumed she would be back there, as she had been sacked from her post in the village. I rose before dawn to milk the cow by lantern light, and left as soon as my morning chores were done. The walk there was into the facing wind, across the mountain tops, and I walked with my shawl pulled up tightly over my head and shoulders. The wind snatched and tugged at my skirts so they billowed like a sail behind me. All I could hear was the wind rushing through the thin grasses, making a continuous whispering hush, hush, hush, until I began the descent and Sian's home came into view on the opposite hill. The whitewashed walls of the cottage shone bright in the autumn sunshine, and the smoke was blown horizontal from the chimney by the wind.

I followed a narrow sheep path which cut through and around jagged outcrops of stone that threatened to snag on my skirts or trip me up. Then I reached the footpath which led up to the door. Long grass, and late flowering dandelions and silverweed grew along the borders of the path and around the front step. I supposed Sian's mother, Gwyneth, had little time for weeding; she had a large brood of children, all of them younger than Sian.

From within came the sounds of children's voices, shouting and squabbling. Gwyneth's voice joined in the shouting, imploring them to settle down or they'd get no supper that night. I summoned up my waning courage to knock on the door. The shouting ceased for a moment, then carried on, so I knocked again, harder. There was another silence, and a little one's voice piped up to ask 'shouldn't we answer it, Mam?'

I heard the latch being lifted then the door opened just a foot. They are people in hiding, I thought, ashamed to face the world outside their door. The face of one of the children peered out, squinting against the bright sunlight behind me. The door closed against me again, and I could hear the little one say 'it's a lady, Mam. What should I say?'

Gwyneth opened the door then and stepped outside, pulling the door closed behind her. Her eyes were red-rimmed and puffed, as if she had not stopped weeping these past days.

"I hope you don't mind, Mrs Pritchard, but I've come to see Sian," I said.

"Megan Jones isn't it? From Carregwyn? You shouldn't have come, Megan," she said, barely able to meet my gaze, as if it were she who was guilty of committing a sin.

"I was at chapel yesterday and I want to say how sorry..."

"Does your Mam know you're here?" she butted in.

"No."

"No. I thought not. You should go, love. You shouldn't go getting yourself into trouble on our account."

"Well, I'm here now. I really would like to speak with Sian. Is she here?"

"She's here alright. I don't know what to do with her, Megan, and that's the truth. The preacher was here, just this morning, says it is our duty to throw her out. Can you imagine? My own daughter? If she'd only do as he asks. I'm at my wit's end."

She began to weep, and dabbed at her eyes with the hem of her pinafore, before going on.

"Her father is going out of his mind. He's talking of murder. I've told him that won't help matters, will it? Her father's all for throwing her out. Livid he is. Says she's ruined us. We'll never find the rent now either, you see, on account of her having lost her job and all. It is a terrible mess she's brought on us, but all she will say is it's not her fault. Not her fault, yet she swears she wasn't forced. I fear she is gone quite mad."

"Let me speak with her. Perhaps she will listen to me."

"Aye. Perhaps you can talk some sense into her. She's down in the orchard, would you believe? A houseful of chores to be done and she's been sat down there since the preacher left, staring off into the distance. I've begged her to come in but she won't come. She won't even speak to me or her father. You'd think it was our fault, the mess she's got herself in."

I followed the stone path which went round the side of the cottage and led to the garden behind. Beyond that was the little orchard of damson and apple trees, the leaves of which were carried along in flurries on the wind. A mountain stream flowed through the bottom of the orchard and was swollen by a recent day's rain. Its rushing noise, as it tumbled downhill, could be easily heard from the cottage. On a wooden bench beneath a gnarled and ancient damson tree, sat the forlorn figure of Sian, looking out toward the hills, her back to the cottage and me.

I felt a surge of rage rush through me at the sight of her. Such a frail looking little thing she was. She couldn't have been more than seventeen, with skin pale as skimmed milk and her body as thin as a willow shoot. The wind was snatching at her fair hair and tossing it round her head, but she seemed not to notice. In a world of her own she was, and I was afraid my sudden appearance would startle her, but she only glances in my direction before returning her gaze to the hills.

"Your Mam is fretting, wants you to come back to the house," I say, sitting down next to her on the bench.

"Preacher sent you, did he? To persuade me to confess my sins? Well, you're wasting your breath," she said with defiance, hugging her shawl tighter around her, defensively.

She may have looked as fragile as a child, but there was hardness in her, and the gaze that met mine was full of hostility. I had wanted to say 'he tricked me too, and I don't know what to do' but I lost my courage, fearing that she was the sort who might go straight to the preacher and tell him 'see, I'm not the only one.' I had been foolish to come, foolish to think I might find in her some solidarity, born of our common experience, at the hands of Iago. I dared not trust her and because of that I could be of no help to her, nor her to me.

Yet, I could not leave for there were things I had to know. Had Iago promised her marriage too? Had he already stopped meeting with her when he first met me? Did he read poetry to her too? Did he say he would die without her? In truth, I hoped her answer would absolve him.

"I haven't come to preach or persuade. I just want you to know that I, for one, do not condemn you," I said, and added "without hearing your side of the story."

I watched a mixture of emotions pass over her face in quick succession; curiosity, suspicion, doubt, and finally, a small glimmer of hope.

"Come for a walk," she says, rising to her feet.

I followed as she leaped the mountain stream, and went out through the picket gate onto the heath beyond. (That picket gate lies rotting on the ground now, and the stone boundary of the garden crumbles.) She led me over the rolling hill, talking as we walked, with only the buzzards above to hear us.

"The way he used to look at me! Like I was something so beautiful he could hardly bear it! I was a fool, I'll tell you that. I fell for the oldest trick in the book – flattery. Knowing what I do now, I think it was more like the look of a crow, circling above a dying sheep, waiting for the moment he can begin to pick her bones clean."

She paused to look at me, gauging my reaction, to see if I was shocked. That's how she felt about him every day now, she said, whenever she thought of him. She told me then, how not a day went by without him appearing, after she first met him. He would sit there, across the road from where she was working, waiting for her to leave the house on some errand for her mistress.

"But I never once felt afraid of him, though I should have, I see that now. He'd grin at me, and doff his hat, then fall into step beside me. And all the while he'd be looking at me like he was head over heels in love."

I knew that look well enough. We had reached the ruins of Hafod by then, and I remembered how, years ago, Morgan and I had played in this ruin as children. We'd ride over here on our ponies. Back then, there were still remnants of a roof and the outside walls were intact. We'd light a fire in the hearth, though the chimney was full of crow's nests. Sian talked as we picked our way round the crumbled walls of the house, stepping over roof slates overgrown with weeds, and stooping to pick up bits of broken china cups and such.

She stopped, and covered her face with her hands for a moment, then began talking again, saying how she was done for now, anyway, and, oh, the irony of it all. Her Da had sent her off to work as a maid because the extra income meant he could keep his blessed farm, and now he would lose it all anyway.

"Let's go and walk on the heath," I said with a shiver. The air around the ruin was chill and damp, overhung as it was with a canopy of trees.

I looked around the ruin with sadness.

"Me and my brother used to come and play here. Such fun we used to have. We'd spend hours playing house. We'd light a fire in the little hearth over there and pretend to cook meals on it. Just look at it now. Within a few years, there'll be nothing left at all to say this place ever existed."

We picked our way out of the ruins and made our way up onto the heath, where the wind tossed our hair and skirts about, as she told me how Iago had duped her.

"He'd be waiting along the road, every afternoon, when I walked back home from the village. I was smitten with him, I don't deny it. Then, one day, he says he won't be meeting me anymore. Out of the blue, just like that."

"And you felt it was the end of the world," I said.

"Yes! That's exactly how it felt. Why? I asked him. Because I know you do not love me, he says. I argued with him. Of course, I love you, I said. Prove it then, he says, show me how much you truly love me."

"I can guess what you had to do to prove it," I said.

"Aye, well. I never saw him again after I did. You think I was a fool now, don't you? It's nothing to what I think of myself. Hate myself, I do."

For the first time since starting to talk, she looks close to tears.

"You weren't to know," I said, and reached out to place my hand on her shoulder.

We reached the top of the hill and stood in silence, facing into the wind, gazing at the landscape stretched out before us. To the east were the great, rolling mountains of Mynydd Morfa, to the west the crags of Esgairwybr. Ahead, was a long, wide valley of fields and scattered farmsteads, winding lanes and woodlands, villages and hamlets.

"I shall hate to leave all this," Sian said, and set off walking again, turning back the way we'd come.

"Have you told the preacher how he tricked you? Surely if he knew the truth, he would not be so harsh on you?"

She let out a short, harsh laugh.

"You think I didn't tell him? It makes no difference to him. I have sinned, and must repent."

She had led us back to the derelict house once more.

"Can you imagine what my life would be like here now? For the rest of my days, they will look upon me with contempt, whether I repent or no. I am a woman with a life-long reputation. No man will want me now."

"It's so unfair that you should take all the blame while…that man goes unpunished."

"Ah, well. The preacher has to make an example of me. To him I am the rotten weed that has rooted itself in his precious Eden. He has to dig me up and throw me out, lest I contaminate the rest. In making an example of me, he is preparing the ground for when he is rid of me, ensuring that no other young women will be tempted to go the same way."

She made a hollow little laugh of contempt and looked at me with a wry twist of her mouth. I could have told her then, that Iago had duped me too. Instead, I say;

"You will always have me as a friend."

I think, she will find out soon enough the reason why, and hope she will forgive me for not confiding in her this day.

"But there is nothing you can do to help me because you are as powerless as I. But thank you, Megan, for coming. You have been a true friend to me this day and I shall never forget it. It will be a great comfort to me when I go, knowing there was one who cared about me."

"But you can't leave! Where on earth will you go? You must stay."

I do not tell her why; that she is the only one I will be able to turn to, when my own hour of need arrives.

"I shall go to a better place than this!" She says and follows with that hollow laugh again. The sun was behind her, low in the sky, filtered by the trees behind the ruin.

"It's getting late. I'll come back again. There are things I should tell you..." I hesitate, before leaning forward to kiss her cheek, then I walk away, leaving her standing alone amid the ruins.

Chapter 9

Megan

The next morning, after my meeting with Sian, we woke to discover that the wind of the previous day had brought bad weather along behind it and left a shroud of cloud hanging over us. It hung so low, it almost obscured the hills about us, so they appeared as no more than dark shadows through the mist. A wet drizzle glossed the cobblestone yard, a drizzle so fine that it irritated, like feathers falling on wet skin. It clung to my skirts and shawl in fine beads. The air was filled with that sharp, pungent scent of recently wetted earth, and the dampness felt chill enough to penetrate my bones. Through the mist, at about mid-day, Sian Pritchard's brother Iwan appeared and rapped upon our door.

"I've been sent to fetch Morgan," he said, wiping snot and tears from his face with the back of his hand. He must have cried all the way from Cefncrug. "She never come home last night, and Dafydd the Mill is setting up a search party to find her. He wants Morgan to search your outbuildings, and if he finds nothing, then Dafydd says can he help come and search the river."

"What do you mean, the river? Why would they want to search the river?" I ask, before the answer to my own question springs into my mind, setting my heart racing.

"Tell the boy to come in, not stand there at the door letting the damp inside the house!" Mam said, and I stepped aside for Iwan to enter.

Morgan came stomping in then, and unaware of the reason for Iwan's visit, he hailed Iwan with a cheerful slap on the back before he realised Iwan was crying.

"Who is saying Sian is in the river?" Mam asks Iwan.

Iwan swallowed a sob and wiped at his eyes with the jacket of his sleeve.

"Mam says she feared this would happen. She's been in a bad way since Sian failed to come home last night. None of us has had any sleep. Mam's crying, the little 'uns are crying, the baby hasn't been fed. Perhaps she's run off with her young man. Da says he wouldn't put it past her."

His eyes searched Morgan's face, looking for reassurance.

"Aye, perhaps she has Iwan, lad. Let's hope that is what has happened," Morgan said, with a reassuring pat on Iwan's back.

"So we don't have to search the river, then," Iwan says, his face brightening with relief.

"I think we'd better to do that, anyway, just to be sure," Morgan says, and Iwan starts up sobbing again.

"You'd better go, Morgan, they'll be waiting for you to join them," Mam says to him.

He shrugged on his coat, and placed his hat on his head, with the expression of a man going to the gallows. He opened the door for Iwan to go ahead of him and they walked out into the mist. As I watched them fade away into the mist, I felt a shiver run through me, as though someone had walked over my grave. Shuddering, I close the door against the cold, damp air that was creeping its way into the room.

"Best place for her," Mam says, leaning forward to poke at the fire with her stick, not looking at me, while I stare at her, aghast.

"Have you no pity?"

She looks at me then, her eyes sharp as needles.

"Aye. I have pity alright-for the poor family."

I turn my back on her, and go over to the barn, slipping on the wet cobblestones. I sit among Morgan's sacks of oats and corn, trying not to panic, trying not to weep. To think of that poor young girl, all alone in this world as she was. I should have confided in her. I should have let her know she wasn't the only one, instead of thinking of my own self, fearing that she might expose me. I remembered what she had told me; that she was going to a better place than this. Is this what she meant? That she was going to end her life? If she had done this thing, I would have to live with the knowledge for the rest of my days that I could have prevented it.

As the hours passed by, with no sign of Morgan returning, I felt I would go mad with the waiting. I scrubbed down the dairy and cleaned out the pig's sty. Then I started on the flagstones of the house, down on my hands and knees, while Mam dozed in her chair. I scrubbed them till they shone blue, and my back was racked with pain. And all the while I silently prayed that Morgan would soon return with good news; that they had found Sian alive and well. I would tell her then, I would. I would go straight over there to Cefncrug. I would. I would.

The morning's drizzle had turned to heavy rain and Mam grew increasingly concerned over Morgan being out so long in such weather. When I took up the yoke and pails to fetch water from the gorge, with the wind and rain lashing my face, I kept looking out for a sign of Morgan appearing through the driving rain. With the growing darkness outside, my anxiety increased and was not helped by Mam constantly asking what those men were thinking of, staying out in such weather.

"If she isn't in the river, she'll catch her death if she's out in this, anyway," she says.

The waiting was such a torment; I had reached the point where I felt I could bear no more. I lit the candles but left the shutters open, so Morgan would be guided by the light from within when coming home in the dark. Then I got my cloak and pulled the hood over my head before venturing out into the rain to shut the hens up for the night. When I was about to run back to the house, I caught sight of a lantern's dancing light coming up the hill. Squinting through the rain, I watched the light get nearer. When I saw it was Morgan and Dafydd approaching, I ran to the gate to meet them.

"Get this lad a change of clothes, Meg, he's soaked through," Dafydd said.

I could not make out Morgan's face in the dim light but I could see he was shaking violently and I could hear the chattering of his teeth.

"Go on Meg, quickly, and get that fire roaring before he catches his death!" Dafydd urged.

I ran into the house, throwing off my wet cloak and racing up the stairs, shouting to Mam that Morgan was home. I gathered together a bundle of clothes and placed them in front of the fire to warm.

"Morgan is soaked through. Dafydd says to get the fire roaring," I explain, to silence Mam's complaint when I throw on kindling, and the fast burning white turf I reserve for lighting the bread oven.

The door swung open with a clatter, and Dafydd was guiding Morgan inside.

"Come on, lad, let's get you upstairs and out of these things," Dafydd says.

Morgan was so stiff with cold, and shaking so much, he could barely put one foot in front of the other. Mam stood up, her knitting dropping to the floor, when she saw him.

"Come on, we'll soon have you warm and dry," Dafydd was saying as he led Morgan up the stairs, leaving a trail of water behind them.

"Whatever is going on? What's wrong with Morgan?" Mam was crying.

I told her to hush a moment while I took the warmed clothes upstairs.

"Good girl, Meg. You get that fire good and hot, now, and heat some milk. Nice hot cup of milk he needs. Don't suppose you've got a drop of the hard stuff?"

He gave me a knowing wink but I had to confess I did not know what he meant.

"Brandy? Whisky? No. Never mind. I didn't think your Mam would have any in the house. Good job I keep some handy for emergencies, medical emergencies that is."

He patted the pocket of his great coat, before taking the bundle of clothes and shutting the door between us, and saying, "right, Morgan, let's get you sorted."

"What's happened to him?" Mam asked again, as I heated a pot of milk over the fire.

"I don't know any more than you! He's soaked to the skin is all I know!" I snapped at her, not meaning to, but I had a growing certainty that we were going to hear the worst possible news. Morgan did not get that wet through and cold from the rain.

"Don't raise your voice to me!" she said, her voice trembling.

"Now, now, Esther, calm yourself. He'll live." Dafydd says, coming down the stairs. "Pull a couple of chairs close to the fire for us, Meg. Is that milk warm? Get a cup for me and all, there's a good girl."

Mam became meekness itself with Dafydd in the house. Morgan came down, hugging himself and still shuddering, though not as violently as before.

"Come on, lad, sit down here by the fire and warm yourself," Dafydd instructs Morgan.

I pour two cups of milk from the pot. Dafydd gets up to take them from me and places them on the table. Then he takes a flask from his pocket and pours a good measure into each.

"There's no alcohol allowed in this house!" Mam says.

"Now Esther, I know, but these are no ordinary circumstances. It'll warm young Morgan here quicker than anything else."

Mam fell silent. She would never lose her temper in front of a visitor. Dafydd handed Morgan the cup, and then Mam asked the question I was so dreading and I felt my body go weak.

"So what happened to you, boy?"

Morgan began to shudder again. Dafydd went to sit next to him and poured more brandy into each of their cups, raising a hand to Mam to stay her protests. Then with a hand on Morgan's shoulder, Dafydd began to tell us what had happened, while the dancing flames of the fire illuminated our faces and cast our shadows against the wall behind us.

"Well, we started our search up beyond Wildwater, though we didn't think she'd have walked that far, but we didn't want to have to back track later, if we didn't find her further down river, if you know what I mean."

Dafydd paused to take a swig from his cup.

"Anyway, like I was saying, we started up there, beyond the Leap. A terrible business, to have to search for something like that. I don't think but one of us spoke a word all afternoon, did we Morgan? Drink up boy, that's it. Have you got some more of that milk for Morgan, Meg? No more milk for me, though. I'll have my medicine as it comes."

Mam tutted but did not protest, so I got up and poured more milk into Morgan's cup, which Dafydd laced with more brandy. Morgan had not spoken a word, sat staring into the flames.

"You know how it is up at Wildwater, so many boulders a body could get trapped under, and the water roaring down from them hills with such violence. I prayed she hadn't gone in there, I can tell you, for she'd be a terrible sight if she had. I think we all breathed a sigh of relief when we got further down, where the river widens and flows a bit calmer, without having seen any signs of her."

"Was her father with you?" Mam asked.

"No, we told him to stay with Gwyneth, and we'd send word to fetch him the minute we had anything to report."

"Thank goodness for that. No father should have to do a thing like that," Mam said.

"We must have walked for hours in that rain. Well, you can see how late it is. We were on the point of giving up when we got near my place, for it was getting late, and we were all tired. Then the wife comes running up to say she'd looked out and thought she'd seen something caught under a branch, down below our mill pond. It was the other side of the river, Mary said. So Morgan, Eli and me set off to see what we could see while the others went to fetch a coracle from Twm's."

I gasped at the mention of Eli's name.

"Eli is back?" I say to Dafydd.

Dafydd paused to glance at me. "Just for a couple of days, while he arranges someone else to take over."

He sighed, then, and emptied his cup. My heart had begun hammering inside my chest.

"Then Eli shouted. Over there! Beneath the tree! It was what we'd been looking for, alright, caught and partially hidden by an overhanging tree."

Tears began to stream down my face as I thought of that poor girl being driven to such a thing. I was not only crying for her but for myself, too.

"I'm sorry, Meg, it's upsetting love, I know," Dafydd said.

Dafydd's sympathy only served to make me feel more wretched, while Mam had begun reciting from the 23rd Psalm.

"Yeah, though I walk through the valley of death, I shall fear no evil......"

Dafydd reached his arm around Morgan's shoulder, for he too had begun to sob.

"Next thing I know, Morgan here had pulled off his coat and jumped right in, and was swimming across the river. Dragged her back to the bank, he did. Pulled her out, and did all he could to revive her. Didn't you, lad?"

Dafydd's voice broke on a sob and he searched in his pocket with one hand and retrieved a handkerchief to dab his eyes, patting Morgan's back all the while. Dafydd swallowed hard before continuing.

"But there was no saving her. She was long past saving."

He continued to dab at his eyes, while I and Morgan wept and Mam continued to recite the 23rd Psalm. Poor Morgan, he had such a big and generous heart, he had not considered his own safety. For all he had said in condemnation of Sian, he still had it in him to feel compassion for the suffering of another soul.

"You should be proud of your son, Esther. He's a brave young man," Dafydd said. "He risked his life, this day, in the hope of saving Sian. There's not many would have."

"Proud? Proud?" she said. "He could have drowned, or caught his death from cold. Do you think I should have been proud of him then? And for what? To save a woman who did not deserve to be saved?"

Dafydd gave Mam a long, hard stare.

"I'll leave you now. Mary will be worrying where I have got to," Dafydd said, getting up a little unsteadily from his chair.

“Take my pony, Daf!” Morgan says, and tries to stand but falls back on his chair.

“I will, thanks, I will. You stay there and keep warm. Megan will see me off.”

I light the oil lamp and lead the way across to the stable. The rain had cleared away and left a damp chill in the air which made me shudder after the warmth of the fire.

“Wept like a boy, he did, when he saw there was no hope of bringing her back,” Dafydd said, taking a bridle from a hook on the wall.

He looked at me, with a firm and steady gaze, by the light of the oil lamp. I wait for him to make his reason clear for wanting me to see him off.

“I wish to God I’d known what she was planning. I’d have taken her in, myself, rather than see her do a thing like that.”

“I feel responsible. She told me she was planning to leave for a better place but I had no idea, no idea….”

“You went to see her? Well done, Meg. I’m glad you went to see her.”

He wouldn’t be praising me if he knew my real reason for going to see her, I thought.

He continued, “a bit more compassion and less laying down of rules is what’s needed around here, if you ask me. You didn’t turn your back on her. Be proud of that. It’s like I said to your Mam, after Sian was shamed in chapel. We’ll have to let Sian know we’re not all against her, I said, or we’ll have another Mary Jones on our hands. I wish I’d acted on my own words a bit sooner, now. Reckon I’ll wish that for the rest of my days.”

He began leading the pony out of the stable.

"Who was Mary Jones?" I asked.

"It was before your time, love, when your Mam and I were young. Long before your Mam converted to the chapel. She wasn't even married to your Da then, I don't think. Mary was a young girl from the village, claimed she'd been raped but didn't know who it was, said it was after dark. No one believed her and her parents threw her out, couldn't bear the shame of it. Next day, they pulled her from the river. What else was she to do? She was ruined."

He led the pony up to the mounting block at the side of the barn.

"I'll tell you one last thing. Preacher can say what he likes. He can be as wrong as anyone else. When all's said and done, each of us has to act according to our own conscience, what our gut tells us is right or wrong, not according to some rules laid down by men for men. The way Sian was treated was wrong, and today was the result of that wrong. I hope we all learn a lesson from it. Good night, Megan."

That night I lay awake, thinking of Sian and wishing I'd had the courage to confide in her, to tell her she was not alone. If I had done so, she may still be alive. I'm so sorry, Sian, I whispered to the rafters over my head. I could never be sure if I could have prevented Sian's death, but one thing I was certain of; as Sian had said, her life here was over, anyway, she was ruined. And so was mine.

By morning, I had decided what I would do. I would take the money I had saved and walk until I reached some place where no one knew me. Then I would pass myself off as a pregnant widow. In my mind, I was convinced that my sudden and unexplained disappearance would hurt Morgan less than it would if he discovered the truth.

It was the arrival of the wool-picking girls from Cardigan which delayed my departure. I knew how much Morgan looked forward to their arrival each year, and how he delighted in their company each evening in the shelter of our barn. Let him have this bit of fun, I told myself, before he has to wake one morning to find you gone.

We had known some of the wool-picking girls since childhood, when they had come with their mothers. Now grown married women, they came with their own babies, wrapped up and strapped to their bodies with their shawls. It would take them three or four days to walk here, sleeping under the stars or in derelict barns by night. They come from the coast, via the ancient road that the monks used to walk from the abbey of Strata Florida. It is a journey of some forty miles, up and down steep mountains and through narrow river valleys.

They'd carry enough provisions to get them here, in sacks tied to their backs, and rely on the charity of us and our neighbours to provide for their journey home. Nobody begrudged them a loaf of bread or a little milk and cheese, for they were good company of an evening, entertaining us with their tales from the coast, or singing the songs of old.

They are as poor as a person can be. Their husbands are poor fishermen, or labourers, or those poor souls that work in the mines and are dead from the poison, long before their time. There are more than a few young widows amongst the wool pickers. Knitting clothes for their backs, and knitting stockings to sell from the waste wool they collect from the mountains of our parish, is the only way they can make ends meet.

That year there were rich pickings. As always, when a hot summer follows a dry spring, many of the sheep had begun to shed their wool before we got to shear them. Not so great an amount from each sheep that we would notice the loss, just bits of wool from around the neck or chest of the sheep that got caught in the bracken and gorse, or rubbed off along the stone walls. It's low grade wool, so the stockings they sell fetch the lowest prices, but the wool picking means their children are kept from the worst of cold and hunger through the winter months. And so they make the arduous journey, year after year, as have generations before them.

They set up camp on the top of our mountain and pick from dawn to dusk. The older children are set the task of picking what they can find on the ground, or of looking after the youngest children. Their mothers pick from the prickly gorse until their fingers bleed. At the days end they come down the mountain to join us. There are too many to fit in our room, a dozen or so plus the children, so we gather in our barn, along with our neighbours who come to join in the fun.

I baked extra bread and made a big pot of broth from the vegetables in our garden, to feed everyone. Then our neighbours arrive to join us each evening, for the talking and singing that last well into the night. That year I sat among them, night after night, harbouring my terrible secret, and feeling I no longer belonged among them, for I was no longer the Megan they believed me to be. I knew that my very presence among them was a betrayal, and it made me feel ashamed, so that it was only with effort that I could look them in the eye.

There was one woman who always started off the singing. Eleanor was her name. Her voice was so low and haunting; it sent a shiver through all that heard it. She'd have been about fifty then, her long, black hair streaked with silver. Her eyes were the colour of bluebells and her face as brown and weathered as the saddle on Morgan's horse. Her mother had been an Irish woman who came over the water and fell in love with a fisherman. They married and had eight children, but only two of them survived beyond the age of two; Eleanor and her brother.

I'd known Eleanor fetch tears to the eyes of grown men, Morgan and all, with her sad and haunting ballads. She would sing the verses, while we all joined in with the chorus. Then quick as a flash, she'd start tapping her feet and start us off singing a series of merry songs that would send our spirits soaring, though of course there would be no dancing. Then, when we were all sung out, and as merry as could be, she would finish with a haunting, sad ballad. While all this was going on, and I no more than an onlooker, all I could think was that I would not be here the next time they came.

Then Eleanor began to hum a keening, wordless tune before she begins to sing again. It was a sound which conjured up for me a feeling of something or someone, lost forever, and I felt the tears which I had yet to cry come closer to the surface. Then Eleanor began to sing the words.

Over the mountains, far from the seas

I hear a man's crying caught on the breeze.
He sings of his true love and her terrible fate
And fears she is knocking upon hell's open gate.
Poor Mary Jones
Hands full of stones,
Eyes brim with tears,
Heart full of fears.
While her true love was gone
And she all alone
The devil he caught her
And left her with daughter.
Poor Mary Jones
Crashed on the stones,
Clothes and frail body
But raggedy bones.
When her first love returned
For his heart for her burned,
The woman he'd left
Was changed and bereft.
She could ne'er tell her past
Fearing stones would be cast
For the lesson to teach her
By neighbour and preacher.
Poor Mary Jones
With pockets of stones
She leapt the wide water
With her unborn daughter.
Poor Mary Jones
Crashed on the stones
We should all shed a tear
For poor Mary Jones.

There was a long and dreadful silence when Eleanor reached the end of the song. Eleanor could not have known about Sian. I looked around at the stony faces of our neighbours, then I noticed Dafydd. He looked at me with tear-filled eyes. Morgan was staring at the ground, arms folded around himself. Then old Kitty let out a sigh, and told Eleanor that was an awful, sad song, and couldn't she sing something more cheery before they left, else they wouldn't sleep tonight. Oh, how I wished that all it took was a cheery song to ensure I slept at night.

The wool-pickers left two days later and as I said my goodbyes, it was with a certainty that I would never meet with them again. I would leave the next day before daybreak. The very idea of leaving all I had ever known filled me with dread and deep sadness.

If only Iago would return and marry me I would not have to go. I could not leave without being sure he had not returned for me. I needed to visit Wildwater, once more, and see the place empty of his possessions before I could shake off this hope. Was it God, or fate, that made me return there and make my humiliation complete?

Chapter 10

Megan

"You're not going up on the hill now, are you?" Morgan says on seeing me leave. "I thought you'd given up that caper."

I cannot look him in the eye and fidget with the strings of my bonnet,

"I've done my work, your supper is in the pot. Why shouldn't I go?" I say.

"For a start there's a storm brewing or hadn't you bothered to look further than the end of your nose. Second, I would have thought you'd want to avoid making yourself ill again."

"It wasn't walking the hill that made me ill," I say.

"What was it then?" he asks, and I see by his expression that he is genuinely concerned.

"I told you. It was the heat," I say, and walk away before he can contradict me.

Lies, lies and yet more lies. Lies without end, because once the first lie is told, the others rush up to cover the first, and then each other, and on and on they go. I was suffocating under the weight of them all. When did I become such an accomplished liar? It was when I began meeting Iago. So in my heart of hearts, I always knew I was doing wrong, but was too hell-bent to allow myself to see it. I lied to Morgan because if I'd told him where I was going he would have stopped me.

The heat was intense as I climbed the hill, and the air was thick and heavy. On the distant horizon, huge billowing columns of cloud were building up, portending the looming thunderstorm which Morgan spoke of. The underarms of my dress were wet with sweat by the time I reached the heath. Sweat gathered between my breasts and ran in rivulets down my belly. I take off my bonnet and fan myself but it offers little relief.

Long before I reach Wildwater I convince myself that he will not be there, yet my whole body is faintly trembling as if my body foresees the destiny which my mind denies. As I turn the bend in the river, and the house comes into view, I see that a pony is tethered by the gate and the door to the house is open. I don't know whether I shall encounter Eli or Iago. Confronting either of them fills me with trepidation and I suddenly fear to go on but know I cannot turn back.

I pause before going further, to try to calm my wits. I take deep breaths of the suffocating air to quell my rising panic and my tears threaten to rise up to blind me. It may not be Iago, but what if it is and he has not come back for me? With trembling knees, I walk up to the door and see Iago kneeling in the inglenook, throwing pieces of paper into the fire. When I knock, he glances over his shoulder at me, then he turns back to the fire without a word of welcome, but not before I have seen in his face that he is not pleased to see me. It feels like the twist of a knife blade in my heart.

I swallow hard and step inside without waiting for invitation.

"I came every day after you left. I didn't know what had happened to you, feared you must have come to some horrible end, or you would have got word to me to explain your absence."

I say all this to the back of his head, my voice trembling.

"I was otherwise engaged," he says, getting up from the floor and brushing soot from his hands.

He does not smile or say he is pleased to see me. He does not rush forward to kiss me. He stands with his arms folded across his chest, with his back leaning against the ingle wall, just as I have always known that he would, known since before my life began.

"I hear you got yourself into trouble with Eli," I say, my heart aching for what I know I have already lost.

"You could say that."

"I have something to tell you," I say. My body has grown so cold, as cold as the grave, now that the time of my nemesis has arrived. He says no words of encouragement, merely raises an eyebrow.

"I am with child," I say.

He laughs then, a cold and cruel laugh, without humour.

"And I suppose you're now going to tell me it is mine," he says, with a smirk twitching at the corners of those lips I so loved to kiss.

My body betrays me with a sharp out-breath as though he has punched me. But I do not take my eyes from his and do not falter when I speak.

"Of course it is yours. Who else's would it be?"

"That is for you to know and not I. How am I to know how many others you lie with when you're not with me?"

Those eyes, that once gazed at me with fondness and desire, are hard and dark with hostility. Still, I do not take my eyes from his, though it hurts almost more than I can bear to see the coldness there. The Iago I have been meeting with these past months no longer exists. Like the spell, he has evaporated, and his place has been taken by this stranger stood before me.

"You are the only man I have ever lain with. You know that as well as I."

"I know nothing of the sort. I do know that if you are as loose with your favours with others as you were with me then you must be in great doubt as to who is the father."

He cannot hold my gaze any longer but looks about the room as he speaks these treacherous words that slice through the heart of me.

"You said you loved me. You said we would be married. Why are you behaving like this?"

I step forward to place my hand on his arm but he flinches from my touch.

"You are just like all the rest; feigning innocence after the event, when you know damned well you wanted it as much as I. You got what you wanted; to feel a man between your legs. I have given you more pleasure than you knew in your life before. If you think I'm going to pay for it and all, you can think again."

Don't run, don't cry, hold fast to the dignity he would deny you. Stand tall and say what you have to say, don't let him see you crumble.

I feel so small, so powerless, and more alone than I have ever been. In my mind I see Morgan on the hill, gathering in his flock. The vision fills me with such a longing to be home that I feel an overwhelming need to cry. I swallow hard and hold tight to the pain within me.

"Is that what you said to Sian Pritchard, too?"

"Don't play the child, Megan. You are more than old enough to know how these things work. You were good company while it lasted. Please don't spoil things now."

It is not Iago who has vanished. It is not the dream. It is my own self, the person I thought existed in his eyes. In my place I see what Iago sees; a wanton whore, a bleating fool, a trifling thing to be tossed aside when no longer of use to him. He has reduced me to nothing, then replaced me with an image I can only detest. All that I was, and the world that was mine, are gone forever. I had lain with the devil and would pay the price.

The light coming in through the door has taken on a sickly, yellow-grey hue. In the distance I hear low rumbles of thunder. Out on the flagstone doorstep, I see the first warning drops of rain. I must reach home before the storm breaks; there is no shelter for me here. I look at Iago for the last time. In his eyes I see something worse than his hostility and contempt. In his eyes I see nothing at all. I have one last thing to say to him.

"I don't know what kind of world you come from. I only wish I had never entered it. Sian is dead because of you. I pity you and will pray for you, for I fear the devil has set up home in your heart. Know this, Iago. One day, before God, you will be made to account for the ruin of two good women."

He laughs that cruel laugh again but now it has a nervous edge. I turn on my heel and walk out of the door, into the gathering storm. The light has grown as dim as twilight, and the birds have stopped singing, though it is early in the evening still. Heavy drops of rain, the size of sovereigns, are falling more frequent. There is a sudden flash of distant lightening which startles me. But my fear of the storm is as nothing compared with the terror I feel at the thought of the future I am walking towards.

Words rush through my mind as I try to calm myself. *Don't cry, Megan, don't cry. No don't, don't cry now, you must get home. Get home before the storm breaks. No don't, don't think of it, do not think of what he said. Get home!*

When I am out of sight of the house, I break into a run. I run as if my life depends on getting as far away from Iago as I can. I run as though, if I run fast enough and far enough, I will reach a place where his evil words can no longer touch me. I run, stumbling over stones, with the rain and tears pouring down my face. With one, deafening crack of thunder, the heavens open, and it seems that all the sins of the world are being heaped upon my head. A blinding, forked bolt of lightning shoots down from the heavens, as if God has pointed his finger at me to strike me down. It lights up the sky, illuminating the tree boughs tossed from side to side by the strengthening wind. The lightning is followed by a crashing of thunder. Then, another bolt of lightning lights up the whole sky. I am surrounded by visions of hell itself, as though God is giving me a foretaste of what is coming for me.

I continue to run, though with each breath I take I feel my lungs will burst. I go on running and stumbling, splashing through the rainwater that floods the sheep paths on the heath. My clothes are soaked through, they cling to me and my sodden skirts weigh heavy on my legs. There is nowhere to run and no hiding place from either the storm, or the images and words of Iago, which I cannot get out of my mind.

You were loose with your favours. You were good company while it lasted. You wanted it as much as me. You're just like all the rest.

And his face, I keep seeing his hard unsmiling face; and his eyes, his eyes devoid of any feeling.

The next day breaks to a dawn of consequences. My sodden clothes lie in a crumpled heap upon the floor. I lie in my bed with the blankets drawn tight around me. I lie curled up, holding my knees tight with my arms, to try to stop the shaking. I cannot tell if I am shivering with fright or from the drenching of last night. I listen to the rain, pouring out of the gutters, and beating out a rhythm on an upturned pail outside the porch. The storm has passed but the rain goes on and on.

I feel that I shall be suffocated by the grief that threatens to engulf me because it cannot loudly cry its name. My body is wracked by the silent sobs I dare not give release. Only a thin wall separates me from mother's prying ears, where she lies in the room next to mine. She must not know, not ever know, this thing that I have done. I think of Morgan and the hurt and anger I would see in his eyes if I told him. His love and respect are all I have worth holding onto. If I were to confide in him, then that too, would be lost.

The first light of dawn creeps through the shutters. I wait until I hear Morgan rise and go out. I dress myself in dry clothes and go downstairs. Mother will not rise from her bed for another hour or so. Morgan will return in a couple of hours for breakfast. I stir the fire into life and feed it more fuel. I hang a pot of water over the fire, to boil. I lay out their breakfast food on the table.

Outside, the rain has stopped, and gaps are appearing in the clouds. Steam rises from the saturated ground as the rising sun warms the air. I go down to the gorge with the yoke and pails to carry the day's water back to the house. I pause on my return, to look out over the valley below, for the last time. Then I milk the cow, apologising for my haste, and carry the pail of milk to the cool of the dairy.

There is no time to do anything else for I must be away before Mam and Morgan appear. I go quietly indoors and take my cape from its peg. I fold it up and place it in my basket so that I shall have something to throw over me at night. I put some bread and cheese in there, too. Then I make my way over to the barn to get the money I have saved. It will last me long enough, till I am far away from here. I shall go to some place where nobody knows me. I shall pass myself off as a homeless widow, looking for work and shelter for myself and the child that is to come. I shall live a life of lies, but at least the child shall live.

Don't start crying now, be brave. There will be time aplenty for tears.

I go to my secret hiding place and remove the stone from the wall. At first, I cannot believe, will not believe, that my purse is not where I left it. At first, I tell myself I must be mistaken for my mind is befuddled. I retrace my steps from the barn door, thinking there must be two stones alike and I have simply looked behind the wrong one. I do this even though I know it is in vain. If the money is no longer here, then I am completely undone.

This possibility is too terrible to contemplate and so my mind refuses to acknowledge the possibility. I return to the hole in the wall and stare at the empty space. Could I have put it somewhere else without thinking? I know the answer before I have finished asking it. I have been so careful with that purse, as though it were a precious, fragile thing. I could not have been careless with it if I'd tried.

I try to think of what to do, where to look, who might have taken it, but panic is scattering my thoughts like chickens trapped by the fox.

Calm down. Stop that crying, mother will hear you. It's not the end of the world, I tell myself.

Oh, but it is. If I don't find the money, my life is over. No means to run, no place to hide, every sin to be accounted for and paid for sooner or later. I shall not be allowed to run, and God will deny me any hiding place. I will be made to face the consequences of what I have done. I would rather throw myself in the river.

'Whatever is the matter, Meg?'

Morgan's voice so startles me that my whole body leaps with fright. I wipe my face with my pinafore and try to compose myself, but the tears go on pouring from my eyes.

"The money! All the money I have been saving! It's gone!" I wailed.

"Perhaps you put it somewhere else without thinking," Morgan says.

'No! It was here! One of the wool pickers must have taken it!'

"Don't be daft. The wool picking girls may be as poor as can be but they're honest. Besides, not one of them would steal from us for fear they would not be allowed back," Morgan says, and I know he is right.

"Then, who? Oh, Morgan! I must have it! If they have not taken it then it must be here somewhere. It must be here, it has to be here!"

I begin scratting about the floor on my hands and knees, like a mad woman, looking under wool sacks, in the hen's nests, amid the implements, knowing I will not find it but not able to accept the fact.

"Stop it, Megan! I have never seen you in such a state!" Morgan says, taking me by the arms and lifting me up.

"If the wool picking girls have not taken my money, that leaves only you or Mam," I say to him.

"It damned well was not me and I do not believe that Mam would have taken it," he says.

'Oh well, no point crying about it now. What's done is done. Let this be a lesson to you, girl; it is for God to decide what you shall or shall not have,' Mam said, as calmly as if I had told her I had spilt a jug of milk.

I knew our Mam well enough to know how she would normally react on hearing that money had been lost. She'd have torn a strip off me, and not let me hear the last of how I could not be trusted, was good for nothing, and so on. She'd have been red in the face, and dancing with rage, to hear that some of the money from the cheeses had gone for nought. Most of all, she would have wanted to get to the bottom of what had happened to it. She'd have been up in arms at the thought of it being stolen. But she sat there with that expression I knew from old. Satisfied, that was what it was. Satisfied.

I realised, then, why Mam had sat back and done little to try to kerb my trips to market. She'd been biding her time, waiting for her moment to outplay me. She'd let me follow the carrot that I pursued, only to snatch it away as I reached it.

"You took it! You stole my money!"

She denied it, of course, and made a big scene about 'how her own daughter had accused her of such a thing and how she would never forgive it'. Morgan knew, I could see by his face, he knew she had taken my money. He knew her as well as I.

"To hell with you then," I told her. "I shall sell no more for you to go and steal my share."

My whole life, I had walked straight in to every trap she set for me. I was about to discover I had done so again. I had reacted just as she had expected me to.

"How are we supposed to manage if you don't sell your cheese at market?" Morgan demands to know, and Mam provides him with the answer.

"I shall go myself, Morgan," she says with a smug smile.

"You? How on earth are you going to do that?" he asks her.

"I'm perfectly capable. You seem to have forgotten, I used to travel every week to market, with the pony and cart, when you were children."

"Yes, but…"

"But what? I won't have forgotten how to drive the pony, you know."

The very next Friday, and every one after that, off she went, as if she had never had a day's illness in her life, but she always came back complaining it would take her till the next Friday to recover her strength. It felt like she had stolen my life from me, but of course, she had stolen nothing. I had thrown it away, all by myself.

I knew that Morgan must have told Mam I had been putting away a little of the takings for myself. He must have told her, though he had promised he would not. Why else would she have gone looking for it?

"Why, Morgan? Why did you go and tell her?" I asked him.

"I don't like telling her lies," he said.

"You didn't have to lie! You just had to say nothing!" I shouted at him.

"Lying is the same as hiding the truth, Megan," he said.

I could almost feel my own lies snapping at my heels as he said the words I knew to be true.

"I must have that money, Morgan. You must tell me what she's done with it."

"I don't know why you're making such a fuss over it. And for what? Some bit of a dress? I think Mam's right. You've taken leave of your senses since Eli left. We're trying to save the farm and all you can think about is yourself."

"That's not true. That's a horrible thing to say. Nobody has worked harder than me for that money. And it isn't for a dress that I want it."

"You told me that was what it was for! You told me that! Was that a lie, too?"

"No. That *was* what I wanted it for…but now I want it, need it, for something more important. What do you mean, was that a lie, too?"

My heart was hammering inside my chest, thinking I had been found out already. Had someone seen me meeting Iago? Had Morgan seen me go over there?

"Because you lied about how much money you were clawing away for yourself, that's why, Megan. There you were telling me you were just taking a little bit when you were taking half, at least."

"What? That's not true!"

"I saw for myself how much was in that purse. Me and Mam counted it together."

Oh, she was too bad, too bad. She must have stolen the purse, then put extra in there, so as to make Morgan think the worst of me.

"Mam put it there. I swear to you, Morgan, I wouldn't have taken more than I said I would."

He wouldn't look at me and his face was a picture of hurt and disappointment in me.

"I would never lie to you, Morgan."

The lie was out of my mouth before I'd known I was going to say it.

"I wouldn't have lied to you about that," I say, trying to undo the biggest lie of them all.

"Aye, well, you can say what you like, Megan, but I won't believe our Mam put all that money there to trick me."

He turned his back on me then, and I knew that I had lost his respect and trust, not because of what *I* had said and done, but because Mam had duped him. I would not try to persuade him of the truth, because I knew he could not bear to believe his own mother would do that to him. I understood him perfectly then, because I knew, only too well, the pain of knowing your own mother would cheat on you.

There was just one person in the world who might help me. Myfanwy, I knew, would not judge me. She might even take me in for a time, until I found employment somewhere. Myfanwy was my only hope.

"Do you remember a woman called Myfanwy at the market? She knits stockings for a living with her daughters," Mam says to me that Friday evening, after she has been to market.

She is sat in her chair by the fire, busily knitting. "She and I are the very best of friends. Her daughters are *very* nice girls, the sort of girls a mother would be *glad* to have around her. Myfanwy and I get on very well. She doesn't bear grudges. She understands it isn't my fault that I have a liar for a daughter."

I feel like the ground beneath my feet has been wrenched away, and I am falling into an abyss.

"Aye! You may well look afraid. She knows all about you, now. She knows you're one of us 'hell-fire and brimstone, Baptist lot'. Not that she minds that one bit. It's that you pretended to be something you're not, that's what really riled her. 'If there's one thing I cannot bear, it is a liar,' were her words."

Now, I was more alone in this world than I'd ever imagined a person could be.

Chapter 11

Megan

God is not merciful; he does not strike me down though I pray all summer that he might. I live each day with dread in my heart of what lies ahead of me. I would face it because I had not the courage to throw myself in the Wildwater. I had not a farthing or any place to seek refuge. I was to be forced to look upon those faces that had looked upon me with fondness all my life, and see anger and hatred where I once saw love. I was to be cast out, never again to take part in the shearings, the harvests, the get-togethers. I was to be taught that to be a sinner was to cease to belong anywhere. I knew this was to be my fate for I had seen the same done to Sian Pritchard.

Haymaking came and went, followed by the corn harvest. How I despised myself that summer, amongst our life-long neighbours and friends. I felt unworthy to sit among them, knowing how I had betrayed them all and no longer deserved their friendship. I had gone against all they believed in and held dear. I had betrayed their unquestioned trust in me to live by the same rules as they. Each smile they bestowed upon me made me feel like Judas himself.

I had nothing to live for but the child which daily grew inside me. I cling to the hope that, when I am cast out, Morgan will find it in his heart to persuade Mam to give me some money to help me on my way. I will take the child as I planned, before my money was stolen, and go somewhere far away. And it will be alright for I won't be alone, I will have the child. When I think like this, I feel stronger and able to go on.

I try to impress on my memory every image of that summer, knowing it shall be my last at Carregwyn. Each evening, when the sun is going down and my chores are done, I go and sit up on the mountain. I look out over the valleys below and to the hills beyond. I take in the dip and rise of every field, the size and shape of every tree and coppice, the shapes and colours of each and every hill. I close my eyes and hold the images in my mind so that I will carry them with me when I leave. I lay back and, with my eyes closed, feel the warm breath of the wind caress my skin; breathe deep the scents of sun-baked heath grass and flowers.

Every flower seems to come out that summer to witness my passing and to make me ache with the missing of them before I am even gone. Rock-roses, birds-foot-trefoil, tormentil and heath orchids smother the short, cropped turf of the hills. Fox-gloves grow up through the bracken. Purple and yellow vetches flower amidst the buttercups, red clover and grasses in the meadows. Meadowsweet flourishes in the damp hedgerows and ditches, its heady scent competing with that of the honeysuckle and dog roses. The deep pink, feathery flowers of ragged robin grow amongst reeds in the boggy areas on the hill.

I gaze on them all, long and hard, and breathe in the scents of summer. I commit them all to my memory so that, wherever my child shall grow up, I will be able to conjure up this place for her with my memories and my words, so that she shall know it and love it as much as I, as much as if she had lived here herself.

When I milk the cow, I close my eyes as I rest my head on her warm flank. I listen to her chewing the cud, to her steady breathing and the sound of each gush of steaming milk as it hits the pail. She is an old friend, who I have known since she was born, without whom I would never have known the delights of the market place.

The summer passes so quickly for there is so much to do. My work in the dairy doubles as the cow puts out great quantities of milk. I do not finish with the butter and cheese making until mid-morning each day. Then there are eggs to collect, the garden to tend, cooking to do, laundering, the house to clean, and the fetching and carrying of water and fuel for the fire. My outdoor chores are a mercy for they keep me away from mother's ever watchful eye as my belly begins to swell.

And Morgan, dear sweet brother that he once was, is so especially kind and considerate to me that summer, that it breaks my heart in two. It is far harder to bear his kindly concern for me, than it will be to suffer his angry and silent condemnation when he discovers my betrayal. Which pain is the greater? To betray or be betrayed? It hurts me as much to know I am deceiving Morgan as it did to be deceived by Iago.

I do not doubt that God shall make me account for spoiling a good man, for my actions changed Morgan as much as Iago's did mine. When still but a child, he became my refuge and consolation from mother's criticism and spite. He was just a boy and could protect me from neither, but his presence was like a salve for my hurts and wounds. Morgan taught me, without words, that I was a person as worthy as anyone of the love and respect of another. If there had been no Morgan, I would have grown up without knowing that. In return, I would teach Morgan that to love is to be betrayed.

'Don't cry Meg, don't cry.' Morgan says, placing his hand on my shoulder. I am eight years old and he six. I had earlier gone up on the hill behind the house and made a little posy from the violets growing there. I had placed the posy on the bleached calico pillowcase of mother's bed, not knowing the little gift would stain the calico.

Mother makes me stand outside with the washtub full of cold water. She says I will stay there until I have scrubbed out every last stain. I rub and rub but the stains don't budge.

'You will have to rub harder then,' she says.

I scrub and rub until the blisters on the palms of my hands burst open, and my knuckles are red raw and bleeding, and I cannot bear the pain any longer. Only when I see there are fresh red blood stains mingled with the purple, do I begin to weep.

'Get out of my sight!' Mother shouts when she sees what I have done, and I run for the hill where little Morgan comes to comfort me.

Don't cry, Meg, don't cry.

Keeping the child, the evidence of my wickedness, hidden in my belly, I become a person I do not recognise as myself. The Megan who existed but a few months ago had vanished, and I sorely grieved her passing. I thought of who I used to be; the Megan I could respect and be proud of; who, though her mother did not love her, was loved by her brother and neighbours; who caught the eye of a good and honest man called Eli, and who hoped for love and marriage; who felt secure and safe in the knowledge that she belonged right where she was.

Attending chapel every Sunday was a quite terrifying ordeal. When the preacher told us that God shall cast out all sinners, and of the burning flames of hell that are the fate of those who will suffer eternal damnation, I feel convinced that he speaks to me personally, and that his eyes are boring into my very soul when he looks out over the congregation.

Geraint confesses that he has succumbed again to his weakness for ale and begs that God forgive him. We all say a prayer for him and do the same for Ceridwen when she confesses that she has committed the sin of avarice. Their sins seem such small, trifling things, compared with mine, and yet they are enough to make them fear God's approbation. My very presence in our chapel, with my sins not confessed, is a sin itself. But the thought of standing up and making my confession fills me with such terror that I fear I will collapse. I should not be there but I cannot stay away without telling my reason. Each time I think of telling, my courage fails me.

Summer made way for autumn and the sun sat lower in the sky, rising later, sinking earlier, and casting long shadows over the landscape. In the mornings, a heavy dew drenched the ground, and the valleys below were transformed into tree-studded islands in the mist. Leaves began to redden, and fruits become ripe. There were apples to pick and store away for the winter. Out in the field, Morgan lifted the potatoes and turnips he had been growing all summer. I picked damsons and elderberries in the orchard, and went foraging for blackberries in the woods and hedgerows. All that I did, I believed was for the last time.

It is while I am out picking blackberries that I feel the first movement of the child stirring within me, like a butterfly beating its wings. From that moment on, I began to see my future life as mother of my child. I could imagine her little hand in mine as she walked beside me. Though I could not know, I felt certain the child was a girl. I could hear myself telling her of a place called Carregwyn, describing the beauty of every place she would never see for herself.

Until the autumn turns to grim December, I think my unborn child must sense my need to keep her hidden, as the shape of me hardly changes. But from then on she becomes increasingly difficult to hide. I wear my pinafores loosely tied over my dress, which is all but bursting at the seams. Yet still, with the truth becoming more evident each day, I cannot find the courage to tell either Mam or Morgan of my condition. I cannot find the right words to so much as begin. There is a gulf so wide between my reality and theirs. I try to prepare myself, try to foresee their reactions if I were to find the words to tell them, but it was beyond the scope of my imagination. It was too different from anything I had experienced in my life so far.

So it was as well, in the end, that Mam saw it for herself shortly after the beginning of the new year. I think the shock would have killed her if she had not known anything until the baby was born. I was clearing the table after our meal and leaned over to pick up Mam's plate. My swelling belly must have brushed against her. I didn't know her meaning at first.

"Is there something you're not telling us, girl?" Mam asks me, her face a stiff mask and a red flush mottling her neck, a sure sign that her anger was up, though as yet I have no idea what I had done to rile her now.

"What have I done now?" I ask her.

"Oh, I think you know, alright. Do you take me for a fool?"

Only then do I suspect the truth is about to come out, and I turn from the table, but Mam grabs my arm so tight I cry out with the pain.

"What in hell has got into you?" Morgan says to Mam.

"That's the question you should be asking her! Take a good look at your sister's belly if you want the answer," she says.

Morgan looks from Mam to me. By now I am crimson with shame but I can see by Morgan's face he still has no idea as to Mam's meaning. I think the prospect of me being pregnant was so preposterous to him that he couldn't see what was staring him in the face.

"Go on! Tell your brother what a filthy slut he has for a sister!" Our Mam shouts at me, rising up from her chair. The next thing I know, she is hitting me about my head with her stick. I stand still as a rat before the cudgel strikes him dead. All the world I have ever known will never exist again after this moment. I stand there, head bowed and shoulders hunched, with my arms at my sides, and let her mete out my just punishment. I feel a warm trickle of blood pour from my brow. Then Morgan leaps from his chair, tossing it aside in his haste. It clatters across the floor and comes to rest below the stairs. He has hold of our Mam, shouting at her to calm down. He pushes her back into her chair, where she sits, panting.

"Calm down, you say!" she says when she has got her breath back. "Calm down, when your sister has done this behind our backs?"

I stand motionless, staring at the floor, frozen with fear and shock now this moment has arrived. Morgan hasn't taken it in yet, can't believe what our Mam is saying about me.

"You must be mistaken, Mam. Tell her she's mistaken, Meg," he says, and laughs nervously as if to say 'listen to how ridiculous our Mam is'.

I remain silent and close my eyes when I see Morgan stare at me, his eyes beseeching me to deny what Mam was accusing me of.

"Now we know why she was walking the hills every night!" Mam says.

"Did he force you? Tell me who he is and I'll go and tear his heart out," Morgan says to me, his voice trembling.

"Nobody forced me," I say, unable to look up at him when I speak.

He stares at me, and then raises his fist to me. For a few moments, I fear he will knock me down dead but then he lets his hand fall. He is shaking with rage.

"Who is he? I suppose you've arranged a date for the marriage without telling us and all," he says, tight-lipped.

I cannot bring myself to answer.

"Well? When are you getting married? You can't leave it any longer, unless you want the whole neighbourhood to know your shame."

"There's not going to be any marriage," I say, my voice barely more than a whisper.Then our Mam starts crying, a high pitched wailing sound, her mouth gaping.

"She's ruined us! She's ruined us! We shall never hold our heads up in public again!"

Morgan starts shouting to be heard over the noise Mam is making.

"Like hell there will be no marriage! He'll marry you, if I have to drag him down the aisle myself!"

I sink down in my chair and hold my head in my hands.

"He's gone back where he came from. He refuses to marry me," I say, fighting back tears.

"Where does he come from? I'll go and fetch him back with my boot up the coward's backside," he says, still believing he can rescue the situation.

"I don't know where he has gone."

"She's no better than a common slut! My own daughter!" Mam wails.

"Did you at least think to ask his name before you laid down with him?' Morgan asks me then, his voice thick with contempt.

"Oh aye, I knew his name, alright, but I shall not ever tell it to you," I say, knowing Morgan would commit murder if he ever caught up with Iago.

The next day was market day. They could not look at me. They spoke to each other but not to me. It was as if I had become invisible, as if I did not exist. It made me shrink inside. Mam went off with the cart, and I went to where Morgan was working in the barn, hoping to appeal to him for some compassion for my plight. He is shoveling the freshly threshed oats of last year's harvest into storage sacks. The winter sun casts my shadow across him, so he must know I am there, leaning against the open barn door, but he does not look up or pause in his work. I swallow hard before I speak.

"It is not like you think. He said he loved me. I believed we would get married," I say.

He drives the shovel into the mound of oats and tips it into the open sack. Then he does the same again, and again, no doubt hoping I will take the hint and skulk off back to the house. Then he stops and kicks the sack at his feet.

"And that makes it alright in your book, does it?" he says, not directing his stare at my face but at my feet. He cannot bear to look at me. "I'll tell you what, Megan. The poor house, the courts, and the rivers are full of young women like you. Women who set out to seduce and trap men, and then claim to be innocent victims when they don't get the promise of marriage they're after. The difference between many of them and you is that you were not brought up in ignorance. You were brought up to know right from wrong, and to live by the Ten Commandments as laid down in our Bible. If ever proof was needed of the consequences of sin, then you are the living, breathing evidence."

He wipes the dust and sweat from his face with the back of his hand.

"I didn't set out to trap him. That is a cruel thing to accuse me of. I thought he was honest, I did not think he was insincere in his feelings for me," I say, and despise the whiny note of my voice.

"Well, then you know exactly how I feel. I once believed you were honest too!"

He turns his back on me and returns to his task.

The barn door creaks as I retreat. As I walk back over the cobbles to the house, I hear him throw down his shovel and begin to sob.

That evening, when I have placed their food before them and they have eaten, they begin discussing my predicament as if I am not there.

"I shall go to the preacher tomorrow and tell him what she's done," Morgan says.

Mam says nothing but gets up from the table with a heavy sigh and goes to sit in her chair by the fire.

"She can face them all on Sunday," he goes on.

I feel like a cold claw has descended into my stomach and clenched it in its fist.

"There's no need to rush into things," Mam says.

"What do you mean? She'll have to confess."

"Do you think I want that? Everyone knowing what she has done? Everyone knowing how she has brought shame on us?" she says, then turns to point an accusing finger at me. "Aye! You'll enjoy that, won't you? You'll enjoy ruining my good name and reputation along with your own!"

She was so full of spite and vengeance herself; she could not imagine any other motive in someone else.

"They'll find out soon enough, anyway," Morgan says, "there's no point in putting it off. We might as well get it over with."

"We'll see. Leave it with me. We'll say nothing for the time being. It won't do any harm to give your sister time to reflect on what she's done, and think about her punishment."

I muster the courage to speak.

"If you will give me back the money you stole from me, I will go. You won't have to worry about anyone finding out, then," I say.

Mam and Morgan both start talking at the same time; Morgan asking how in hell did I think they were going to run this place without me, Mam denying any knowledge of my money.

"Alright, if you didn't steal it, you're making plenty now from the cheese I make. So give me some of that, and I promise you I will be gone before morning," I say to Mam.

"And where do you plan to go? Chasing after him, I suppose?" Morgan says.

"I told you, I don't know where he is. I will go far away from here, where no one knows me, as far as my feet will carry me. I just want enough to keep me until I find work," I tell him.

"You've taken leave of your senses, again. Who is going to employ you in that state?" he says, pointing at my belly. "And what work will you be fit for? Have you thought about that?"

"I could get work as a dairy maid or a house maid. If I can do the work here, I can do it elsewhere just as well."

"And what are we supposed to do? Hire a maid to replace you? That will take care of our profits, won't it? But I don't suppose you were thinking of us when you were making your plans." Morgan is spluttering with anger as he speaks.

"Now you know, boy," Mam says to him. "How many times have I told you, your sister can't be trusted and thinks of no one but herself? Perhaps you'll heed me now."

"Oh aye, I'll heed you, alright," he says.

"If you both think so little of me, you should be glad to see me go," I say to both of them.

"Oh, I'd be glad to see you go alright, if it didn't mean our poor Mam here would have to do your work instead."

"As if I haven't suffered enough….." Mam says with a tremulous voice.

"That's right, Mam, and now this."

Morgan glares at me with a hatred and contempt that breaks my heart.

"You make me sick. After what happened to Sian Pritchard and all. I can't believe I'm standing here talking to you. You're going nowhere. You'll stay and face up to your shame, that's what you'll do."

"Malicious spite. That's why she's done this. To spite us. Just like her father before her, there's nothing she'd like better than to show me up and besmirch my good name," Mam says to Morgan.

"Well, Mam, you would think that, wouldn't you?" I say. "Because malice and spite are all that you are made of."

"I will not sit here and be insulted in my own home by a common slut," she says, haughtily, rising up from her chair and announcing;

"I am going to my bed."

"So am I," says Morgan, with a harsh glare at me.

I sat a long while, gazing into the flames of the fire, its light throwing flickering shadows on the walls of the room. We are all alone in this world, I whisper to the little one in my belly. We are as despised as two creatures can be. I know not a soul who will help us.

The thought of going on living in that house was unbearable. How could I live through each day with two people who despised me? I knew why Mam was in no hurry for my sins to be made public. She saw my shame as a reflection on herself. She had so readily condemned Sian's parents, she feared that same condemnation would now be turned on herself. And she knew how hard the waiting for my punishment would be for me.

As I contemplated all this, it was with a feeling of overwhelming sadness. That I had brought it all on myself was indisputable. That I had been reckless and stupid, likewise. But what of Iago? Had he not been reckless, stupid and selfish, too? Yet he was off to a new life, probably a new girl, and would never be punished as I was being punished. God would be the only one to judge him and his actions, no one else. Not his mother, brother, neighbours or friends. I had committed no greater sin than him. It seemed I was not being punished for my sin but because I was a woman.

As soon as it was light, I began ransacking the house in search of money. I went through every drawer and chest and, once Mam was out of her bed and Morgan out and about his work, I lifted the mattresses from their beds. Then I started again downstairs in the vain hope that I had overlooked it somewhere.

"You won't find what you're looking for, if you look from now till kingdom come," Mam said, watching me.

I was in the process of emptying the dresser drawers for the second time. I got up off my knees, exhausted, my belly aching. I stood with my arms at my sides, my hands clenched into fists.

"Please give it to me then, Mam. I shall go, with or without it. Do you want to be responsible for me and your grandchild starving on the road?"

She began to weep then. Not the pretend tears she put on when she couldn't get her own way but quiet tears that rolled down her cheeks from closed eyes. She held a hand to her mouth but her shoulders shook with the sobs she was trying hard to suppress. The sight of this genuine display of grief shocked and frightened me more than all her tantrums. I couldn't remember the last time I had seen her truly upset, and to see it was to know how badly I had wronged her.

Tears welled up in my own eyes and I wanted to run to her and say 'I'm so sorry, Mam, so sorry. Please forgive me'. But I stood rigid as the handle of Morgan's rake. I watched her fumble in her skirt pocket for a handkerchief. She dried her eyes and let out a shuddering sigh. Then she opened her eyes and looked at me with such sadness, it made me feel worse than all her anger and condemnation.

"You mustn't go. I cannot manage without you. We shall just have to find a way to deal with this," she said, and her face began to crumple again and more tears flowed.

In all the years, when she had done nothing but find fault with me and everything I did, she had never before admitted she could not manage without me. My heart swelled with the idea that she must love me after all, or she would never be so upset at the thought of my going.

"I'll stay then, Mam," I said with a sudden rush of sympathy for her.

The next day I went into an early labour.

"Fortune! That is what we shall name her, for that is what she'll cost us, one way or another," Mam declared, on discovering my child was a girl.

I had laboured all night alone to bring her into this vale of tears. Of course, Mam refused to send Morgan to fetch the midwife because the whole parish would have heard about it by the next morning.

"It is for God to decide whether they live or die," she said, in answer to Morgan when he made the request for help on my behalf.

"It's no place for a man," she said, when he asked to be allowed to help me then, claiming he could do as well as any midwife, he'd pulled enough calves and lambs in his time.

This conversation took place out on the landing, beyond the closed door of my bed chamber, the gist of which I caught between my screams of fear and pain and pleas for help. Fortune arrived with the dawn and her cries competed with the birdsong outside my window. As I looked into her eyes for the first time, I felt overwhelmed with love of her.

I emptied the chest in which I kept clothes and bedding, and this became her crib, lined with the sheepskin cover of my bed. Morgan must have loved her a little because he carved two pieces of curved wood and nailed them to the bottom of her crib, so I could rock her to sleep at night.

That week, the first snows arrived to hide away my shame. They came swirling in, one evening, on a northerly wind. The next morning, we awoke to find the snow blown under the front door, in a drift which reached the bottom of the stairs. On opening the door, Morgan was confronted with a wall of snow which he had to dig out before he could get out to check on his sheep. He'd sniffed snow on the air the day before, he said, and had the wits to bring his flocks down from the topmost hills. Mam said it was a godsend, for we wouldn't have to worry now about anyone coming up here and discovering my shame.

"Take it away from me!" Mam said, when I asked her if she would like to hold Fortune.

"Look how perfect she is!" I said to Morgan.

He looked softly on her for a moment, before turning away and saying gruffly that he had work to get on and do.

"If you think I'm going to tend that thing so you can go about your chores, you have another think coming," Mam said.

I bound Fortune to me with my shawl. With her tiny head resting on my breast, she slept while I trudged through the sparkling snow to carry water. On she slept, as I churned the butter and milked the cow, only stirring occasionally to open her sweet little rosebud mouth to yawn. When I paused from my work to feed her, her eyes would lock with mine as she sucked on my breast, as though she was looking deep into my soul. Like this we spent our days until my chores were done. Then I would retire to my room with her, and sit beside her in her cosy crib, away from Mam's disapproving gaze.

Fortune was some two weeks old or more when Morgan came up to my room on one such evening, offering to carry the crib downstairs, so I could sit by the warmth of the fire.

"You can't go on sitting up here every night in the freezing cold," he said to my protest that I did not want to sit where I was not welcome.

"Look at you. You're shivering with the cold up here. You're coming down," he said and lifted the crib with Fortune inside it, and carried them down the stairs.

"I won't stand for Megan sitting upstairs all evening in the depths of winter. It's not right," he said to Mam, placing the crib on the ground, when she asked what did he think he was doing, bringing that thing in the same room as her.

"Her little nose is cold," he said, leaning over the crib and stroking Fortune's nose with the back of his finger.

Fortune's eyes sprang open with alarm. She had not been touched before by anyone but me. She stared up at Morgan, her wide eyes searching his face. Then she grasped his finger in her tiny fist.

"She's a strong one! Look how she's got hold of me!" he said, turning to me with a smile of delight.

I felt overwhelmed with gratitude and joy that Morgan was as delighted by Fortune as me. I thought then, everything is going to be alright, Morgan has taken to her and Mam will too, with time. I could bear the condemnation of the whole parish if I only had them to support me.

Following that first evening, Morgan's interest in Fortune grew, and he would offer to hold her for me while I prepared our supper. It made me smile to see him fussing over her, talking to her and rocking her to sleep. Mam would sit in stony faced disapproval throughout, averting her gaze from Fortune. I thought it would just be a matter of time before she swallowed her pride and relented.

Chapter 12

Morgan

There are some things a person should never ask of another, and to the end of my days I will solemnly wish our Mam had not asked what she did of me. By day, I can tell myself I only did what Mam asked of me. But at night God shines his lantern, and its penetrating light seeks out and illuminates the hidden places of my heart, so that I must face the truth I try so hard not to think about by day.

Back then, I told myself Megan was lucky. If it wasn't for our Mam, she'd have been turned out of the house with nowhere to go and not a soul in the world prepared to take her in. She'd have found the door of every neighbour slammed in her face. She'd have had no other recourse but to throw herself in the river like Sian Pritchard had done, or to make her way to the poor house and be separated from her child, anyway.

In the middle of my sleepless nights, I see that Megan's deception is just another hook on which I can hang up my conscience. By day, I can say, if she had not deceived me then I could have forgiven her. By night, I know that I did not have it in me to forgive her. I have come to believe, of late, that it was my test in this life to find it in my heart to forgive Megan, and I have failed it. Each restless night, I wake from dreams that are memories of that time. I see myself, sullen and speechless, punishing Megan with my silence. I turn in my bed, away from this vision only to see another, of

Megan as alone as any person could be, alone with her fate, and not a soul to confide in or to ask for help.

Mam was doing right by Megan, that's what I told myself. Our Mam was rescuing Megan from the terrible consequences of her actions. Our Mam went out of her way to cover up Megan's sin. I saw it as an act of supreme forgiveness on the part of our Mam. Not until the time came to carry out Mam's wishes, and take Megan's baby, did I question the rightness of what we were doing. I have had cause to question it ever since.

Mam had the strength of mind which I lacked. While she stood strong, there were times when I started to weaken, and feel compassion for Megan and her plight, until Mam reminded me how Megan had betrayed us.

"Don't you see the kind of person your sister really is?" Mam asks me.

Megan is up in her room where she has spent her evenings alone since Fortune was born. She is hiding away up there with her shame. The only times I see her are when she quietly places my meals on the table before me.

"To think what she was scheming all those months! You've always thought butter would not melt in her mouth. Well, now you know better!" Mam says, looking at me with her 'I told you so' face.

"Just imagine how she must have been laughing at you, coming back here and playing the innocent after what she'd been up to."

"Aye, I can imagine it, all right. There's no need to rub my nose in it!"

"I'm just surprised, that's all, that she did not come to you and ask your advice about this man, given she was supposed to think so much of you."

She had an uncanny knack, our Mam, of knowing exactly what a person had on their mind. It was the very question I'd lain awake all night asking myself. Why hadn't Megan come to me before it was too late?

"She couldn't have really thought much of you, could she? Not a word about it to you, and you always having treated her so well and all."

I stare into the flames of the fire, my heart aching with the hurt of it, wondering what kind of deluded fool I was, to think Megan was the good and honest sister I'd always believed her to be.

"You must see now, Morgan, why I've always had to be hard on her. I saw the bad in her from the beginning, saw what you've always been blind to."

By the flames of the fire, I look at Megan in a new and ugly light which illuminates every blemish. I see memories of instances when I felt her fondness and respect. As I look, they become nothing more than ploys to gain my sympathy and I want to spit on the fire.

"She's been playing you for a fool all these years, boy, but if I'd have told you, you'd have refused to see it. Well, now you have seen it for yourself."

"Aye, alright, you've had your say, Mam. Will you leave it now?"

"It's a pity you didn't see it sooner is all I can say. If you had, this would never have happened. If you hadn't been so soft on her, she would never have dared to go behind your back. She'd have had some respect for you, as the man of the house. But there we are, what's done is done."

It had not occurred to me that I might be to blame for Megan's ruin; that it was all down to my lack of authority as a man. I never thought of it as a failure on my part until our Mam let me know it.

"So it's my fault now, is it?" I say, my anger rising to take the place of my hurt feelings.

"There's no point blaming yourself. How were you to do your duty while your sister was prepared to take you for a fool? It is all down to her that you have failed in your duty," Mam says, letting me know that I have failed but offering me a peg, in the form of Megan's deception, on which I can hang my guilt.

I gladly hang my guilt on that peg in the weeks that follow. Megan had no one but herself to blame. Whether Megan did what she did to get back at our Mam, or she'd set out to entrap the man into marriage, to have her revenge on Eli, either reason meant she deserved no sympathy for the plight she was in. I had no desire to hear her version of events because I knew I could no longer trust a word she said. Megan had broken my trust and I'd be a fool to wholly trust her again. Even if I might forgive, I could never forget. While I lived, I would always remember how she had deceived me. Trust is such a precious, fragile thing.

Mam could not have sent Fortune further away without taking her out of the country. The further she goes the better, she said, where nobody will know her. She'd seen Nesta Harding's name mentioned in a newspaper, and it was I who had fatefully brought that newspaper home. I'd been to attend the chapel service, alone, riding the four miles through the snow on horseback. It was the only chance, with the snow on the ground, to see neighbours and friends and hear any news. Megan had given birth some two weeks before. Our Mam said how lucky we were that the child came in the midst of winter. It meant we did not have to continue making excuses for Megan's absence from chapel.

The newspaper belonged, of all people, to the preacher. He'd left it behind, in the stable by the chapel, where he housed his pony during the service. A breeze had snatched its pages and was carrying them down the lane below the chapel. They stuck to the snow, giving me time to chase after them and gather them up. I rarely got to read a newspaper so was damned if I was going to let the thing blow away.

"Why pay for a newspaper when I can walk down the road and get all the news I'll ever want for free?" Mam used to say.

Among the articles about the prices recently fetched at market, and the details of a court case involving the prosecution of horse thieves who were to be transported to Australia, Mam found the piece which providence itself seemed to have led her to. It was another court case, about a fallen woman trying to extract money from the father of her illegitimate child for the breach of promise of marriage. She said she needed the money to pay a Nesta Harding of Tyravon Cottage, in the parish of Henllan, for the upkeep of the child. It was that or not be able to work and end up in the poor house. She claimed to have been a respectable woman, the innocent victim of a devious seducer. Yet, when asked to provide witnesses to her secret meetings with the accused, she could provide none. The case was thrown out, the alleged father stating that any one of a dozen men could have been the father.

Megan did not have an inkling, of course, as to what our Mam planned for her. I don't know what she thought might happen. She asked our Mam for money several times, before the baby came, to see them on their way to God knows where. She asked me too, but like I told her, Mam held the purse-strings, I had no money of my own to give her. If I had my time over again, I would gladly steal the money to give to her, rather than take part in what came after. I suspect that Megan may have thought our Mam was simply going to let her stay and face the shame. One thing I know for certain, she never imagined her own Mam was going to steal her baby away from her. I could hardly believe it myself when Mam told me what she had planned after reading that newspaper.

"It is a gift from God!' Mam said. 'We will not have to suffer the shame and humiliation of Megan's ruin."

"What are you talking about, Mam?"

We were sat alone by the firelight. Megan and the child were upstairs.

"We will send Fortune to this Nesta Harding who is mentioned in the newspaper!"

She said this as though she were talking of selling a cow at market.

"Don't be bloody daft! You can't take the child from her now," I say, hardly believing she is serious, thinking it is just a silly idea that's come into her head and will as quickly go.

“Well, you didn’t think for one minute she was going to be able to keep it, did you?” she says, as if it must be me who has taken leave of my senses.

“But you can’t take it from her now!”

“Would you see your sister ruined then? Would you have this one mistake blight the rest of her life? Do you care so little as all that?”

“No. I don’t want to see her ruined. But it’s a bit late in the day is what I’m saying. What’s done is done. The baby is here. There’s nothing we can do about it now.”

“But there is, boy! Here in this very paper you have brought to our door is the answer! Heaven sent it is! God, in his mercy, has sent this to us so that Megan may not bring ruin on herself and shame on us all!”

“You can’t take the child from her. You’ve seen how she dotes on her.”

“She’s only had the baby two weeks. She’ll soon get over it. It’s not like it is a proper grown child yet. Your sister is not in a frame of mind to make the right decisions for herself. It is our duty, before God, to make the right decisions for her. She will come to see that what we have decided is the right thing in the long run. Think Morgan, what her life will be like if she keeps the child. She will be shunned by all. What is it she’s always wanted? To marry. That will never happen if she keeps the child.”

Mam had Megan’s best interests at heart so I thought she knew better than I. I thought she was right, it did seem like a gift from God himself, until the day Megan found her baby was gone. It didn’t seem so much as a gift from God then, it seemed more like he had sent us a taste of what hell is like.

Following this conversation with Mam, I encouraged Megan to come down of an evening with Fortune, and sit with us by the fire. I thought if our Mam saw more of the child, she would grow attached to it and forget any ideas of sending her away. I was mistaken. Mam refused to acknowledge the baby's presence, would not so much as look at her, and when Megan was out of sight and hearing, Mam impressed on me the importance of taking the baby soon.

"The sooner you do it, the kinder it will be on your sister," she said.

"Kinder? I don't see anything kind in what you're suggesting," I said to her.

"You wouldn't be so quick to take your sister's side if you knew what she says about you."

"What are you talking about now?" I snapped at her.

I was tired of her nagging at me to do what I could not do.

"Forget I said anything. I don't want to go making trouble," she said.

"No. Come on. I want to hear what you have to say."

"Well, if you must know, she blames you for her predicament."

"Blames me? How the hell did she come to that conclusion?"

"I knew I shouldn't have said anything. I knew it would get your anger up. I'll say no more."

"Get my anger up? It's done that alright. Come on! What exactly did she say?"

I had to drag the truth out of her. She knew the effect her words would have on me. She didn't want to tell me but I wouldn't let it lie.

"She said if you'd looked out for her as a brother should, then, well, it would never have happened. She has a point."

"Has a point? I'd like to know how I could look out for her when she was such a liar, pretending she just 'wanted some time to herself', when all the while she was meeting him, whoever he was."

"There's no need to shout at me! Keep your voice down, unless you want the whole parish to hear about it."

"How dare she blame me?!"

"Ay, I know, I did think she had a bit of a cheek. But then, what you don't realise is, that is your sister all over. Always pointing the finger of blame at someone else so she doesn't have to take responsibility for what she's done. You don't know the half of what she's said ever. You don't know her like I do. Remember how she was squirreling away all that money for herself. Selfish, through and through, she is."

"Well, if she thinks she can blame me for this she can think again!"

I was boiling over with anger, to think Megan had said such a thing behind my back. To think I had been ready to let the past lie and accept her bastard child. She could go to hell now, I thought. I thought of all the times I'd stuck up for her against our Mam, and this was how she repaid me.

"Go now, boy. Go and get the child," Mam says to me one evening, a few days later, and my supper curdles in my stomach.

Fortune had cried all day. Maybe she sensed her fate. Megan had paced up and down our kitchen since breakfast, rocking the baby, singing to her, cooing to her. Nothing would placate her.

"It will be wind," Mam says, by way of explanation.

It does nothing to ease the lines of worry from Megan's face.

"What is the matter, little one?" Megan asks Fortune, over and over.

Fortune finally stops crying, half way through the evening. Exhausted, she lets Megan give her the breast and then falls soundly asleep.

I am still in that place where hope digs in its heels, refusing to budge. I think our Mam will surely change her mind. Despite the bawling, and my anger with Megan, I'm liking having the little one in the house and cannot bear to think of her going. What the hell does it matter what people think of Megan? To hell with them all, I think, we can damned well manage without them, though I knew very well we could not. The truth was, I was caught between the devil and hell, and didn't want to have to choose either.

Our Mam was such a strong woman. She didn't weaken an inch. She was the same with Megan as she was with our old dog Rowan, when she took each litter of pups from her. To her it was no more than a job that had to be done. There was no room for sentiment.

"Go now, boy, while they are sleeping," Mam says, when Megan has retired to her bed early with the baby, worn out from the day spent pacing up and down the kitchen.

It comes as a shock to hear her say it, even though I have been given fair warning that this time was coming.

"No. I won't do it. I can't do that to Megan and the little one, no matter what Megan has done," I say, digging my hands deep into my pockets, as if I fear they will do our Mam's bidding against my will.

"You've already agreed it is for the best. You can't go back on your word, now."

I can't recall having agreed to it, but I hadn't disagreed either and that was agreement enough for Mam.

"Why not give Megan the little money she asks for?" My voice sounds whiny and pleading. Weak.

"Have you not listened to a word I've said these past weeks? Where do you think she'd end up, a woman with a child in tow? The gutter is where girls like that end up. Is that what you wish for your sister?"

The thought of Megan having to do God only knows what to support herself and the child near curdled the blood in my veins. I was squeezed into a corner. No matter where I looked, I could not see any other way out for Megan than what our Mam suggested.

"Let what will happen be, then. Let Megan keep the child and face the consequences."

"Don't be stupid, boy. Can you imagine what it would do to Megan? You know how she is. She's never been strong. It would break her, mind and soul, to be cast out, treated like a leper, shunned by neighbours and friends. You saw what it did for Sian, and then there was Mary Jones when I was a girl, she ended up in the river along with her baby. They were washed up under the bridge below the village. And even if Megan didn't take her life, can you imagine the life Fortune would have? You may wish such a fate on your sister, but do you wish it, too, on that child?"

Of course, I did not wish such a fate on either of them. I made my decision, our Mam was right, there was nothing else to be done. Mam handed me a purse full of coins with which I was to pay Nesta Harding. I put the purse in my pocket, and feeling like Judas himself, I ascend the stairs to Megan's room. It does not occur to me until later, much later, that it was Megan's own money that went to pay for what we did to her that night.

My legs feel like they are refusing to do my mind's will as I climb the stairs. They are stiff and unbending with each step. They are fumbling, shaking hands that lift the latch on Megan's door. I stand in the open doorway. The only light in the room is the moonlight shining through the cracks in the shutters. A shaft of light shines across the baby's crib but her face is lost in shadow. I see the shape of Megan's body under the bedcovers but her sleeping face is hidden in darkness. I walk across the room and pick up the crib from beside the bed. The baby stirs, grizzles and rolls onto her back. She makes little sucking motions with her mouth but does not open her eyes.

If Megan will only wake, I think. If she will only take fright, sit up in bed and ask 'Morgan? What are you doing?', then mother's plan will be thwarted and I will not have to do this thing. Then, responsibility for whether Megan and her child survive or die will lie with nobody but Megan. Megan stirs and turns, and her sleeping face is captured in the shaft of moonlight. I feel a stab of pain where my heart used to be. The dirty deed is not yet done but already I am filled with pity, guilt, remorse. I'm sorry Megan, I say, silently, to her sleeping face. She does not stir from that slumber where she does not dream such a nightmare as this could befall her and her child.

Downstairs, mother is ready with sheepskins to swaddle the child against the freezing night air. Still, she does not wake and scream for her mother to come and rescue her. You cannot do this, I tell myself, as I strap the crib to the seat beside me on the cart. You cannot do this, I tell myself as the cart trundles through the snow along the winding track down the mountain. You cannot do this, I tell myself as we travel along the frost sparkled country lanes, my breath clouding the crisp night air. The whole landscape about us was frozen, glowing and sparkling in the moonlight. My hands and feet ached with the cold and I was chilled to the marrow of my bones, but Fortune slumbered on in her cosy sheepskin nest, rocked by the motion of the cart. You cannot do this, I tell myself as I finally reach the bridge below what I think must be Nesta's cottage, hours later.

I could turn back right now, I say to myself as I tether the horse to a tree near the little footbridge. But I carry the child in its crib to Nesta's door, and then she is taking the crib from my arms, and telling me not to worry about a thing, the baby will be well looked after, she will love her as her own. And it was for the best really, wasn't it? And did I have the money, and thank you, that was lovely, and the door shut behind her, and the thing was done. As I walk away, I hear Fortune's cry and the sound all but tears the heart clean out of me. It is a sound I shall never forget till my dying day. It is a sound that haunts me still and, whenever I remember it, I want to die.

The longest journey I ever made was that journey home by the light of the waning moon. I do not see the frost covered road ahead. I see instead, through a veil of tears, all the things that would never now happen. I see Fortune learning to crawl around our kitchen floor. I see her take her first steps and toddling out of the door. I see her playing out in the orchard, running on the hill, as Megan and I once did before her. And of course, in every image, I see Megan smiling, doting, and proud.

At some point on the journey home, I pulled up the pony and cart, thinking I would have to turn round and go back for Fortune. Then a vision of Mam's wrath confronted me, and the scenario of me having to go through all this another night because Mam would never relent. And the fearful thought crept into my mind that perhaps Mam would do worse than that.

I'd heard tales of new-born babies being found in town rivers, thrown there by mothers who were desperate not to be found out. There were plenty of fallen girls locked up in the county jails for the crime of infanticide. If a mother could do that to her own child, I was sure Mam was capable of it, if denied the option of sending Fortune away. It was plain that Mam detested the very sight of the child. Did she hate her enough to drown her?

A memory came to me then, of a time when Megan and I, as children, had found our sheepdog with a litter of new-born puppies in the barn. Nell, the dog's name was. She had made a nest amidst the hay. Unknowing, we ran over to the house, all excited, to tell Mam what we had found. Mam went out to the scullery and came back with a sack which she took over to the barn. I didn't realize what was going to happen until Mam began dropping the puppies into the sack, while the dog was running around in circles, and whimpering, and Megan was screaming at Mam, pleading with her to stop. Then Nell picked up one of the puppies in her mouth and ran out of the barn. Mam didn't see it happen and went off down to the gorge to drown the sackful of screeching puppies swinging at her side.

It goes without saying, we never told Mam when we found Nell's new hiding place in the hollow of the old oak tree above the house. We would sneak morsels of food from our plates to take up there for Nell. As the puppy she had saved grew, we grew more fearful of Mam discovering him. When he started to want to follow his mother around the farm, we knew it was only a matter of time before Mam saw him. So we carried him down to Eli, who gave him back a few years later when Nell died of old age. He is the dog I have still.

I flicked the reins and set off for home, and by the time I arrived back at Carregwyn, I felt some part of me had died. I felt a hollowness in the heart that had swelled only yesterday with the love of that little babe.

How easy it is to stop a life in its tracks. It was a kind of murder we committed that night, Mam and me. We murdered the Megan who was Fortune's mother, murdered her as surely as if we'd taken a knife to her throat. And we murdered Megan's baby, as surely as if we had drowned her, like Nell's new-born pups, when we took her away and made her someone else's child. I have often wondered what our Mam would have done if

I hadn't taken that damned newspaper home. Would Fortune really have ended up being drowned like Nell's pups?

It is not far off dawn when I return. Like the guilty murderer I was, I put away the horse and cart, then take a broom to brush the snow over my tracks, trying to kick over the traces of my involvement. It was a daft thing to do, the brush strokes themselves were like bold capital letters, spelling out the truth. Then I go and sit in the barn and sob my heart out, like I had not done since I dragged Sian's limp body from its watery grave.

I need not have worried about my tell-tale brush strokes in the snow. A fresh and heavy fall of snow came in that hour before dawn and it continued to snow for an hour after that. It seemed the heavens themselves conspired to cover up our crime, though I am more inclined to think, now, it was the devil himself who guided our actions that night. By the time Megan rises late from her sleep, the snowstorm has passed over and left a blanket to cover my tracks. Outside our door, the snow is pure and white and unbroken, so that it seems the child might have been spirited away by the fairies themselves.

It was Megan's own stupid fault I told myself after, when she begged me, over and over, to take her to Fortune. I would never have had to do such a thing if she had not gone and got herself in such trouble. I did what our Mam herself did, I heaped all the blame on Megan's head so that I could absolve myself.

Chapter 13

Megan

That terrible, fateful morning, when I rose from my bed, and finding Fortune's crib gone, went downstairs, it was with the expectation of seeing Fortune's crib lying next to mother's chair. Fortune had been unwell the day before. Usually so quiet and undemanding, she had cried and cried the whole day long and nothing I did appeased her. I thought Morgan, or Mam, must have come in the night to take her downstairs when she cried, so that I could get some rest. As I descended the stairs, I was imagining Mam or Morgan sat by the fire, rocking the crib to keep Fortune from waking. If it was Mam, I was already seeing myself thanking her for helping. God help me. I was all ready to thank her.

There was no crib by her chair. She sat stony faced, her arms folded across herself. Her gaze avoids mine when I look at her. Then I know something is not right, but as yet I have not been flung into the pits of hell by the knowledge of what is amiss. My eyes scour every inch of the room, looking for the crib.

'Where is Fortune?' I ask, no panic in my voice as yet, because I am telling myself she is alright, she has not died in the night while I slept, for that is the terrible idea that is trying to worm itself into my mind. Please God, don't let her have died.

Mam says nothing, but picks up her bible from the stool beside her chair. She places the bible on her lap. She opens the bible and begins to silently read.

'Mam! Where is Fortune?'

I ask louder this time, thinking she has either not heard me or cannot bear to tell me that Fortune has died.

'She's gone. Let that be an end to it. You will thank me for it one day,' she says, without looking up from her bible.

Her words so chill my blood that my heart stops racing and slows, slows, slows. I can hear and feel my heart go thud, then pause for many seconds, then thud again, and so it goes on, as if my heart itself has run into a corner to hide; as if it dares do no more than the occasional beat to keep me alive. It is hiding, hiding from what it knows it cannot survive.

'Where is she gone to? Is she with Morgan?'

The voice that asks my question sounds almost light-hearted to my own ears. Where is she, I ask, as if the answer will be that Fortune is just in the next room, as if there is no need to worry. Mother turns a page in her bible and sighs an exasperated sigh, as if I am being a nuisance with my questioning.

How long I stand just staring at her I don't know, but in those moments I feel something break inside of me. It is a sharp, cracking thing, like a branch breaking in a storm. It is not my back that is broken, for I remain standing. It is an inside thing, my spiritual spine, I think now, that breaks. For when it breaks there is a sensation that my very self is collapsing inwards upon itself, somewhere deep inside and yet, at the same time, not of my body. The force of the break sends me reeling, so that I am suddenly propelled from room to room , out into the scullery, back into the kitchen, up the stairs, in and out of my room, into mother's room, Morgan's room, and all the while, I am reeling, I am tearing the place to pieces, pulling furniture out from the walls, overturning beds, searching, searching in even the most unlikely places, to find a baby sleeping contentedly in its crib.

There is a terror building inside me which, if I do not find Fortune, will devour and destroy me. Like the poor pigs who sense when they are about to be slaughtered, inside myself I am silently screaming with fright. And because the threat to my life is not a physical one, there is no place for me to run to escape it. And so it is my mind which is running scared, flying about inside my head like a trapped animal looking for escape, terrified of the agony which awaits.

Then Morgan has hold of me, his arms pinning my own to my sides, like a vice. I scream and wriggle and kick at his shins. He loosens his grip from my arms but as I make to get away, he grabs me around my waist. My arms now free, I flail my arms, punching at his arms, his head, but he does not flinch and will not let me go until I have no strength left in me to fight him. Then when he thinks I am broken, like his horse out there in the stable, he lets me go and I am hurtling again, down the stairs, to where mother has been stirred enough to get out of her chair.

'Morgan!' Mother shrieks, grasping the edge of the table.

Morgan is onto me too fast, pinning my arms at my sides again. I struggle with every ounce of strength in my small body but, even in my madness, I am no match for the strength of a full grown man.

'Please stop, Meg, please stop,' Morgan says, over and over, and he is sobbing, tears running down his face, dripping on my head.

'Where is Fortune?' I scream at him.

'She's gone Meg ...to a woman who takes in ..... bastard children. Surely you knew you would not be able to keep her?' Morgan says, his face puzzled, as if he truly believed I should have expected them to do such a thing.

Oh. The pain of it. The agony. The wrenching, tearing, clawing agony it is when the heart is torn out of you. The terrible, howling noise a body makes when its soul is being murdered. No, the body cries out, no, no, no, please, God, no, the body pleads for mercy. How can one being inflict such pain on another? How could she, my own mother, sanction such atrocity? And how could he, my own brother and one time friend, go along with such evil?

How long was I like that I do not know. It seemed like an eternity, like I was suffering the eternal hell and damnation our preacher so often warned us to beware of bringing upon ourselves, but hell being the domain of the devil himself, it was my own mother and brother who helped the devil put and keep me there.

Was it hours or days later, I don't know, but at some point I began to think that all was not lost, that if I pleaded and begged loud enough and long enough, then mother or Morgan would relent and tell me where I could find Fortune.

'I shall forget what you've done, Mam, and forgive it absolutely, if you will only tell me where she is. I shall go away, far away, and take Fortune with me. I promise you, dear Mam, not a soul shall ever know what happened. I shall disappear without a trace. I'm so sorry, Mam, so sorry. I should never have done what I did.'

I all but prostrated myself on the floor at her feet. I hated her, loathed her, but would do or say anything to persuade her to tell me where Fortune was.

'You'll forgive me, you say? I have done nothing but the best I can for you and your bastard. But I shall never forgive *you* for the trouble you have brought to my door, and for which I shall now have to pay for the rest of my days.'

I had to swallow it all, every cruel and heartless word that came from her mouth. I could not speak my mind, not retaliate, nor condemn. I had to be kind, I had to be sweet, for it was my only hope of getting Fortune back.

Morgan will help me, I think. Morgan has only gone along with this thing because mother has poisoned him against me. He would never have done such a thing, otherwise. Not Morgan, not my own sweet brother Morgan. Morgan will understand he has done a terrible wrong to me.

'It is not too late to put right the wrong, Morgan. You have only to tell me where Fortune is and need not trouble your conscience any longer.'

'What do you mean? I have nothing troubling *my* conscience. I have done nothing but help our Mam put right your mistake.'

'I'll go far away where nobody knows us. There is no need for this.'

'I told you when you asked me before. I have no money to give you.'

'I'm not asking for money. I will manage somehow. A crust of bread here or there on my journey, I'm sure I will find. I only need to know from you, where you have taken Fortune. That's all. And then I will be gone, and neither you, nor mother, need to worry, anymore.'

'Please don't ask me, Megan. You know I can't tell you. I can't go against our Mam. She's doing what's best for you, don't you understand?'

Still, I am not defeated because to admit defeat would be to die. I ask mother again, I ask Morgan again. I keep on asking nicely, politely until my patience runs out. My breasts throb and ache and ooze with the milk that is made for Fortune. Is she hungry? Who is feeding her? Is she crying for me? I know she is just a babe, but does she feel I have abandoned her?

I try a different tactic with mother.

'Mother, Mam. You must tell me where I can find her. You must. For if you do not, I fear for your soul. What you are doing is wrong, it is evil. Please, I beg you, tell me where Fortune is. You cannot truly believe you are doing right. You are doing a bad, bad thing. Tell me, for I fear if you do not, your soul will be eternally damned.'

'You dare to try to tell me right from wrong! You! Sinner and slut that you are!'

I fear I am losing my mind, for it seems that my hands are screaming to be allowed to tear and claw at that throat, and that face which shows no regret, no remorse, no compassion.

Morgan is my only hope, and in my despair, I am able to convince myself that he will relent. He is not like mother. He has a good and kind heart. He will tell me where Fortune is. I go out into the snow to search for him. I follow his tracks up to the hill.

'Morgan. Our Mam is not right in this. Ask yourself. Can it be right to torture another soul as you are torturing me? Can it be right to take a child from its own mother? I know you think I have done a terrible wrong but I ask you, what wrong did Fortune do to make you take her from her own mother?'

'Shut up! Shut up! Shut up! I won't do what you ask! I cannot! You! You are the cause of all this! You! Why will you not leave me be?!'

Spittle flies from his contorted mouth as he screams at me.

And then I know I am never going to find Fortune again, and the loss of her, oh, the loss of her, my daughter, my child, my reason for living. It feels as though the scree on the north side of our hill has come tumbling down the mountain to bury me. And it was Morgan's shouting at me that disturbed and loosened the stones and set them in motion, and once they began to tumble downwards towards me, there was no stopping them. There was no place of shelter, no time to run for cover. All I could do was let his words, the cruel, hard, unrelenting stones, come tumbling down upon my head and bury me along with all hope of finding Fortune.

And there I remained, beneath the rubble which was all that remained of my life. It was a dark and lifeless place I inhabited, where nothing moved my senses. There was no beauty in the flowers, the trees, the fields or the hills. There was no pleasure in feeling summer sunshine on my skin. No joy in the company of those whose rejection I had so feared. Some neighbours and friends have died in these past six years, some have married, some have had children born, some have had children die. Their lives have gone on following the paths allotted them, for better or worse, while I barely registered their passing.

For the life of me I cannot remember any of the events that have shaped these people's lives in the past six years, for I have no memory of them happening. I only know they happened because Morgan will say; Do you remember when 'such and such' happened? And I pretend I remember for myself, but the truth is I remember little of what has happened since Fortune was taken from me. It is as if I have been elsewhere, and have only now returned, but I cannot say where I have been or what I did when there.

It was as if Fortune had died but not as children sometimes do, from accident or disease. To me it seemed like a murder, for mother had willed that Fortune would cease to exist in my life. She had taken Fortune's life from me as surely as if she had drowned her like a puppy in the washing pool. And Morgan had been her accomplice. My life stopped when Fortune went. Six years of my life have been erased, and that is why I say, they did not only steal Fortune, they stole my life from me.

Now Eli is returned to me and perhaps God might grant me another child to love and cherish. I can never replace Fortune but it may help to heal my broken heart. Every day, week, and year that goes by, I have longed to know where she is, if she is happy, if she is well. As time has passed by, she has grown alongside me. In my mind I have seen her walk, talk and grow as if she is right here beside me. It is my only consolation, for I know I can never have her back. I would be a stranger to her now, and the only mother she has known, or will remember, is the one they took her too.

I wonder that Eli does not see the layers of dust and dirt, and the scars and the hurt. It must be because Eli is still in love with the Megan he left behind. When he looks at me, he does not see me, he sees her. I am not loved as I'd like to think. Not I. Not the Megan who fell so far she thought she could not survive the fall. Not the Megan who picked herself up and gave birth to her child, all alone in that room upstairs, terrified and bleeding, with no one to hold my hand or reassure me that the agony will not tear my body asunder. There is no one but me who loves that Megan, for I am the only one who knows and can forgive her. That must be enough.

Chapter 14

Morgan

If it had seemed to me like a chapter had ended on Megan's wedding day, I needn't have troubled myself. Megan has been married less than a month and has already walked up our hill a half dozen times. To give Beulah a hand, she says.

"There's little to do at Wildwater. Gwen insists on doing it all, as she has always done, and I don't want to tread on her toes. I can't even make the butter or cheese, there is a milkmaid to do all that," she tells Beulah and me on her arrival, wearing a fine new bonnet and shiny new leather boots.

"You're surely not going to help me while wearing that lovely dress," Beulah says to her.

I hadn't noticed the dress was new as well.

"Oh! This! This is just my everyday dress! You don't have to worry about this," Megan says, pulling a face and looking down at her dress as if it were some old rag.

It is certainly a nice life for some. It makes me mad as hell. There's Beulah so tired she falls asleep in her chair before bedtime, her chin slumped on her chest. I wish Megan would keep her mouth shut, or else Beulah will be getting ideas of casting about for a wealthy farmer and an easy life of her own. If our Megan can do it, Beulah should have no trouble.

"I don't know how Megan managed to run this place on her own," Beulah tells me of an evening. "There aren't enough hours in the day. I swear with all the running back and forth I do, one of these days, I'll meet myself coming back."

We rub along as well as any two people thrown together by circumstance and need. She needs the work and I need her to do it, nothing more to it than that. But I'm afraid it's more than Beulah can cope with, and she will pack it in, and leave me high and dry. I tell her it will get easier come the end of the summer.

"Oh yes, I'm looking forward to carrying the water up from that gorge in winter, slithering about in the mud," she says with her usual good humour.

She'll make a joke about anything, will Beulah.

While Megan swans around, without a care in the world, I haven't had a proper night's sleep in weeks. First, I worry that Beulah will hand in her notice. Then I roll over and worry I can't afford her anyway. I'm damned if Beulah goes and I'm damned if she stays. There's been no income from the dairy since Mam died. There's shearing coming up, and I have to find the money to pay for food and drink for the neighbours who will help me get the job done. I know I'll get it back when I help them out in return but I have still got to find the cash to keep up my side of the bargain.

I thought I'd have a word with Megan when she comes again. I don't want to dim the newly-wed sparkle in her eyes but I can't put it off any longer. The God honest truth of it is, I need the money put aside for the little one to pay Beulah's wages and the rest. If Eli will foot the bill for Megan's mistake then I'll manage. I daresay Eli won't like paying for another man's child any more than I do, but it's not like he has to have her under his roof and rubbing his nose in it. He's taken our

Megan on despite her sins and I take my hat off to him, really, but having taken her on he has to take on the rest, too.

It's that or I'll end up losing the farm and I'm damned if I'll let that happen. I've tilled this soil through back-breaking toil. I've picked every stone from these fields with my own bare hands. I've worked from dawn till dusk, and by moonlight, since I was eight years old. I know every inch of every acre. I know which of the mountain springs never dry up, not even in the hottest summer; where the skylarks make their nests on the heath; where to find watercress in summer; where the best blackberries are to be found in autumn; where to find the willow for making Megan's baskets; where the badger setts are on the hill. I was born of this farm and I wish to die on this soil.

Megan turns up again, this time to help Beulah with washing the bed linen. That was one job Megan loved in the summer. She'd carry the whole lot down to the stream in the gorge. She'd keep a big copper pot down there all summer, to boil the water in. Then she'd light a fire under it, with bits of dead bracken and gorse, and spend the day down there. She said it was easier than carrying water up to the house. I think what she liked about it most was it got her out from under Mam's nose. She could get on with the job without our Mam nagging, have you done this, have you done that, and let me see if you have done it properly. When the washing was clean, she would drape it out on the gorse and heather to dry. When the sun was going down, she would return with the washing, all folded and dried, and her face glowing from being out in the sun all day. Throughout the summer, I'd get into bed at night with it smelling as sweet as a hayfield.

I ask Megan if she'll give me an hour to help round up the lambs for marking. I could do it with just Swift for help but I need the excuse for some time alone with Megan. She says she'll come as soon as she's shown Beulah how to get the fire going under the pot. I watch them head off to the gorge with their baskets of laundry on their hips, chattering and laughing like a couple of woodpeckers.

Megan leaves Beulah tending the fire and we head up to the heath, following the sheep paths through the crumbling remains of last year's bracken, and the fresh green shoots of new growth which snap and crush under our feet. Where the bracken runs out, and the grass is crisp and short, white bedstraw flowers grow so thick it looks like snow on the ground. Megan picks sprigs of wild thyme, rubbing them between her fingers to release their herby perfume. She breathes it in and sighs. She is silent all the way up, with a faraway look in her eyes. I decide to bide my time until we get to the top, before broaching the subject of money.

The boulders of rock, on this side of the mountain, are marbled with quartz and glisten and sparkle in the sunlight. Even the sheep paths under our feet are scattered with small, sparkling shards of it. When Megan was little she'd come up here to fill her pockets with it. Then she'd hide them, like treasure, in what she thought was her secret hiding place in the hollow of the old oak tree behind the house. I'd see her hide all sorts of things in there; a handkerchief that a neighbour embroidered for her with her initials on it; little posies of wild flowers she'd picked; a handful of brown hazel nuts picked from the trees in the coppice below the house. All sorts of things, I can't remember the half of them now.

When we were older, I told her I'd known about the hiding place she had as a child, and asked her why she left those things in there. She said she used to leave them for the Tilweth Teg, the little people of legend which some people still believe in. She said she left them gifts in the hope they would take her to live with them. Hurt me that did, to know she would have gone away with the fairies and left me here.

Up on the heath, where the grass sighs and whispers in the breeze, I send Swift out wide to gather the flock. He's a good dog, knows not to get too near to them, and drops down on his haunches the moment he hears me whistle, when the sheep run too fast. Then up he gets, moving left to right, keeping the flock to a narrow path.

"Oh look, Morgan!" Megan calls to me. "The heartsease is in flower! Let's pick some for Beulah. She will love it."

As if I have the time, or inclination, to go picking flowers.

"You pick some if you like and catch me up," I tell her.

I leave her on her knees among the yellow blooms and follow on behind Swift to make my way down the hill. Megan comes running to join me half way down.

"Aren't they beautiful?" She says, holding out two posies for me to admire.

"Hmm."

"There's so much Beulah has not seen yet. You should take her around the farm. I just know, if she gets to see how many beautiful places there are, she will fall in love with the place and the work will come easier to her."

"Didn't stop you from leaving," I snap, the old bitterness in me still quick to surface.

Without a word, she carefully places her posies in her pinafore pocket and we get the flock down into the holding pen behind the barns. I think, I shall tell her now, but the very next moment I lose courage and think I dare not bring up the subject of the little one again. I know what Megan is going to think, that I'm still making it up, just to make things awkward for her.

We separate the sheep from the lambs by driving them through the narrow double-gated channel. I have rigged it up for the job, from hazel hurdles. Megan drives them down through the hurdles while I operate the gates, sheep through one, lambs through the other, into separate pens. As the last of the sheep runs into the pen, my stomach begins to churn. I have to do it now or else the chance will be gone. She turns away to go and rejoin Beulah, not wanting to stay any longer, no doubt fearing her clothes will get spattered with blood when I begin cutting my mark in the lambs' ears.

I clear my throat.

"I need to talk to you a minute."

I don't know where to begin, the words stick in my throat.

"Is there something wrong, Morgan?" she asks, a little furrow of worry gathering between her brows.

"Aye, you could say that."

I hesitate. The words don't come easy, but in short, broken sentences.

"The little one - Mam - she must have scraped to find the money. And now, with Beulah to pay, well, there's nothing over to pay for the little one's keep."

"Oh."

Colour floods her cheeks.

"I thought perhaps Eli might find his way to pay for her from now on, seeing as he's taken you on, and all."

She stares at the ground before her for a good few moments while I wait for her answer, fearing another tantrum.

"That's not possible."

She looks up at me with her brown eyes filled with fear and sadness, like a rabbit caught in one of my traps, knowing what is coming and unable to do a darned thing to stop it.

"Why not, Meg? God knows, he can afford it better than me. It's not like he has to have her under his roof, after all."

There is another long silence before she answers. She cannot look me in the eye.

"Eli does not know about her," she says, her voice barely more than a whisper.

It takes a few moments for her words to sink in, and my first reaction is disbelief, but I can see by her face that it's true.

"God in heaven, Megan! You didn't let him go marrying you without knowing a thing like that? What in hell's name were you thinking of?"

I want to kick every damned hurdle from here to kingdom come, such is my anger and frustration.

"Please, Morgan, don't be angry with me. How could I tell him? He's waited all these years for me. He loves me. He never wanted anyone but me. How could I tell him without breaking his heart? I could not."

"Could not? Or would not? You should have turned him down from the start if you weren't prepared to tell him the truth."

I glared at her with hatred in my heart. I could barely believe she would deceive Eli just like she had deceived the rest of us.

"I did try to turn him down, I did! Too much time has passed, I said to him, I'm too old to be thinking of marriage. And there's Morgan to think of. He could never manage without me."

This elicits a snort of disbelief from me. I didn't believe she had given me a second thought once she had Eli's proposal. I think of how I would feel if I were Eli and I found out after the marriage. I would think her a cheating whore and want to strangle her.

"It'll be more than his heart that's broken if he finds out you have lied to trick him into marrying you."

"It wasn't like that. I told no lies."

"Well, you haven't exactly told the truth either, have you?"

"I never set out to deceive him."

"That's what you've done, nevertheless."

I take off my hat and throw it on the ground. I could tear out my own hair.

"What a bloody mess!"

"Please don't swear."

"You're worried about me swearing? You have no right preaching to me when what you have done is a damn sight worse. God Almighty, Megan, is there no end to the trouble you cause?"

She hugs her shawl tight around herself, and starts pacing back and fore, talking all the while, talking fast.

"I never meant any harm, never in my life. Do you think I wanted things to happen the way they did? You have no idea, no idea. All you've ever done, you and Mam, is to dwell on the mistakes I've made. Neither of you ever gave a thought to what it was like for me. It was so terrible, awful; I don't think I shall ever get over it as long as I live."

Her face crumples and tears well up in her eyes. She puts a hand over her mouth to stifle a sob. For a moment, I feel her sorrow tug at my heart, remembering what it was like, how much she suffered. But I am too angry with her and hold back from placing a comforting hand on her shoulder.

"I do know what it was like for you. How could I forget? But it does not change the fact that you brought it on yourself. You were old enough to know what you were doing and what the consequences might be."

It was about time she heard the truth and took some responsibility, I thought.

"I may not have been a young girl but I was stupid and gullible. I trusted people that I never should have. And for that I am to be punished for the rest of my days? If it is a sin to be stupid, then there'll be a long queue in front of me at hell's gates."

Her voice is thick with emotion, and with a defiant motion she swipes the tears from her eyes with the back of her hand.

"That's as may be, but I'm trying to deal with the consequences, here and now. I haven't got the money to pay and I'm not going to give up the farm on account of you. You're going to have to come clean and ask Eli to pay."

That terrified look comes in her eyes again. I can see she's in a tight corner, and I am sorry for it, but we're talking survival here. I can't afford to be sentimental.

"I'll throw myself in the Wildwater before I'll tell Eli," she whispers.

That scares me.

"Don't talk daft, Megan. You know you don't mean that."

"I mean it. It would finish him if he found out now. I won't do that to him. And I want you to promise me, right now, that you'll never tell him, either."

"Alright, alright! I promise I won't tell him, but will you tell me how in hell's name I'm going to get the money to pay for Fortune?"

"Hush! Beulah's coming! I'll think of something. We will speak again."

She wipes her face with her apron and takes deep breathes to compose herself.

"You two have been gone so long I was wondering what happened to you." Beulah approaches us with her slow, swaying stride, looking with curiosity, first at Megan, then me, wondering what the matter is but not liking to ask.

"I was just on my way," Megan tells her with a shaky smile.

"Water's been boiling for over an hour."

"Oh! I nearly forgot! I picked these for you," Megan says, taking the posy of flowers from her pocket. "I'll just go and put them in water before we go back down the gorge."

They head off back to the house, Beulah asking wherever did Megan find such beautiful flowers and Megan saying to ask me to take her up there to see them. She's a great pretender, our Megan. She can turn on a smile and chat, even while her treacherous heart is quaking.

Chapter 15

Morgan

So Eli isn't the saint I thought he was. Damn it to hell. To think how I praised him up at the wedding. I don't even like him much. If I'd known Megan hadn't told him, there's no way I would have let her go through with it. She must have taken leave of her senses, again. If Eli ever gets wind of it, God only knows what will happen. It doesn't bear thinking about. How can she keep that to herself, keep it from him? But then, she's had practice aplenty at deception, has our Megan.

My hopes are dashed, now. I can't depend on Eli paying for the little one. Megan says she will think of something, but she knows as well as I that she can't ask Eli for money without telling him what it is for. He provides for her upkeep, her food, her clothing, and keeps a roof over her head. Whatever she wants, she has only to ask, but she can never ask him for that. Stupid, selfish sister of mine! It seems I am bound forever to pay for her sins.

I can't get together the full annual sum for the child's keep before it's due. I'm going to have to go to the vile Nesta Harding with a small amount to tide her over, until I can find the money. I cringe at the thought of going cap in hand to Nesta. I don't know what the hell I'll say or do when I get there, but I'm hoping the crone will give me more time to come up with the full amount. She'll have to give me more time. If I haven't got it, I haven't got it. I can't conjure it out of the air. I'll tell her that, if she kicks up a fuss.

I tell Beulah I'll be gone for the day. I say I'm stopping at the blacksmith to shoe the pony, and I have to collect a barrel of cider for the forthcoming shearing, and that I'm making a few visits roundabout. She's not to know any different. Beulah wraps some bread and cheese with muslin so I don't go hungry. She's not such a bad old girl. I leave her in the dairy churning butter. The exertion puts some colour in her cheeks. The cow is putting out a lot of milk and I'm hoping we can go back to selling at market. She's learned to make good butter, has Beulah, pale and creamy with just the right amount of crunchy salt thrown in. I haven't broken it to her yet, that I'll need her to go sell it too. She can't cope with her workload as it is. I fear she will give me her notice.

I'll be an hour at the blacksmith and another picking up the barrel of cider. Then it will take me three hours with the pony and cart to get where I'm going, then another three back, and that will be half the day gone. I should be out weeding the potatoes and barley. In the run of fine weather the weeds grow faster than I can hoe them. It's a fine summer's day for a cart-ride and, if it weren't for my destination, I'd be enjoying sitting up here on the board in the sunshine with a warm breeze blowing.

Along the south side of our track, the sycamore leaves flutter in the breeze, their silky surfaces glistening in the sunlight. Purple and yellow vetches, red clover, buttercups, dog-roses and honeysuckle colour the hedgerows and banks along the lanes. The meadowsweet is in full bloom, its heady perfume scenting the air. If this were a different journey, I'd have liked Beulah sat alongside me. She'd enjoy a ride out on a day like this and it would be a welcome rest from work. In her stead, I have Swift, sat up on the board beside me, his tongue lolling out the side of his mouth, the picture of canine contentment.

If it's a fine day on Sunday, I'll take Beulah out for a ride when I come back from chapel. Beulah's family is church and she doesn't go but once a month. I tell her she won't go to heaven. She answers with a cheeky grin, saying she'll take her chances. A ride would put some colour back in her cheeks, too. She's lost weight since she came to Carregwyn, all the running about she does I expect. Her hips don't sway quite like they did and her smile is not as broad. I wish I could do something to make things easier on her.

Out of the range of the hills and valleys of our parish, the countryside opens out into river plain and lush meadows. It's dairy country, where men can make a living and more without breaking their backs to do it. Cows graze languidly, or lie in the sun, swatting the flies off their backs with their tails. So well fed they are, that they have the luxury of time to rest from scraping to get enough to eat. They have an easier life than I do.

The meadows are rich with red clover, buttercups, daisies, cornflowers and more flowers than I can name. A few fields along, a couple of milkmaids sit on their stools, milking the cows where they stand. They are bent forward with their bonneted heads resting on the cows' flanks, the steaming white liquid gushing out into the buckets beneath. Perhaps, if God will forgive me my sins, in the next life he will have me be born on a farm with lush river meadows.

At the ford, I cross the wide river. After weeks of good weather with only light showers, the river is low and slow moving. A duck paddles downstream with a brood of ducklings following behind, and the sound of the cart splashing through the water startles a pair of wild geese foraging in the reeds. They take off slowly, with staggering wing beats lifting their cumbersome bodies out of the water. I watch them fly away, their haunting, plaintive cries carrying on the air long after they are out of sight.

A mile or so down the lane, the hedgerows end and I cross a now rare piece of open, common land, one which had escaped enclosure by the landed gentry. I watch the skylarks rise and fall in the air, their warbling notes rising and falling with them. Buzzards circle overhead, watching and waiting to swoop on one of the hundreds of rabbits that chase each other in and out of the gorse.

A little way along, on the edge of the common, I pass a small hamlet of cottagers' dwellings. The hovels are poorly built, mud and dung for walls and floors, their roofs thatched with reeds from along the river. These are the Ty-yn-y-nos, 'house in a night'; homes built according to the old law which said that if you had a fire burning in the chimney by morning, then the house was yours. And the amount of land you could farm around it would be determined by how far you could throw an axe from your door.

A group of dirty-faced children run to greet me, their hands outstretched, arms and legs like sticks. Swift stands up on the board and barks excitedly at them, his tail wagging. Outside her front door, an old woman sits at her spinning wheel, her back bent, the skin of her face as wrinkled and weathered as my pony's saddle. She looks up as I approach and smiles at me with a toothless grin. She takes a pair of knitted stockings from the basket beside her and waves them at me, calling out "stockings for sale" with a croaking voice.

Two dwellings along, a young woman sits on a stool, rocking back and forth with a weak, whimpering baby in her arms. She does not notice me ride by, her eyes are focused on some distant place and clouded with the dreadful knowledge that her baby will not survive. I think God must be showing me a sign; for all my complaints, there are plenty worse off than me.

I head on out of the hamlet and pass a bare-foot girl, dressed in rags, tending a small flock of cottagers' geese on the common. She'd be about six years old, our Fortune's age, and I am reminded of my destination; Nesta Harding's filthy hovel where Fortune must live out her life. I ask myself, is she any worse off than the goose girl? Is Mam, yet again, being proven right? Fortune's life was no worse than it was for most children, she had said.

As I near my destination, I see Fortune in my mind as I last saw her. Every year, it cuts the heart of me to see her grown and not have witnessed the growing. I don't know how Megan bears it. I think the pain was too much to bear, so she buried it deep inside her, so deep that you'd have to cut her wide open to get to it. It was that or do herself in. I think she came close to that, too.

The child is my flesh and blood but she does not know it. To her I'm just the man who brings money each year. The money man, that's what she calls me. I heard her shouting it to Nesta, the last time I went there. "The money man's coming! The money man's here!" It cut to the heart of me that did. She thinks she is an orphan. That's what Nesta told her and I didn't contradict it. It seemed less cruel than telling her she had a mother somewhere, leaving the poor girl wondering where and why she did not come for her.

My haunches are aching and stiff, from sitting on the board for the past three hours, and Swift is getting restless. I decide we will walk the last half mile, and I tether the pony to the branch of an oak alongside the dusty lane. She will graze the grass along the hedgerow until we return. Swift runs along beside me, sniffing at the scents of the countless, nameless animals that have passed this way before him.

Now I am almost there, I feel an ambivalent mixture of emotions. I feel excited at the thought of seeing Fortune again but sick at the thought of yet another encounter with Nesta. She makes out she takes in illegitimate children for the love and pity of them, but it's clear as day she is only in it for the money. She is given enough to feed and clothe the girl, and a good deal over for her trouble, but the bulk of it she spends on herself. A woman does not get so fat without eating more than her share. But it is her slyness that most irks me. That way she has of making out she is doing me a personal favour. Each time I leave, having placed the money in her hand, she winks at me and tells me not to worry, she will take care of my little one for me.

I know what she thinks, that the child is mine. Nesta said to me once, "left it on your doorstep did she?" I didn't waste my breath arguing. There are people like Nesta in every parish, they believe what they want to and it's usually the worst. They don't give a jot for the truth, because the truth is less entertaining than what they can make up. I could deny till I was blue in the face, but Nesta would never have wanted to believe the child was not mine.

Mam understood, if Megan didn't, how much it hurt me to suffer the humiliation of going to pay that woman while, somewhere in this world, Fortune's father walked free of his responsibility.

"I'm sorry to have to ask you to do this for your sister, boy, but the time has come round again. I know it hurts you as much as me, to have to toil in the fields to pay for another man's child."

Each time I had to pay, it would open the wound and I would fester with resentment, and punish Megan, even though it was our Mam's decision to send the child away and pay someone else to keep her hidden. It wasn't what Megan wanted, Megan asked only for a little money to help her and the child on their way. Yet Megan it was that got the blame for that and all. Megan it was who felt the lash of my anger, because it was I who had to work to pay for the upkeep of another man's child.

I think our Mam was afraid, and it was fear that hardened her heart. She couldn't allow herself to weaken. She had to be strong to hold our family, and our lives, together. I believe she truly thought she was doing the best thing. She wasn't a bad woman. What Megan did - that was a terrible thing to do to our Mam. It was the worst humiliation our Mam could suffer. Mam never forgave Megan, of that I'm sure. She thought Megan had done it to spite her. I don't know about that, but our Mam must have thought she'd wronged Megan or why would she think Megan wanted revenge? I think Megan was always a thorn in our Mam's side because Megan reminded her of our Da, and the humiliations she suffered over his drinking and womanising. That was why she was so hard on Megan; too hard. Though I have sometimes despised Megan for all the trouble she brought to our door, I can see why she longed to be married and away from here. I just wish she had given one thought to the effects on us if it all went wrong.

I'm not a bad man or, at least, never used to be. I was once a good and kind brother to Megan. Megan had hurt me, betrayed me and deceived me. I went along with blaming Megan for everything else and all, because it did not seem to matter what I beat her for, just so long as I beat her. I don't mean I laid a hand on her, but I may as well have. I beat her as much with angry words or sullen silences, just as some men beat their wives and daughters with sticks.

In my heart I know it could have been different and that I had the power to make it so. I could have refused to do Mam's bidding. I could have faced the whole damned parish, and told them I would not turn my own sister out, whether they turned their backs on us or not. If I am honest with myself, I can't even put it down to cowardice, or to truly believing Mam was right. The one and only reason I did not stand up for Megan was because she had deceived me, and I could not forgive her that.

Thus I am tormented, remembering it all as I stand here on the footbridge about to pay Nesta, yet again. I look up at Nesta's hovel. I do not have much to be proud of. Even my plan to reunite Megan with Fortune was more to salve my own conscience than anything else. It is not to be and perhaps that is how it should be. I did a terrible wrong the night I stole Fortune away. I should pay some price for that, I think, and wish Megan the good luck and happiness I have begrudged her these past months. What Eli doesn't know will never harm him.

As I step off the bridge and onto the track, I see Nesta's front door open, and a man appears, his image framed against the dark interior. He is buttoning the flies of his breeches. Then he shrugs his braces up over his open necked shirt and comes down the track towards me. As I stand aside to let him pass, he winks at me and grins.

"Bed is still warm for you!" he says.

He's gone over the bridge before I understand his meaning. When I do it, feels like he's swung a punch at me and my legs almost give way beneath me. I cannot believe what I've been a witness to, in broad daylight. And it's taking place in the house where little Fortune lives. Swift sits at my feet and looks up at me and whines.

I order Swift to stay, and charge up the path to the cottage, and bang on the open door with my shaking fist. Through the gloom I see Nesta descend the stairs, adjusting her low cut bodice over her enormous breasts. The fatty rolls beneath her chin tremble as she speaks.

"Oh it's you! 'Bout time you turned up!"

Her gaze slides past me in the direction her visitor took.

"Who the hell was he?" I jerk my head in the direction of the bridge.

"A paying guest, you might say."

She gives me a grotesquely coy smile and twirls a tress of her greasy hair around her little finger.

'You're a filthy whore!" I say, my voice trembling with rage.

"Got to make a living somehow, especially seeing as you are so slow in paying." She pokes her tongue in her cheek as if she thinks she's got one over on me. I want to tear the greasy hair from her head. I want to knock her to hell and back.

'I pay you to take care of Fortune. Is this what you call taking care of her? Raising her in a whore-house?'

"Don't you come all high and mighty with me! You're no saint yourself! Fortune is evidence of that."

"Where's Fortune?"

I bury my shaking fists deep inside my pockets. I've never physically harmed a woman in my life but I want to take this one by her fat throat and drown her in the river.

"Ooh, don't worry!" She pulls a face, dragging down the corners of her mouth, mocking me. "I sent her to fetch some milk from the farm up the road. She's a bit young to learn the tricks of the trade, yet. It'll be a few years, yet, before she starts paying her own way."

I make a step towards her, ready to knock her filthy mouth shut.

"You lay a finger on me and I'll turn her out! Then who will you find to hide your little bastard?"

Nesta has always known and made use of her power over me. From the start, she could say what she liked, safe in the knowledge that I was powerless to do much about it. I needed her far more than she needed me. She thinks I will still do nothing, even now, because she is right; I don't know anyone else who will take Fortune. Of one thing I am certain, if I turn my back and walk away from Fortune now, knowing what I do, I will be paving my own road to the gates of hell.

"There will be no need to turn her out. She's coming with me. Go pack her things!"

Nesta snorts with disbelief.

"You don't fool me! You've got nowhere else to take her!"

"I'll take her to where she belongs. Now go pack her things."

Now I have made the decision, I feel calmer. This old bitch will never have the better of me again. She stops her smirking and narrows her eyes.

"I want my money. She's going nowhere unless you pay me."

"You're paid in advance. I owe you nothing."

"She won't go with you! She don't hardly know you!"

Swift barks, and through the open door I see Fortune coming over the footbridge, carrying a churn of milk. Swift runs to greet her with a wagging tail.

"She'll come with me," I say, and I don't know why, but I'm certain she will.

I go out to where Fortune is making a fuss of Swift.

"Go and pack your clothes and things, Fortune. We're going for a ride in the cart."

"I got nothing to pack."

She doesn't look at me when she speaks, but continues to pat Swift's head.

I reach out my hand and she places her hand in mine. Nesta comes out and starts shouting.

"You'll soon change your mind! She's nothing but trouble! You'll be bringing her back before summer is out!"

I keep right on walking, without a backward glance, but Fortune twists round to take one last look. When we reach the pony and cart, Fortune climbs straight up after Swift to sit on the board beside him. As I take the reins and turn the pony around, she looks at me for the first time.

"Where are we going?" she asks.

"We're going home," I tell her.

She places her arm around Swift who returns the gesture of friendship by licking Fortune's ears and making her squeal with delight. I see her ears are in need of more than a licking. I'll wager she's not seen a bath in a long while. Her hair is a mess of filthy tangles and her bare feet are caked with dirt.

"Where are your shoes?" I ask her.

"Don't have no shoes. No point in buying shoes for feet that is still growing."

On our journey home, my anger subsides, and in the sober aftermath I contemplate the consequences of my hasty actions. I'm going to have to think up a story fast. The whole parish will want to know who Fortune is. It's a nightmare of my own making. For Megan's sake, I have to think of some answers but the more I try to think, the more panicked I feel, so I can't think straight.

What in hell's name was I going to tell Beulah? As for Megan, I have no idea how she will cope with it. Rightly, she's terrified of the truth coming out, of Eli discovering what she did and kept secret from him. I've got to go and tell her what I've done. She will never forgive me. I've dug one hell of a hole for myself, now, and when Megan finds out what I've done she'll gladly bury me in it. Right now I'd like to bury myself rather than face the mayhem that is coming.

Megan didn't believe me when I told her how Fortune was living, she's even less likely to believe my reason now for taking Fortune from that place. She will think I've done it out of spite because I didn't want to go on paying for Fortune. I know I've done right by getting Fortune out of that place, and I'm glad of that, but in doing right by her, I may be about to smash Megan's world to pieces. I feel like I've just heaved one great weight from my shoulders only to see it go rolling down the hill, heading straight for Megan, who doesn't even know it's coming her way.

"Are you taking me home because you're my Da?" Fortune asks me, knocking the breath from me with the directness of her question.

"No. I am not your Da," I say, keeping my eyes on the road ahead.

"Nesta says you are and that's why you pay her to look after me."

"Then Nesta is a lying bit.....then Nesta didn't tell the truth," I say.

The child goes quiet beside me. An idea starts forming in my mind, an idea that might save us all.

"I'm taking you to a nice place, my home. There is a nice woman there, called Beulah, who looks after my house for me. I need you to do something for me. It's very important that you listen, and remember, what I'm going to tell you."

Chapter 16

Megan

I am out in the garden, sobbing because some creature has crept in during the night and torn up all my beautiful seedlings. Then I hear a shout, and turn to see Morgan marching down our hill. Eli is out in the field. I see him wave to Morgan. Morgan is calling out, saying I need to speak to you, Eli, there is something you should know. I run, tripping and stumbling over the tussock grass in my haste to get to Eli before Morgan does. When I reach Eli, I grab his hand and pull him, beseeching him to come with me. He says Morgan is calling, wants to speak to him. I say no, come with me now, there is no time to waste.

He runs with me, shouting, slow down, Megan, you'll do us an injury. But I can hear Morgan shouting, coming after us and getting closer. I have to get Eli far enough away that he cannot hear what Morgan is wanting to tell him. We are racing headlong towards the river with nowhere to turn. We have to leap the Wildwater or Morgan will reach us. With Eli's hand still in mine, I jump off the edge. We are not going to reach the other side. We are falling, falling, falling towards the crashing water and rocks.

I wake as we hit the water, gasping for breath as if drowning. The pillow beside me is empty. Eli is already gone to work in the fields. I bury my face in my pillow to stifle my sobs, for fear that Gwen will hear me crying. The dream was so terrifying, I cannot shake off the feeling of doom it has left hanging over me. In my mind, I keep seeing us falling, and I fear the dream is an omen of disaster lying ahead, waiting for us.

I am so afraid, every day. I cannot rid myself of the fear that Morgan will not rest until he sees me undone. Does he not think I have been punished enough for one mistake? I thought that once Eli and I were married, that would be an end to it, that all would come right. A line would be drawn under the past. Then Morgan, telling me after all these years that Fortune is being neglected. Did he think I would believe him? What a terrible, cruel thing to say to me. And then wanting Eli to foot the bill for what he, along with mother, once deemed was worth paying for. He asked that Eli pay the price of HIS decision.

Morgan is too fond of reminding me of my mistakes, while wanting to absolve himself from the consequences and cost of his own. If only they had let me go with Fortune when it was what I begged to do. But no, they would not allow that, would not allow me to make my own way in this life, for better or worse. And now, excuse my crying but it hurts so much, Morgan would ruin my marriage, my whole future, too. What did I ever do against him, really, for him to treat me so cruelly?

I get up and look out of the window and see the sun is already above the hills. There is a stifling feeling of weight on my chest, so that I feel I can't get my breath. I open the window and the chill air of early morning creeps in and makes me shiver. I wash my face and make our bed. I empty our wash basin out of the window, pick up the water pitcher and place it in the empty basin. It is a matching white porcelain set with little pink rosebuds for decoration. I go to the mantle-piece and with my fingernails, pick at the wax that has spilled from our candle. I straighten the patchwork quilt that covers our bed and plump up our feather bolster.

I walk out onto the landing, the polished floorboards creaking under my feet. I open the doors of the smaller rooms which stand either side of ours. They have unmade beds and an atmosphere of expectancy. They await the arrival of our hoped for children. Across the landing, behind a locked door, are the rooms where Gwen and the dairy maid sleep. Their access is up wooden steps that lead off the back of the kitchen. I have not been up there, fearing my curiosity would be an intrusion.

I go down the main staircase which descends into the hallway with its heavy, oak front door. To my right is Eli's study, where he keeps his accounts which I am not to concern myself with. I believe he keeps money in there to pay his workmen, money I could give to Morgan for Fortune's keep. But I dare not take a penny of it. Eli is so careful in everything he does, he would be sure to miss it, and then there would be calamity as he would rightly think it stolen.

The doorway on my left leads into the room where Eli and I spend our snatched moments together. A small fire still burns in the inglenook. Gwen lights it each evening because the evenings are still chilly. Sunlight pours in through the south-facing window and reflects off the polished surface of our dining table. Gwen keeps everything so sparkling clean.

On the far wall, next to the door which leads into the kitchen, hangs a painting of Eli's late mother and father,

Eleanor and Rees. Eleanor is sat on a high-backed chair which I recognise as the one Eli sits on at our table. Rees stands to the side of Eleanor with a protective hand laid on her shoulder. They are dressed in black and their demeanour, also, is sombre. They appear to stare at me with disapproval wherever I am in the room.

"They know you've cheated him, that's why."

I hear mother's voice as if she were in this very room. I wonder if this is what people mean when they talk of being haunted by the dead. I had thought when I moved here, away from all the reminders of mother, that I would cease to hear her voice. But still she goes on, her words casting doubt and fear in my mind, just as they did when she was alive.

My day stretches ahead of me, and I do not know what I shall do with myself to keep me from thinking. I long to head up to the farm for the distraction of physical work and Beulah's uplifting company. I have not been since my talk with Morgan, and I fear going again a while, lest he begin badgering again for money that I have no power to give him. Instead, I pick up my spinning wheel and carry it outdoors.

The garden is my only sanctuary, as it was for Eli's father in his twilight years. It lies to the back of the house, facing south, so it gets the best of the sun. I have sown carrots, parsnips, peas, beans, summer cabbages and salad vegetables in the vegetable patch. I am relieved to see the soft green seedlings are intact and still growing in their neat little rows. There is a small herb garden, too, where self-heal, comfrey, coltsfoot, mint and mallows grow, so the household is never without remedies for any mild ailments which may befall us.

Beyond this kitchen garden, is a small orchard of apple, pear and damson trees. I set my spinning wheel by the seat under an apple tree. From here I have a view back to the house and in the other direction, the hills beyond the small hazel coppice at the end of the garden. The air is full of the sound of bees, bumbling through the blossoms. I am spinning what is left of last year's wool. I have a notion to dye it yellow from the gorse flowers that are blooming up on the hill. I thought I might weave it into a cheerful shawl to wear on summer evenings. Mother would never have allowed me to wear anything so brash, but Eli will not mind it.

I take a handful of wool from my pinafore pocket and turn the wheel with my free hand to set it spinning. The yarn on the spindle grabs the fibers of wool and twists them as I tease them out. Eli can't watch me spinning without falling asleep like a babe in a rocking cradle. He says his eyelids begin to droop as soon he hears the rhythmical, padding sound of the pedal and the soft humming of the wheel. So it is a good thing I have time to spin when he is not here.

In the long grass beneath the trees, daffodils grow in springtime. Now there are speedwell and daisies growing there. Eli breaks my reverie with a kiss on top of my head.

"You were miles away," he says, sitting down beside me on the seat below the apple tree. "If the weather holds, we'll have a good crop of apples this year."

He looks up at the blossom laden canopy above our heads and reaches up to pluck a blossom which he tucks behind my ear. Then he sits beside me, and places his arm around my shoulder, leaning back in the seat. I rest my head on his chest and smile up at the face which is so dear to me.

"I do so love you."

"And I you," he says, kissing my brow. "I wish I could spend all day sitting here with you."

Eli works long hours on Wildwater. With the help of his labourers, he's making many improvements; draining the lower fields and repairing the stone wall boundaries. He says things were left to decline when he was away on his uncle's farm. He snatches these small excursions back to the house, just to see me, if it is only for five minutes. He knows the hours seem long to me because I'm not used to having so much time to myself, with little to do but tend to the garden, or do a little sewing or spinning. He says, make the most of it, I'll have no time to spare when the little ones start coming.

"Are you going up to see Beulah today?" he asks, not knowing that the merest mention of the place has the power to turn my spine to water.

"No. Not today. I thought I might go for a walk upstream and look for the waterfalls you told me about."

And then he is off again to his fields.

I walk along the Wildwater, towards the great mountain of Carregdu and the river's source. At times my journey takes me through small woodlands and coppices, their undergrowth still smothered in bluebells. Wood anemones nestle under mossy tree trunks, and wild strawberry flowers sneak along the paths. The hawthorns are in flower; their exquisite clusters of pink-edged, white blossoms are stirred by the breeze and fall like snowflakes on my hair. Their sickly-sweet perfume drifts on the air in waves. Despite my perfect surroundings, my thoughts are as much in turmoil as the broiling torrent of water I walk beside.

I come to a place on the Wildwater which I instantly recognise from Eli's description. It is called the Giant's Leap. Two great slabs of rock overhang each side of the river. Between them, is a gap of some six feet. Beneath is a black pool of eddying water that Eli says is as deep as the height of our house. Many years ago, two young brothers were drowned here when challenging each other to jump across the divide with their ponies. The one boy's pony slipped on the wet rock, pony and rider fell into the water. The other boy jumped in to try to save his brother, and both drowned. Eli told me this story, among others, so that I would know the history of Wildwater as if it were my own.

Dear Eli. He has made such efforts to make me feel I belong here. I never imagined how difficult it would be for me to be happy here. I did not set out to trick Eli as Morgan describes. I truly believed that to omit to tell the whole truth is not the same as to tell a lie. I tried to tell Eli the truth, I really did, the day he asked me to marry him.

"I don't deserve you, Eli, and you deserve someone better than me," I told him, and he laughed, telling me not to be so daft.

"No, you must listen. When you went away, it broke my heart to think you'd met someone else. I'd never loved anyone else but you. But I thought, well then, I shall show him and do the same, and to blazes with Mam. I couldn't bear the thought of you coming back with some pretty young other on your arm, and me sat here, the poor, lonely spinster. And so I did something recklessly stupid, something I never should have….'

Before I am able to say another word, he has crossed the room and scooped me up in his arms.

"I knew it! In my heart I was so sure you must still love me too, else I'd never have dared come here! Let's not waste any more time, Meg! I'll go to the preacher tomorrow and ask him to read the banns on Sunday."

All he heard was what he wanted to hear; that I had loved him as much as he loved me.

"No, Eli, I haven't finished…"

He told me to hush and kissed me, then leaned back to look at me, his face beaming with happiness, before kissing me again. He lifted me off my feet and twirled me in a dance around the kitchen table, his happiness so infectious that I was swept up in the moment and began laughing too. For those moments we were together in the kitchen there was no past, there was only me and Eli, together, as we were always meant to be. He was so happy to be marrying me at last, I could not bring myself to spoil it all.

Later, as I watched him ride off, I told myself I could still be the 'little Meg' of years gone by. I was still the girl that Eli had always loved, for all that happened in between. The past was another time, and I would bury it along with all the pain it had caused me. All that mattered was our future together, and I would do everything in my power to make Eli happy, and to atone for my sins.

I know I had other chances to tell him, after that day he came to ask me to marry him, but from then on it seemed there was no turning back. I believed what he didn't know could never hurt him. And I was probably right in that. What I never considered was whether I could tolerate the pain of knowing what he did not. That I betrayed him here in his own house makes my treachery all the worse. It haunts me every day.

Not until our wedding night, did I feel the full weight of my omission bear down upon my conscience, when Eli my virgin husband believed his nervousness and inexperience to be matched by my own. I cannot ever forgive myself for that, just as Eli could never forgive me, if he ever found out that we did not meet that night as equals. I feel the treacherous blade of guilt twist inside my heart, every time I think of it, and I loathe myself for that cruellest of all deceptions. Now, it is a secret burden I will carry alone with me to my grave. If he were to ever know the truth, he will think of our wedding night and know how cruelly I deceived him. I will give up my life before I will hurt my Eli. Morgan thinks I jest but I am in absolute earnest.

Nearby, I hear a cuckoo calling and am reminded of that other cuckoo with whom all our troubles began. If not for him, Sian Pritchard would still be alive and I would have gone on waiting for Eli's return. One man had caused the destruction of so many lives. If I were to see him now, I would thrust a knife into his heart. I wonder if it is as great a sin to think of murder as it is to commit it. I know in my heart of hearts that I am capable of it.

I have been so lost in thought that I have almost reached the source of the Wildwater, without knowing. Looming ahead of me is the great mountain of Carregdu. Deep gorges run down the mountain's sides and from these gorges, streams cascade to meet, and merge, and create the Wildwater. I sit on a damp, mossy bank close to the falling torrents, the sun shining through the spray and creating rainbows above my head.

As I watch the rainbows appear, fade, and reappear, in the mist of the spray, the strangest thing happens. The noise of the water recedes and the birdsong fades, as does the bleating of nearby sheep. All seems far away and yet I have the curious sense that I am the water, the birdsong, the sheep, the rocks, the mountains and the air I breathe, and they are me, and there is no difference or distance between us, we are all as one, and God is within all and all within God, and whatever will be was always to be, and is right and is truth, in the past, the present, and the future, for all eternity.

Like one waking from a dream, the sounds of the water and birds return and I look at the rainbows above my head. I am reminded of the fleeting nature of all things, and I believe it is God's sign that nothing, good or bad, will last forever. This time will surely pass, and Morgan will let things lie, and the past will be covered over again, like the moss covered rocks around me.

I make my homeward journey in more cheerful spirits. I tell myself that Morgan's money troubles cannot be so bad as he describes. He was just trying it on, knowing Eli is better off than he. I'll wager he never mentions it again. And even if it were true that Morgan was short of money, surely this woman who has looked after Fortune so long, would not turn her out for lack of payment. Fortune must be like her own child to her now. The pain of my loss and the weight of my guilt will become lighter with time. I pray God, and God willing,

Eli and I shall have a child or two of our own before too long.

Chapter 17

Morgan

By the time we arrive back on the farm, I and Fortune have rehearsed our story. If we stick to it as planned, I think I can wangle things so I don't drop Megan in it. What I'm thinking is, as long as nobody discovers Fortune's true identity, then the truth will never get out. Fortune herself doesn't know it. I just have to warn Megan that I've brought her home and why. I reckon, that once she's got over the shock, she'll be over the moon.

Beulah is carrying water up from the gorge when we arrive.

"I found her on the road," I say to Beulah, jerking my head towards Fortune who is clambering down off the cart.

Beulah lifts the yoke from her shoulders and looks at me as if I have grown two heads.

"On the road? What do you mean you found her on the road?"

"She was wandering, lost, with no place to go."

I wheel the cart into the shed, so I don't have to look Beulah in the eye.

"Well, I'd take her right back where you found her, if I were you. Her parents will be looking for her," she says, following me to the cart shed.

"I got no parents. I is an orphan!" pipes up Fortune, right on cue.

She's a smart little thing. The lies trip off her tongue with ease. She's her mother's daughter, alright.

"That's right, an orphan. That's why I picked her up," I say, walking the pony into its stable.

"Got no home to go to."

Fortune says this with a slow shake of her head, suddenly finding a particular interest in the cobbles at her feet.

I lead the horse to the stable and take off her harness.

"You must have come from somewhere. Where were you going when Morgan found you?" I hear Beulah ask Fortune.

"Money man found me on the side of the road when not a person in this world would open their door to me."

I never thought to tell her not to call me that.

"Money man? Who is this money man she's talking about?" Beulah asks me.

"I think she's delirious with fever," I say, "I can't make sense of half she says."

Beulah places the palm of her hand on Fortune's forehead.

"Doesn't feel hot to me. What's your name then? You must have a name."

"My name's Fortune. I'm six years old and I'm an orphan."

"Who has been looking after you, Fortune? Who gave you your name?" Beulah asks her.

Fortune chews on her lip and stoops down to ruffle Swift's head. I steer Beulah to one side as though I don't want the little one to hear.

"Best not to say too much. She's had a tough time," I whisper.

"Oh! Alright," Beulah says, wide-eyed with curiosity.

"That's right. I came across her wandering the road," I tell Beulah, filling her in on the whole sorry story when Fortune is bathed and tucked up in bed.

"There she was, no shoes on her feet, and looking as though she were lost. So I asked her if I could give her a lift to her home. That's when she started crying 'I got no home to go to.' Pitiful it was. I couldn't leave her there, could I?"

"There's plenty would have, Morgan. It was good of you to pick her up."

It seems Beulah is looking at me with new eyes and seeing Morgan the hero. I'd thought she would be furious when I brought the little one home, but I think our little story has tugged the maternal heart strings.

"Well, I suppose so. Anyway, that's when she told me about how her parents were travelling people. They both died within a week of each other. The way she described it, I'd say it was the cholera. She's been wandering the roads alone for a month or more, begging for food where she could get it."

"The poor thing! What a terrible thing to go through. Just think, Morgan, if you hadn't happened along, she could have ended up spending the rest of her childhood in the poorhouse."

"I know. It just doesn't bare thinking about," I say, and shake my head sadly.

"Poor little thing," Beulah says again. "It's so hard to take in."

"Mm. It's best not to question her too much, I think, it upsets her so much to talk about it."

"Oh yes, I'm sure! No! I won't say a word to her. She'll talk about it in her own good time, if she feels like it."

"That's right! Though she'll want to forget about the whole thing, I should think.

"I'm sorry to land this on you, Beulah, but I couldn't leave her there and come and ask you first."

"No. Of course you couldn't. I understand why you had to bring her. It was a bit of a shock but I think it'll be nice to have a little one about the house," she says.

And I'm home and dry.

"You're a good woman, Beulah. I knew I could depend on you," I say. "And she could be a big help around the house."

Beulah has washed Fortune's dress and hung it over the rail by the fire to dry.

"Fortune hasn't got a thing to wear but this thing she was wearing. It's hanging together by a thread. I don't know what we're going to put her in. I'm no good with a needle else I'd cut down something of my own."

"I was wondering if you would go down to Mary Williams, tomorrow, and ask if she'll give us something her girls have grown out of."

"I'd rather pull my own teeth, Morgan, than go visit Mary, the Mill," Beulah says, making me laugh out loud.

Beulah had apparently met Mary at Megan's wedding and they hadn't exactly got along. Stuck up busybody, was how Beulah described her later. Mary had told Beulah, to her face, women only became housekeepers when they were not good enough for any man to marry. Naturally, that didn't go down too well with Beulah.

"I'll pop down there myself after breakfast, then," I say.

It's all going so well that I feel very pleased with myself. I'll go and see Mary, first thing, tell her I found this waif on the road and taken her in. Then I'll go and tell Megan I've brought Fortune home but she's not to worry because nobody will ever know who she is. I feel so relieved to have finally found a solution, I fall asleep as soon as my head touches the pillow.

When I come in for breakfast, next morning, Fortune is up and sat at the table, and for a moment I feel I have spun back in time and it is our Megan sitting there. Beulah has tied Fortune's hair back with one of her own ribbons, and now she is tidied up, she looks the spit of our Megan when she was that age. I only pray to God that nobody else sees the likeness.

"Now, remember what I told you and mind you're a help to Beulah."

I wink at Fortune.

"Yes! I can scrub and peel potatoes, carry the milk, carry wood for the fire…" Fortune ticks off the chores on her fingers.

"And help churn the butter," I butt in, to remind her.

"Well you are clever being able to do so many things," Beulah tells her.

"Yes, I did lots of things to help because Nesta can't do very much on account of she's as fat as a pig."

Fortune's hand flies up to her mouth, and she looks over at me with fright when she realises she has said too much.

“Is she indeed? As fat as a pig?” Beulah says, raising one eyebrow at me with a questioning look.

“Oh yes, Fortune told me about her, didn’t you, Fortune? Took Fortune in for a couple of days but Fortune ran away because she beat her.”

“That’s right! She was a nasty fat old thing! She’d have probably eaten *me* if I’d stayed much longer!” Fortune says, letting her imagination get the better of her, and straying from our story.

“Oh, I don’t think that’s true, Fortune,” I say, trying to rein her in a bit. “Right, I’m off. Remember what I told you. Don’t go getting on Beulah’s nerves with *saying* too much.”

I can only pray she’s bright enough to understand my meaning and keeps her mouth shut.

I never thought lying would come so easy. I know it is a sin to lie but it has surely got to be better than the alternative. I can’t believe God would want me to ruin one life in order to help another. It is not like I haven’t impressed on the little one that these are exceptional circumstances; that it wouldn’t normally be alright to lie. I’ve told her if she’ll just go along with my story, she’ll get to stay in my nice house with a room of her own and some good boots to wear on her feet. I’ve also told her, that if anyone finds out she already had a home before she came here, she’ll be straight back to Nesta with a flea in her ear.

Coming so hot on the tail of my recent worries, the relief of having rescued Fortune, while escaping the consequences of Megan being found out, is so great that I feel quite light-headed during my ride down to Mary’s. Oh, you clever man, Morgan Jones, you clever man, I tell myself. I can't remember the last time I felt so good. And what a smart little thing Fortune is. When I think of how long I have wanted to bring her home. It seems that God, or fate, in the form of Nesta's whoring has played a hand in making that dream come true. Finally, I am able to make amends. I can hardly wait to tell Megan but first I have to get some clothes for the little one.

"The master and missus have gone to market for the day," the maid tells me when I arrive at the mill.

I ask her would she know if Mary had any clothes that one of her older girls may have grown out of. She comes back from a forage in the trunks upstairs, carrying an armful of clothes.

"I should ask the missus, really, before I let you take them. She may be keeping them for patchwork."

"Don't worry. Tell her Morgan said it would be alright."

"May I tell her what they are for?"

"Aye. Tell her they are for a little visitor we have staying with us," I say.

When I return home with the bundle of clothes, Fortune races up the stairs with them, to go and try them on. I can tell that Beulah is not in the best of moods, the moment I walk in. She doesn't give me that broad smile she usually does when I come in. In fact, she ignores me altogether, except to ask when am I going down to tell Megan.

"Or does she know already?"

My stomach curdles at the thought of going to tell Megan what I've done.

"No. I haven't had time to go there, and all. I can't go today, anyway. I'm behind with my chores now. I'll tell her soon. There's no hurry is there?"

Beulah folds her arms and narrows her eyes at me.

"I'll go tomorrow," I say.

I tell myself that I need to work myself up to it, gather all my courage, though I know in my heart that a lifetime wouldn't be long enough, and it won't be courage that takes me down there but that I have no choice other than to go.

Beulah's mood is no better that evening. She is unusually quiet after she has put the little one to bed.

"Fortune tucked up in bed, is she?" I ask, worried the little one has let something slip.

Beulah answers a curt yes and bangs my dinner plate down a little too hard on the table.

"She's taken a real shine to you," I say, trying to make light, though fear has crept into my stomach and cowers there.

Still she says nothing, but goes to the fire and throws on a lump of peat with a little too much force, sending ash and sparks flying into the room.

"Has she said anything about it at all?" I ask, trying to sound only mildly curious.

"Oh. No. Not a word," she says.

I breathe a little easier, knowing Fortune hasn't dropped us in it.

"You're a good woman, Beulah. I'm glad I can depend on you," I say, giving her a warm, appreciative smile.

"Oh, I'm sure you are. Good old Beulah. I'll tell her a heart-rending story and she'll feel so sorry for that poor little mite, she'll take her under her wing. You must think I've the brains of your horse out there in the stable, Morgan."

"I don't know what you mean by that," I say, suddenly finding it hard to swallow my supper for the feeling of panic rising in my throat.

"Well, then, Morgan, I'll explain. Something was troubling me from the moment I saw Fortune. You see, she reminded me of someone, but at the time I just couldn't put my finger on who."

I laugh, shaking my head, as if I think she's being silly.

"Really? Well, it must be just coincidence. There are no travellers in these parts."

"Mm. That's what I told myself. But then, when she was all cleaned up, and her hair brushed and in ribbons, it struck me again. The uncanny likeness."

I look up from the supper getting cold on my plate to find Beulah watching me closely. I swallow hard and think fast.

"Well, it's funny you should say that, I had the same feeling myself. I thought how much she reminded me of our Megan when she was that age. That's uncanny I thought but, obviously, just one of those incredible coincidences that sometimes happen. Because, of course, she is no relation to us! Or at least, I don't think so. I can't say for sure, mind. Perhaps, somewhere, way back, there might have been travellers in the family. Who knows?"

I smile at her and return to trying to eat my cold supper. Beulah nods her head slowly and sits down opposite me, where there is no avoiding her gaze if I look straight ahead.

"Oh, I see! So you're saying it's no more than coincidence that she is the spitting image of Megan!"

"Well, yes. What other reason could there be?"

I get up from the table and go and sit on the settle so I have my back to her. But she gets up and follows, and sits in the chair by the fire where she can get a good look at me.

"A real family likeness then!" she says. "You see, Morgan, what I was thinking was, how much you and Megan are alike. So if Fortune looks the spit of Megan, then she looks the spit of you, too."

I can feel her eyes boring into me, searching for the truth. I look up to find her staring at me and I quickly look away.

"I don't know what you're getting at. Is there something wrong, Beulah? For you have been acting strange all evening and I can't think for the life of me what notion may have entered your head."

She leans forward in her chair, her face up close to mine, so I cannot avoid her.

"Don't you indeed? Well, let me tell you something, Morgan Jones, which you clearly don't know for yourself. You are a damned poor liar. And if I can see right through your lies then so will everyone else, for they have known you longer and better than I."

"Aye, well, there you are, you've said it yourself. You don't know me well, so you suspect I am lying when I am not. I'm hurt, Beulah, truly I am. I didn't know what a low opinion you had of me."

"It's getting lower every time you open your mouth! And let me tell you for why. You are playing me for a fool, that's why! You make up this cock-and-bull story and get the child to go along with it. And let me tell you, I don't think much of you doing that, either, and all so you can use me to look after your illegitimate child for you!"

"My what? *My what?* She's not mine! God Almighty, what kind of man do you take me for?"

"A liar is what I'm taking you for at this moment, Morgan Jones, a man who I know I can't trust to tell me the truth."

"Alright, then! I'll tell you the truth! That child up there was living with a whore. I am supposing you know what that means? She was living with a woman who beds with men for money. I couldn't leave her there, knowing that, could I?!"

"Oh, my God! It gets worse." Beulah stands up and clamps her hand over her mouth but sadly she doesn't keep it there. She points towards the stairs and speaks in a loud whisper.

"Are you telling me you fathered that child with that sort of woman? Does Megan know about this? Did she know what you were planning? If she did, I shall never forgive her. She told me what a good and honest man you are, how I wouldn't find a better man to work for."

"Did she? Did Megan say that about me?"

Beulah puts her hands on her hips and nods her head at me. "Oh ho, look at you! All surprised to hear someone say something good about you! Well, I'm off down the road in the morning. You can find someone else to tell your lies to."

"No. Beulah. Please. Don't leave me high and dry. Please! Oh, God help me. If I swear on that bible over there to tell you the truth, will you swear too on that bible that you will never tell another soul what I tell you?"

She hesitates, and gives me a long, hard look before going to the top shelf of the dresser for Mam's bible.

"I swear I shall never repeat what Morgan tells me this night," she says with her hand on the bible, standing in front of me.

She passes the bible to me. I do not take my eyes from hers as I speak.

"I swear to tell Beulah the truth – on condition she will never tell another soul what I am about to tell her."

Beulah sits back down in the chair by the fire. Our Mam's old chair as it happens. I don't know where to begin. Beulah nods at me, telling me with her eyes to open my heart to her. I begin by telling her that Megan and Eli would have been married long ago if it weren't for our Mam. I tell her about our Mam, how she treated Megan, and how she tricked her. I tell her how Megan rebelled, and tried to trap another man into marriage by getting herself pregnant, even though Sian Pritchard had ended up in the Wildwater after getting herself the same way. I relate that summer when Megan's money went missing, and how I knew now that our Mam had stolen it, and the shock when we discovered that Megan was pregnant.

Beulah has been silent all the while I have been speaking, just occasionally nodding her head, encouraging me to go on.

"But how did Megan's baby end up with this terrible woman?"

I don't know how to tell her the rest. I don't want to see her condemn me. I stare into the flames of the fire. In the flickering flames, I see Beulah leaving in the morning, leaving because she has lost all respect for me. I have sworn on our bible, so I have to tell of the part I played in taking Megan's baby away. But I tell her too how it hurt me to do it, how I begged our Mam to change her mind and let Megan choose her own fate. I tell Beulah this, knowing how weak and pathetic a man she will find me. I tell her how much I have longed to make amends to Megan for taking her child away, and how I had given up all hope when Megan didn't believe me, when I told her how Fortune was living. And now, Megan won't believe this latest news about Nesta either, for I can hardly believe myself what a terrible woman we sent her baby to.

It is close to dawn when I finish telling Beulah the bare bones of the truth.

"I'm sorry, Beulah, we didn't set out to deceive you. If I hadn't been forced into bringing Fortune back with me, well, nobody would have known. You do see, that if word got out about what Megan did, then her new found happiness would be ruined? I just want to do what is right, for both of them, Megan and Fortune. Fortune shouldn't suffer for something that is no fault of her own. And Megan, well, I think she has suffered enough for what she did. But others won't see it that way. Eli. Can you imagine if Eli was to find out now?"

"Yes. I can imagine too well. Oh, Morgan. What have you done?"

"I know. I know. I should never have agreed to take Fortune away. Let me assure you, I am well aware of that."

We sit in silence for what seems like an eternity, until the birds outside the window begin to herald the dawn. Finally, Beulah begins to speak, and I am sure that when she is finished speaking, she will go and get her few things and go back from whence she came to me.

"I can't blame you for taking Fortune away. What else could you do? It was what your mother asked of you. You shouldn't blame yourself for that, Morgan. Honour thy mother and father. That is one of the commandments, whether you are chapel, or church, as I am. Nowhere in the bible does it say "honour thy mother and father so long as they are worthy of that honour". Your mother asked you to choose between herself and Megan. And in asking you to choose her way, she asked you to choose wrong over right. That isn't your fault, Morgan. She should never have asked that of you, it was cruel of her to do so. Oh, don't. Don't cry.'

I don't know what is wrong with me. I didn't used to be the crying sort. But I have no power in me to stop the tears pouring from my eyes.

"Come here, you soft, silly, man," Beulah says and comes over and sits beside me, her big arms around my shoulders, and she stays there until I am all cried out.

"Now," she says, "we need to think of what is the best we can make of a terrible situation."

"Can't we just tell everyone I found her, as I told you?"

"Oh Morgan, don't be daft. If I can see right through it, the rest of them will."

"I'm not taking her back to that whore!"

"No. I know. It is too late for that. Oh, Lord, it's so unjust. Poor Megan."

"Poor Megan! It was Megan got us into this mess!"

"Lord, help us poor women! All the sins of kingdom-come heaped upon our heads since the time of Eve! There you have the greatest injustice of them all. Women are damned if they give you what you ask, damned if they don't. All women are the great seducers of weak and innocent men. That how you see it, is it, Morgan? That's what the hell-fire preachers teach you in that chapel of yours?"

"What is wrong with that? It's the truth!"

Beulah gets up from her chair and stretches and yawns. She puts a log on the dying embers of the fire. A glimmer of dawn light creeps through the shutters.

"Nothing, I'm sure, from your point of view. It means men can do what they damned well like and never be brought to justice. What happened to the man who brought about Megan's ruin?"

"He went back wherever it was he came from."

"I'll bet he did, and I'll wager he has not lost a moment's sleep over Megan since. And I'll tell you something else. Even if Megan had been raped, which you say she was not, she would still have been blamed. They'd say she must have done or said something to provoke an innocent man. Its men that make the rules and the rules are there to protect themselves."

Beulah goes to the window and opens the shutters. Outside, the birds are starting to sing and the cockerel crows from the barn.

"You have to have rules, and the line has to be drawn somewhere between right and wrong. I suppose you'd like women to be able to make up any stories they like so as to get a ring on their finger."

" I'm not saying you can have no rules at all, I'm saying they must be just and not simply there to benefit some at the expense of others. It's not Megan you should be blaming. You should be blaming the rules that allow feckless cheats to walk free while good people are forced into wrongdoing for fear of being cast out. If the rules had been different, Megan would not have been abandoned, she would not have had to suffer her pregnancy alone, your mother would not have sanctioned evil and you would not have been party to it. All of that; it happened because you were all so afraid that Megan's 'mistake' would come to light."

She goes out to the scullery with the kettle and returns to hang it over the fire to boil.

"You remember my grand aunt Suzannah? Well, she never set foot inside church nor chapel, after the age of eighteen. To hell with the lot of those bible bashers, she used to say, I'd rather not belong anywhere if belonging means going along with the persecution of innocent people. There was another sister, you see, other than my grandmother. Her name was Mary.

A shiver ran through me. "Not Mary Jones?!"

"Ay. Mary Jones. Mary threw herself in the Wildwater too, along with her child, when she found herself abandoned. The man responsible dragged her off the road one night, when she was walking back from market. Mary was hauled up in front of the congregation at chapel and condemned as a sinner and defamer of a good man's name."

"You don't know they weren't right. There's plenty cry rape after the event."

"Oh, you think so? When did you ever hear a girl say she was raped and be believed? I never did. How many girls do you think would say it when they know they won't be believed, and know it will only mean more humiliation heaped on their heads? That happened to Mary nearly fifty years ago. She was just sixteen. And here we are, all these years later, and attitudes haven't changed much, have they?"

Beulah goes out to the larder and brings back bread and cheese, then she goes to the dresser and lays our breakfast plates on the table. She pauses, her hands resting on the back of her chair.

"Suzannah gave me some good advice, which your Mam would have done well to give to Megan. She said; never trust a man who asks for anything before marriage, and never trust that a man will marry you until the ring is on your finger. I don't believe Megan set out to get herself pregnant. It's a ridiculous notion. She would never have risked it, knowing the consequences if it went wrong. No, I'd lay money that she was duped, tricked into believing she was going to be married. What wrong is there in wanting to believe you are loved? What wrong in wanting to marry and have a life of one's own? What wrong in trusting the word of another, for where would we all be without trust?"

Beulah knows how to talk. Now she's begun, it seems like she will never stop. She does talk a lot of sense but, hell, we can't have women thinking they can change the world or God only knows where we will end up.

"You have thought Megan a selfish, scheming woman who brought ruin on herself. That is the greatest injustice you have done Megan. That is what you should be wanting to make amends for. Though, God bless her soul, she seems to have forgiven you for it. That's what your hell-fire preacher should be telling you all to practice. Forgiveness. For that seems to be what is in shortest supply in these parts."

"Aye, well, you may be right about that. But what am I going to do about the little one sleeping upstairs? If you are right, and people will guess who she is, then Megan is ruined. Whether you like the rules or not, that is Megan's fate if her secret comes out."

"I know Morgan, I know. What I don't know is what we can do to prevent it."

"I thought I had it all worked out," I say, feeling ragged with the tiredness of not having slept and the sharp bitter taste of disappointment in my mouth.

"Whatever happens, we must stand by her. We must let her know, that whatever others may think of her, we still hold her in the highest regard. I don't want Megan ending up in the Wildwater like Mary and Sian. I really could not bear for that to happen."

Beulah rubs her eyes with her fists then yawns loudly into her hands.

"It's impossible to think straight when I'm this tired. Right, first things first. You need to let Megan know. It would be terrible if she turns up, and sees Fortune without prior warning. So let Megan know she's here, and tell her to come up and see me. Then we can all sit down together and decide what is best for all."

Chapter 18

Megan

As I return from my walk along the Wildwater, our house comes into view in the distance, and I see Mary the Mill riding up the path, like a crow, with her black cloak billowing out behind her. The only thing I ever liked about Mary was her ability to rub mother up the wrong way. So different from Dafydd, Mary has not a charitable bone in her body. She is also a busybody, rummaging about in peoples' lives, looking for tasty morsels of gossip, like a pig rooting for acorns. That was her purpose this day, and when she tells me her news, I feel the end of my life rush towards me.

"Oh! Hello, Megan! I've just popped over to ask you, who is this little girl that Morgan has staying with him?"

"You're very quiet this evening, Meg," Eli says to me later, "is everything alright?"

I take his hand in mine, and say I think I may be coming down with a cold and will go to bed early. I can hardly bare to look at him, it hurts so much. Such a short time we have had together.

When Eli comes up to bed, I pretend to be asleep. I lie awake all night, wide-eyed in the darkness. Even when I close my eyes, it is as though there is another pair of eyes in my head and they are wide open. My mind is wide awake but empty of all thoughts but one.

I lie next to my poor unsuspecting Eli, who thinks this is forever, and I listen to his breathing. My body too is wide awake and waiting. I feel suspended in the darkness, as though hanging by some invisible thread. There is no pain, no tears yet, at Morgan's betrayal. This body of mine is holding it all for as long as it can, knowing I have not the strength of mind to bear the pain, if it is true. And I shall not fully believe he could be this cruel until I have seen Fortune with my own eyes.

When the first signs of dawn appear, I roll onto my side with my back to Eli, so that he will not know I am awake. I hear him stir and feel his tender kiss on the nape of my neck. I shut my eyes tight against the tears, and bite my lip, for his tenderness is too much to bear. He strokes my hair before getting out of bed and goes quietly out of the room.

I wait until I hear him leave the house and hear Gwen moving about downstairs. Then I get up and dress. I tell Gwen I am going up to Carregwyn and don't know when I will be back.

"I wouldn't go up that hill today, if I were you. I can smell rain on the air and the wind's picking up. I wouldn't be surprised if we have a storm."

"I'll take my cloak. I'll be alright. I'm used to all weathers up there."

"Won't you be having any breakfast before you go?" she asks, as I make to go out of the door.

"No, I'm not hungry this morning, Gwen. Perhaps I'll have something when I get there."

I leave her tutting and muttering that a body needs food for a climb like that. There is a chill to the wind which is blowing up from the east, and I pull my cloak tight around me. The branches of the trees in Eli's wood are tossed from side to side. The wind roars through the leafy canopies, and leaves fly on the air as if it was autumn.

Upon the hill, the bracken waves back and forth, and the wind whistles through the grasses on the heath. Everywhere, there is movement, and yet inside me there is a deathly stillness. I go to sit among an outcrop of rocks, above the house. Hawthorn and rowan long ago seeded themselves in the crevices and have grown outwards to form a sheltered canopy, overhanging my hiding place. From here I can see the house and the gorge below, but I am hidden from view. I pull my cloak around me and draw the hood up over my head. And wait.

I do not have to sit long before I see Beulah emerge from the house with a little girl by her side. When I see her, my heart leaps in my chest. It is all I can do to stop myself racing down the hill to her. My mind cries out. Oh my child, my child! She has long chestnut hair like me. She carries my old basket and has her face turned up to Beulah. She is likely chattering away, and though I cannot hear a word from here, I find myself straining to hear, just this once, the sound of her voice. A gust of wind catches Fortune's hair, hurling it around her head. She and Beulah duck their heads, and race across the cobblestones. They go into the barn and re-emerge after a short time with a basket full of eggs. They go back into the house and close the door behind them.

It is her, it is her, I know it is her. My whole being knows her and yearns to go to her. What am I to do? I notice movement, then, and see Morgan is in the field below the barn, setting up makeshift pens of hazel hurdles, in readiness for the forthcoming shearings. Oh Morgan, what have you done to me, now? And why now? Why now, and not before I had pledged myself to Eli? I wonder how he can work there in the field, carry on his life as normal, when he must know that he has brought an end to mine.

Now I see Mary the Mill, riding up the track, undeterred by the turning weather. I see Morgan has also witnessed her arrival, and watch him walk up to the house. I wonder if he is telling Mary, at this moment, the true identity of Fortune, to ensure the whole parish will know by nightfall. He must have told Beulah already. She will think ill of me, no doubt. She will have heard Morgan's version and think me a scheming, selfish liar. As will Eli, very soon.

Don't cry, Megan, don't cry.

God works in mysterious ways, the preacher says, his wonders to perform. I cannot begin to understand why God has chosen such a life for me. I did no wrong before Iago came along. With my face turned up to the darkening sky above, I ask God if I have not been punished enough. Was it not enough to be deprived of my child? Would you have Eli suffer, too, for my sins? I ask him. Eli, who never harmed a soul in his life?

Mary does not waste any time. She mounts her pony and leaves, minutes after her arrival. She is in a hurry, no doubt, to spread the news. Morgan was once a good and kind man. Whatever happened that he should choose to harm not only me, but Eli too? Speaking of the devil, Morgan comes out of the house and goes to the stable. I watch him mount his horse and ride off in the direction of Eli's wood.

I am alone in this world and about to be attacked from all sides. There is not a soul I can turn to for help. Eli is the only person who cares for me and the one person I can never tell of my anguish. If I could only go down to the house and see Fortune; touch her, hear her speak, and tell her I never chose to give her up. I would have liked her to know that. What will they tell her about me? That I abandoned her? Will they have her grow up thinking her own mother didn't want her? Yes. They have proved themselves unjust enough to do that.

My day of judgement is coming for me, and I would gladly let them throw their stones of condemnation, and be done with it all. But I cannot bear to see the look of hurt and betrayal in Eli's face, and his love for me turn to hatred, when he learns the truth. No matter how much he may refuse to believe when tongues begin to slander me, he will know the truth for himself when he sees Fortune. I do not want to be in this world when he does.

I take the long way down to Wildwater for I do not want to run into Morgan. I don't ever want to see him again. It begins to rain and the wind lashes my face with it as I head down the mountain, so that I cannot tell where my tears begin or end. He loved me once, did Morgan, when I was a good and pious sister. I pray he will love Fortune as much, and that she will never do anything to destroy that love, as I have done.

When I get back to Wildwater, Gwen tells me that Morgan called by.

"I told him you were on your way up there already," she says, "he was worried where you must have got to for he hadn't passed you on his way down."

"I changed my mind. I don't feel up to it, after all. I think I will go and lie down."

"You don't look well. That's what comes of going out with no breakfast."

"Yes, I think you are right, Gwen."

I go and lie down on our bed and watch the rain pour down the windows through the holes in the broken guttering which Eli plans to repair. At least the rain will delay Morgan's shearing, which is when Eli will be confronted with the consequences of my sins. All hell will not be let loose just yet. I wonder if I should write him a letter, try to explain. But I would not know how to begin. There are no excuses for what I have done.

When he comes to judge me, this man who has loved and known me all my life, he will measure the weight of my sin against all the else that I am, and all the good that is in me will count for nothing against it. My name, my reputation, all that I have been in his eyes, will be destroyed. And then I will cease to be, for there will not be a soul left in this world who sees the true Megan, anymore. It will be like dying. There is no point in going on. Better to die quickly of my own volition, than to die slowly, as Eli turns his face from me and shuns me along with all the rest.

"*An eye for an eye. Your life for your sin.*" I hear mother say.

Chapter 19

Morgan

"No, I won't go this early. I don't want to run into Eli and have him say, 'hello boy, a bit early to be visiting, isn't it, is there something wrong?'."

I say this to Beulah, when she says she cannot be still until she knows I have put things straight with Megan. Her pacing up and down the kitchen is wearing me out, but I won't relent. The last thing I need is to have to answer awkward questions from Eli. I'm wrung out as it is, from having no sleep, and it will take all the strength I have in me to go and tell Megan what I must.

"I'm going down to prepare the bottom field for the shearing. I'll go as soon as I'm done down there."

Mercifully, Fortune awakes then, for Beulah is sorely in need of distraction.

I've been down in the field less than an hour when I see Mary, the Mill, ride up to the house. She didn't waste any time to come nosing around. I walk up to the house. When I walk in, Beulah gives me a beseeching look that says she is not best pleased by Mary's visit.

"I've just been chatting with your visitor. She tells me her name is Fortune!" Mary says to me. "I was saying to Megan, yesterday evening, Morgan has a little visitor, a little girl."

Beulah and I exchange looks. I hadn't imagined Mary would be so quick to go fishing for information from Megan before I'd had a chance to explain. God alone knew what must be going through Megan's mind.

"Megan didn't seem to know anything about it," Mary goes on, staring intently, first at Fortune, then at me.

"I didn't have time to tell her, yet. I found Fortune wandering the roads. She's an orphan."

"An orphan, is she? Well! I never!"

She looks at Fortune again, and maybe it was my imagination, but I was sure it was with suspicion.

Beulah steps forward then.

"That's right. And Morgan here has decided to give her a home. It was that or take her to the poorhouse."

"*Very* kind of him, I'm sure."

Mary runs her finger along the shelf of the dresser and inspects her finger for dust. I have to suppress a smile when I see the look of outrage on Beulah's face.

"You should be going, Morgan. You were going down to Wildwater, remember? And I have chores to do."

Beulah stands with her hands on her hips, waiting for Mary to take the hint and leave.

"Nice seeing you, Mary, and thanks for lending the clothes. You shall have them back just as soon as I can get Fortune some of her own."

"Not at all. Keep them. It's not every day I get to help an *orphan*," she says, with another glance at Fortune and me, before going out of the door.

Beulah goes to the window, to make sure Mary is out of earshot, before she speaks.

"I don't believe it! What must poor Megan be thinking?"

"She'll be thinking I've gone behind her back, that's what."

"That busybody will have told half the parish about our little visitor before nightfall. We must speak with Megan and decide what to do."

"Are you going to send me back to Nesta with a flea in my ear?" Fortune asks, her eyes brimming with tears.

She is standing at the bottom of the stairs and has been eavesdropping.

Beulah takes her hand. "No! Never! Don't you worry, you're staying with us from now on, whatever happens," Beulah says, and I agree.

When I get to Wildwater, it is only to be told that Megan has already left for our place.

"Are you sure Megan said she was going to Carregwyn? I should have passed her on the way," I say to Gwen.

"That's what she said, but you know Megan. She's probably wandered off to pick some flowers on her way."

That'll be it, I think. That's why I didn't see her. So I'm expecting to find her at Carregwyn when I get back.

"She's not been here," Beulah says. "but I'll keep an eye out for her. You'd better do the same. She must be coming to see you know who."

Beulah motions her head towards Fortune who is sat at the table munching oatcakes which Beulah has made for her.

By mid-afternoon, it is certain that whatever Megan's original plans, she is not coming here.

"I haven't been further than the dairy all day so I couldn't have missed her if she'd come," Beulah says.

"I'll go back down to Wildwater. If she's not there I don't know what else I can do. I wouldn't be surprised if she's avoiding me. She will probably never want to speak to me again."

"You could write her a note and take it down with you, just in case, to let her know how things stand. I could do the same, just to let her know I will remain her friend, whatever happens."

I go to the drawer for paper and quill and sit down to write.

Dear Megan,

I am writing this note in case I don't find you at home. Please believe me, I had to bring Fortune home. I did not do this to harm you. Please come up and see us. We will work something out between us.

Your loving brother,

Morgan.

I hand the quill and paper to Beulah who looks at me, shame-faced.

"I can't read nor write. You'll have to write mine for me."

"I'll teach, you if you like. Not now, mind - when things have settled down, like. If you stick around, that is."

Her gaze meets mine.

"If I stick around, Morgan, yes, I would like that very much. Thank you."

"Will you teach me and all?" Fortune pipes up, reminding us that she is listening to everything we say.

"Aye, I'll teach you to read and write, too. It'll be like a regular Sunday school up here. But first I will teach you not to be so nosy!" I say, gently cuffing her round the ear and making her laugh out loud.

"This is what I want you to put from me to Megan," Beulah says, her face all serious, looking at the paper in front of me.

Dear Megan,

Please, please, come up and see us so we can work out what is the best thing to do. I am and will always remain your friend and will stand by you, whatever happens.

I send you my love and understanding,

Beulah."

I seal the letters with wax from the candle.

"Who's Megan?" Fortune asks us.

Beulah looks at me, waiting for me to answer.

"Megan is a good and kind person who also happens to be my sister," I say, my voice quavering, and not taking my eyes away from Beulah's.

"I'd better go," I say.

"Yes. Hopefully you will find her home. If you do, say it well, Morgan, say it well."

"I will," I tell her with a confidence I don't feel.

On my second trip this day down to Wildwater, it's as much as I can do to sit upright on the pony. What I would give, to lay my head on her neck and sleep. My eyes feel as though they are full of grit, and my body is crying out for rest. The blustery wind and sudden sharp showers are the only things keeping me awake. In a way, I hope Megan is not there, for I feel too tired to fight my corner with her, if she still refuses to believe I mean her no harm.

Gwen answers the door to me with a look of surprise.

"Oh! It's you again, Morgan! You've struck lucky this time. Megan is home but she's not well, mind, so I hope you're not thinking of dragging her up that hill."

"No, Gwen, I just wanted a word, that's all."

Gwen goes upstairs leaving me standing in the doorway. When she returns, it is to apologise for not asking me to wait inside. She ushers me into the hallway and points to a chair, saying Megan won't be long. I remove my hat and sit down. Gwen bustles away, and I sit listening to the tick of the grandfather clock which stands inside the front door. It's a grand hallway, with a high ceiling, and a lovely old carved staircase leading upstairs. Megan may have fallen but she landed on her feet when she touched the ground.

Then I see her come round the bend on the stairs and she looks not like she landed on her feet so much as crashed, and I fill up with tender concern at the sight of her. She is wearing her cape, with the hood pulled up, as if ready to go outdoors. Her face is pale and drawn and I think, Beulah and I were not the only ones who got no sleep last night.

"Gwen says you're not well. Should you be going out?" I say, getting to my feet.

She gives me a withering look.

"I don't want to talk to you here," she says, and each word is clipped short.

I notice the trembling in her fingers as she turns the door knob, and I want to reach out and take that hand in mine and hold it tight until it is still. But I stand back for her to open the door, feeling like an awkward, unwelcome visitor in her house.

I follow as she takes the narrow path along the roiling Wildwater. I have always hated this part of the river, the constant noise and turmoil of it. What with that, and the wind howling through the canopy of trees overhead, I cannot hear my own thoughts. She does not stop until we have gone round a bend and are out of sight of the house.

I hear Beulah's words telling me to say it well, Morgan.

"Megan. I am truly sorry. I can see you think ill of me, but I want you to know, I would not have brought Fortune home if there had been any alternative."

She does not look at me as I speak, but at the ground beyond me. I reach out to place my hand on her shoulder but she flinches and takes a step backwards.

"I caught a man leaving that woman's house. She was a whore, Megan."

Her eyes flick up and lock with mine for only a second but it is long enough for me to see her scorn.

"I'm not making it up. You can ask Beulah. I swore on the bible it is the truth."

"You mean to tell me that you and mother paid a whore to look after my child?"

"Yes. No. I did not know, until I went there this time, that she was doing that. I suspected Fortune was being neglected and ill-treated but I never suspected that."

"Did mother know? Did she know Fortune was being neglected? Did she know just how great a mess she made of things when she decided to take my life into her hands?"

"I told her I didn't think the place was good enough for Fortune. I wanted to bring Fortune back home. I was too weak to stand up to Mam, I know that. All I've wanted since is to make amends, Meg. But I swear I didn't want to make things difficult between you and Eli. I would never have chosen to do that to you."

"Do you understand what you have done, Morgan?"

She looks directly at me now, her eyes boring into my soul is what it feels like.

"Yes, Meg, I do and I am very sorry for it but you must believe me, I would not have done this to you for the world, if I'd had anywhere else I could take Fortune."

"No, Morgan. I am asking do you understand what you have done by bringing her home NOW, instead of years ago? Do you not think, if people must suffer in this life then it should at least be for some purpose? Do you not think that there might be some comfort from knowing one has not suffered for nothing? Can you understand how futile one's existence might seem if one knew it had all been for nought?" Her voice rose with each sentence, rising to a shriek.

"Please, Meg. Don't talk like this. I can't bear to see you like this. You're trembling, come on, come back to the house."

I reach out to take her hand and she pulls away.

"No! I don't want you talking to Eli!"

How did I ever manage to so destroy all her trust?

"You surely don't think I'd do that, do you? Come up to us, Meg. Come with me now. Beulah is longing to see you. She's on your side. She has nothing but sympathy for you. I have a note from Beulah, herself, read it if you don't believe me."

She reads it and hands it back to me.

"Looks like your handwriting to me."

I explain that Beulah can't write.

"And what is it that you both imagine is 'the best thing to do'?"

"We'll stand by you, Meg. Whatever happens, you will have a home with us."

She turns her head sharply away from me.

"Wasn't the whole point of stealing Fortune from me that I should not bring ruin on us all? Is that not why I was made to suffer, and why Fortune suffered too?"

"Well, yes. I suppose it was."

"So if I were to bring ruin on us all, now, then as I say, all these terrible years would have been for nothing."

"But it can come right now! You and Fortune can be together again!"

"And at what cost, Morgan? At the cost of that good man back there," her voice wavers, and she nods her head in the direction of the house. "…and to the cost of you and Beulah, and Fortune. You must know that you will all suffer if you stand with me."

"Suffer indeed!" I say, as if she was talking nonsense.

"It's the truth, Morgan. You love Carregwyn as you would love your own child. You couldn't bear to have to give it up on account of me. And that is what you would have to do if you did not shun me. You know how you struggle as it is. We all rely on our neighbours. Without each other, not one of these farms would survive."

"Eli seems to manage alright."

"Eli owns his own land. He does not have to pay rent. He does not have to rely on his neighbours' help because he can afford to employ labour."

"I'll manage. Together we can manage. You, me, Beulah and the little one."

I tell her this, though I know we never could. When she looks into my eyes, I see she doesn't believe it either.

"We'll all stick together, anyway, whatever happens. I can always start over somewhere else. If they all turn their backs on you for one mistake, I wouldn't want to stay here anyway. They can all go to hell."

"But you belong here, Morgan. HERE. I know how you've near broken your back to make that farm pay. That land is as much a part of you as your own skin and bones. And Fortune belongs here, too. She was made here and born here and wherever else she has been till now, she will feel she has come home. She will love Carregwyn as I did. She deserves to grow up there. You know what it is to feel born of a place, knowing your ancestors lived and died there too. You feel as much a part of the place as you do your own kin."

She knows that I know she speaks the truth. I would rather cut off my own arm than give up Carregwyn. But if that is what I must do, I shall do it. For I truly believe that nothing less will make amends.

Say it well, Morgan, say it well.

"I know I haven't been much of a brother to you these past few years but I intend to make that up to you now. You can say what you like. I'm standing by you. You don't know how much I have regretted not doing that in the past. If I had my time over, I would have done it back then and never agreed to take Fortune from you."

Megan kept glancing over her shoulder, towards the house. Was she listening? Had she heard all I said to her? I pray that she has.

"Megan! I am deeply sorry for it and shall be until the day I die. There are more important things than land or places, Megan, and they are the things we do for each other. I failed you once, I don't intend to do it again."

God help me, I must have taken leave of my senses. I am prepared to give up all I have strived for all my life. And gladly. So gladly, I feel light-headed with the prospect of being free of the heavy weight that has been my conscience all these years.

She says;

"You must go now. Eli might come looking for me. And say thank you to Beulah for me, for being a friend to me in my hour of need. We will speak again."

She ushers me away, urging me to go, quickly, before Eli returns and starts to worry where she has got to.

"You will come up tomorrow? Come and see Fortune. Oh, Meg! She's such a bright little thing. Really clever. And she's the image of you. You will come, won't you?"

"One way or another," she tells me, with a sad little smile.

"You said it well, Morgan, you couldn't have said it better. I'm proud of you," Beulah says when I tell her how it went, after she has put Fortune to bed.

"She'll be up tomorrow to see the little one."

"I have been thinking, while you were gone, and I want you to hear me out before you say anything for I have thought of something which will solve all our problems."

I think that will take nothing short of a miracle, but I hold my tongue and wait to hear her out.

"You know how I thought, when you brought Fortune here, that she was yours?"

"Aye, I won't forget that in a hurry," I say, huffily.

"But if she *were* yours and not Megan's, no one would hold it against you, would they?"

"No. Perhaps not. Well, the women of the parish would be up in arms, I expect. But she isn't mine. I don't know what you're getting at."

"What if you were to say that she was yours? That you've been paying for her upkeep all these years, but have now had to bring her home because the woman looking after her has died? No one would have any reason to think you weren't telling the truth. They'd never suspect she was Megan's, and even if they did, they could never be sure. There'd be no need to give up the farm."

I stare at her while it sinks in.

"What do you think? Would you do that, pretend she was yours for Megan's sake?"

"You clever bloody woman!" I say, grabbing her by the shoulders and kissing her. "Aye, I'll do it, alright!"

We stand there grinning at each other.

"I can't believe it! I don't know why I didn't think of it myself. God. I can see them now, Rees and the rest. The nods and the winks and the slaps on the back, saying how they didn't know I had it in me. The womenfolk will be a bit taken aback, but they'll decide I was not to blame, that I was seduced by some woman who was no better than she should be. It's the perfect solution.

Beulah! It was a grand day when Megan asked you to come here!"

"Oh, get on with you!" she says.

I never saw her blush before.

Chapter 20

Megan

There is a roaring inside my head, and I cannot be sure if it is the sound of the raging torrent below me or my own rage at this treacherous world. My rage overwhelms me; rage at the mother who did not care what kind of place my child went to, just so long as she went; rage at Morgan for agreeing to leave my poor little Fortune with that woman, year after year. Knowing that Fortune suffered; it tortures me so, that I double over and cry out with pain, every time I think of it.

I take a step closer to the water, out onto the great stone slab which reaches out like an accusing finger across the Wildwater. It would be quick, I tell myself, as fear, panic and regret rise up to destroy my courage. The force of the plunging water would drag me under and the stones would keep me there.

It seems fitting that I should end my life here, where the mountain's streams converge, just as all the wrong paths I have walked in this life have conspired to bring me here. I am weary of carrying the burdens of my own secrets and lies. They have pulled me down, just like these stones which line my pockets would pull me deep beneath this torrent.

Everything and everyone has a price, mother once said to me. Now I am to pay the price for all the lies I have told. I was right when I told Eli he deserved much better than me. I should never have let him go on believing I was still the Megan he left behind. I should have told him the truth when I had the chance. Instead, I thought I could turn back time and pretend the past did not exist. The truth has caught up with me now and there is no place to run to, no place to hide.

I'm so sorry Eli, I whisper.

Chapter 21

Morgan

I go to my bed wrung out from lack of sleep but more happy than I've felt in years. I can make amends to Megan without giving up all. If I were not so tired I'd ride down to Wildwater, right now, so eager am I to tell Megan of Beulah's brilliant plan.

I sleep like a dead man, can't even remember falling into bed, until that hour before dawn when I start to toss and turn, drifting in and out of dreams that are recollections of past times and conversations with Megan, all mixed up together with no dividing lines of time. I feel aware that I am dreaming but am so tired I barely wake from one dream to another, and all the while, Megan's voice drifts in and out of my dreams.

We are in the barn and she holds out an empty purse to me. *At what cost Morgan, to that good man?* she says, and drifts away.

Eleanor, the wool picker, takes Megan's place. She is singing her song about poor Mary Jones, pockets of stones, and raggedy bones.

Megan reappears beside me, sitting in our Mam's chair, by the fire.

"What was the point of it all?" she asks, and I open my mouth to answer but cannot speak.

"Fortune will love this place as much as I did."

We are up on the hill and Megan is picking the purple and yellow heartsease. It is the day she tells me Eli doesn't know about Fortune. And the words she speaks bring me wide awake and shouting her name.

I'll throw myself in the Wildwater before I'll tell Eli.

"No!" I shout out loud, and leap from my bed. She would not. She could not.

As I pull on my breeches, hopping from one foot to another, and drag my shirt over my head, Eleanor's song is going through my head. But she is not singing about Mary Jones now, she is singing about Megan.

I run out of the house, still buttoning my shirt. I run to the stable then change my mind, thinking it will be quicker to run. I can't gallop the pony downhill.

Poor Megan Jones
Hands full of stones,
Eyes brim with tears,
Heart full of fears.

The damned song goes on and on as I race through the oak wood. Please let Megan be alright.

While her true love was gone
And she all alone
The devil he caught her
And left her with daughter.

Please, God, Megan, there is no need, I'll tell them she's mine.

Poor Megan Jones
Crashed on the stones,
Clothes and frail body
But raggedy bones.

I'm being daft. She will be having her breakfast, and she will look up, surprised to see me coming so early in the morning.

She could ne'er tell her past

Fearing stones would be cast
For the lesson to teach her
By neighbour and preacher.

I leap the stone-walled boundaries of Eli's fields. Whatever is the matter, Morgan, she'll say to me. Has something happened?

Poor Megan Jones
With pockets of stones
She leapt the Wildwater
O'er the loss of her daughter.

Please God, don't let me be too late. I'll do anything, anything you ask of me, but please let Megan be home when I get there.

Poor Megan Jones
Crashed on the stones
We should all shed a tear
For poor Megan Jones.

I trip and stumble as I run across the tussock grass, my lungs bursting and the sound of my own heart pounding in my ears. Gwen will open the door and say, I'll just go and get her, Morgan. And later, I will tell Megan what a fright I had, thinking she had thrown herself in the Wildwater. And we will laugh about it and she will say, thank you, Morgan, for doing this thing for me, for saying she is yours. I am so relieved that all will come right now.

When the house comes into sight, I stop, bent over double, fighting to get my breath. If I had any breakfast in me I'd be throwing it up. When the feeling of nausea has past and I have recovered my breath, I go up to the door, and knock, resisting the temptation to burst right in. I'm out of my mind. Of course Megan will be here. I knock again, afraid I have not been heard.

The door opens and Gwen appears.

"I'm sorry, Gwen, to disturb you yet again, but I need to see Megan."

"Oh! She's gone out, I'm afraid. The master has gone out too, to town, on business. He won't be back till this afternoon."

"She's gone with him!"

Thank God. Thank God.

"No, no. She said she was feeling a bit better today and it is going to be such a fine day, she is gone to pick some pretty wildflowers she's seen growing along the river. You know how she is!"

"Which way did she go?" I ask, trying to keep the panic out of my voice.

"Oh. Now. Let me think."

I want to shake her and shout, quick, woman, quick.

"I really can't say for sure. But she usually goes upriver. She said not to expect her back soon. Now, did she say they were growing beside the Giant's Leap? I insisted she took some bread and cheese with her if she was going to be gone all day. She doesn't eat enough, I'm sure that's why she's been under the...."

I leave her talking and break into a run. She's alright, she's just gone to pick some flowers, because it's a nice day, she isn't planning anything stupid. I tell myself this, while fear is driving me to run like I've never run before in my life. I shout her name as I run. Megan! Megan! I have something to tell you! But she will never hear me, I fear, above the noise of the river.

I leap over a fallen tree trunk, and duck under overhanging hawthorn branches. When I round the bend of the river, I will see her. In my mind I can see her already, crouching down to pick the flowers. She will be there, and she will look up and smile and say, look, Morgan, aren't they lovely. And I will say yes, Megan, yes they are. And I will tell her all those things I never could before; like how glad I really am that I have a sister who never fails to see the beauty of flowers.

I see a flash of bright blue, and then another. Megan has dropped some of her flowers in the water. They ride the surface of the water as it crashes and tumbles over the rocks. Then I am sure this is all a bad dream, for then I see her bonnet is caught on an eddying whirlpool, spinning around and around upon the surface.

Any moment now, I am going to wake up, get out of bed, and go down to Wildwater, to tell Megan she has no need to worry, anymore. I can see her now, her face lit up with happiness. And she'll say thank you, Morgan, God bless you, Morgan, you are the best brother in all the world.

Chapter 22

Morgan stands with one arm stretched out, gripping the trunk of a hawthorn tree. His body is doubled over and he continues to retch yellow bile. After a minute or two he stands up, turns, and rests his back against the tree, his arms hanging limp beside him. Then he slowly slides to the ground. He sits with his back against the trunk, eyes closed, his legs splayed out in front of him. He hasn't got his breath back yet, and continues to take great gulps of air into his lungs, as if it is he who is drowning.

"You gave me such a fright," I say, when he begins to recover, "I heard you bellowing my name and I dropped my bonnet in the water. It was a new one, too."

He opens his eyes and squints up at me, rolling his head from side to side.

"I gave *you* a fright?" He closes his eyes. "I thought *you* were dead."

"I'm sorry."

He opens his eyes and runs his fingers through his hair.

"I got this thought in my head that you were about to... when I saw your bonnet coming down on that torrent, I thought I was too late."

"I'm so sorry, Morgan."

"No need for you to apologise. I don't know what I was thinking of....you wouldn't do that, would you Meg? Promise me you won't ever do that?"

I go and sit down beside him and he takes my hand in his.

"I've got something to tell you, Meg, something that changes everything. It was Beulah's idea and it's the answer to everything."

He tells me then that he is prepared to pretend Fortune is his own, so no one need ever know about my past.

"So Eli won't ever have to know about what happened, Meg," he says, grinning with glee.

I take my hand from his and get to my feet.

"I can't let you do that," I say.

"I don't mind doing it. Hell, I won't be very popular with the women of the parish for a while but, like Beulah says, they'll forgive me anyway, and decide I was the innocent victim of some evil seductress."

I pick at a piece of the hawthorn bark behind him. "Remember when I wanted to go and you and Mam wouldn't let me?"

"I'm not likely to forget that, am I?" He says, looking contrite.

"Mam said to me that a person has to belong somewhere, that people are no different from sheep; isolate one from the rest of the flock and it won't survive long, she said."

"Have you thought she might have been right?" He must see the hurt in my face for quickly adds, "about that, I mean, not about the rest. No person can survive alone in this world."

"I did! I went on living with you and Mam, and in this parish I'd belonged to all my life, but I felt as alone in this world as any person could be," I snap, and am immediately sorry. I don't want to blame him, anymore.

"I know, and I'm truly sorry for it, Megan. I shall be sorry for it for the rest of my days."

He gazes out at the Wildwater , his eyes filled with sadness.

"I'm not blaming you. I realise how hard it must have been for you to refuse our Mam's bidding; harder for you than anyone. That's why she asked you. She knew you had never refused her anything in her life." I reach out a hand to help him to his feet. "Let's start walking back, it looks like there is rain coming."

I pull him up and notice he is shaky on his feet, still not wholly recovered from his race down here to save me.

"What kind of place is this to belong in anyway? Where women are driven to suicide out of fear of retribution, while men go unpunished, whatever they do."

"Beulah said much the same thing."

"I was prepared to die, Morgan, rather than speak the truth. It can't be right, can it, that a person has to live a lie so as to live among people."

We follow the bend around the river and Wildwater house comes into view in the distance. I tremble at the thought of what I have to do when I get there.

"I hear what you say, Megan, but it's the way it is. There's nothing you can do about it. We have to tell them Fortune is mine, it's the only way."

"I can't do it, Morgan. I can't go on living this lie. Every time I look at Eli, I see how I am betraying him. I can't bear it any longer."

"Well, you'll have to bear it, Megan. You can't tell him now. He'll never forgive you," he says, stopping in his tracks and laying a hand on my arm to hold me back.

"And if I don't tell him I will never forgive myself," I say, pulling away.

"You'll just have to live with that, then."

He is cross with me now, has that sulky expression, like when he was a boy and couldn't have his own way. I continue walking and he has no choice but to follow.

"I thought you'd be over the moon," he says with a crestfallen look.

"All I know is that no good ever came out of lies. No good will come from my continuing to deceive Eli. He deserves to know the truth, even if it is the last thing on this earth he'll want to hear."

"I think you're making a terrible mistake," Morgan says.

"No, I already did that." I say.

"He'll throw you out on your ear."

"Then tell Beulah to have my bed aired."

"I don't know how you can be thinking of doing this. You know what they're like. When this gets out you'll be shunned by the lot of them, and us along with you, if we don't do likewise."

"I thought you said you'd stand by me."

He is silent a little too long. "That was before I realised there was another way out, when I thought there wasn't any choice."

"You'd have me live a lie, then, go on pretending to be someone I'm not, for the rest of my days; to Eli and everyone else."

"It's better than the alternative."

"Better for whom?"

I stop walking, not wanting to reach the house before I've sorted this out with him.

"Damn it, Megan!" he shouts, kicking the ground in exasperation. "Why must you always pull at the reins?"

"Because they are there."

"There will always be rules we have to live by!"

"Then they should be just ones!" I say, quietly.

"If you tell Eli, he'll be off down to the preacher to let him know. That's what I would do. I'd want the whole parish to know. He'll want revenge."

"He won't need to do that. I'm going to chapel this Sunday and I'll tell them all, myself. And I'll tell them how their rules don't just destroy lives, they destroy the good in people too."

He is turning this way and that, grasping his head in his hands, and groaning like a man in pain.

"Oh! Oh! God! I don't want to even think about what's going to happen when this gets out. Don't you remember how the preacher shamed Sian, in front of the whole congregation and all? Is that what you want to happen to you? And then he'll be on at us to turn you out or we'll be damned along with you."

I swallow my words of recrimination. He wasn't thinking like this, a short while ago, when all he could talk of was bringing Fortune home. He wasn't thinking of what our neighbours would do or say to me then. He was too wound up, with absolving himself of guilt, to think of consequences then.

The mention of Sian reminds me of what Dafydd Williams said to me in our stable, that night when Morgan had pulled her from the river.

"You know, Morgan, not everyone was against Sian back then. Dafydd wasn't."

I tell him what Dafydd said, about there being too many rules made by men, and the need for more compassion, and how the preacher could be as wrong as any other man.

His face contorts with disbelief.

"Dafydd said that? Dafydd?

I nod. "And he said everyone should be guided by their own conscience, not fear. That is what I am doing now, following my conscience. So, not everyone will turn their backs on us, Morgan. And even if they did, I would gladly leave, anyway. It's what I should have done a long time ago."

I think of the friends I once made in the market place, friends who were more compassionate and tolerant of human failings. Mam had told me Myfanwy no longer wanted to know me, but I think now that was probably a lie too, to make me feel I had no one left in the world to rely on.

"But what about Fortune? Have you thought about her?"

"I haven't stopped thinking of her, these past six years. If I have to leave, then I will take her with me, just as I should have been allowed to do, when she was a babe."

"But I don't want you to go! And I don't want you to take her! We've grown very fond of her, Beulah and I."

"Perhaps it won't come to that. Anyway, Morgan, don't you think it's time you married Beulah and started a family of your own?"

I stop long enough to see his jaw drop open, then I head on up to the house without him. Eli's trap is out in the courtyard. My heart begins to pound. These will be the hardest words I'll ever say;

"I'm so sorry, Eli, but I have something I must tell you."

Acknowledgements:

A big thank you to Heidi Lloyd; for proof reading, and introducing me to the modern, digital world!

About the author:

Jenny Lloyd lives in Wales with two dogs and two black sheep. This is her first novel. She is currently writing the next book.

Connect with me online:

Twitter: jennylloyd@jennyoldhouse
My blog: jennylloydwriter.wordpress.com
Facebook: www.facebook.com/jennylloydauthor

If you have enjoyed reading this novel, please take a few moments to leave feedback.

Made in the USA
Lexington, KY
01 May 2013